# Praise for the Works of Howard Engel

"Mr Engel is a born writer, a natural stylist...This is a writer who can bring a character to life in a few lines." — Ruth Rendell

"Engel can turn a phrase as neatly as Chandler ... Benny Cooperman novels [are] first-class entertainment, stylishly written, the work of an original, distinctive, and distinctively Canadian talent." — Julian Symons

"Benny Cooperman is a lot of fun to hang out. I'm delighted to see him getting into trouble again." — Donald E. Westlake

"Benny Cooperman is a character who somewhere in the collective literary unconscious of this country was crying to be invented. Canada needed its own private eye and Howard Engel was clever enough to see that he would, of course, have his comic side." — Philip Marchand, *Toronto Star*

"The great Canadian detective did not exist until Howard Engel invented Benny Cooperman." — Andrew Ryan, *The Globe and Mail*

"The Cooperman novels are heavy on full-bodied characters, sharp dialogue and rich humour. Benny just plain charms the socks off anyone he meets." — *Booklist*

"Engel keeps the pace up with lots of plausible funny material about a commercial broadcasting world where 'heart attacks were as common as head colds'." — *Washington Post*

"One of the series' best ... Engel has spent decades at the CBC. He knows all the inside stories about television; that makes the story sparkle." — *The Globe and Mail*

"His wittiest case ever ... Deliciously wicked twitting of the TV industry and a droll homage to *Laura* produce a comic standout." — *Kirkus*

"Engel tells his story with a lot of wit, and the book bubbles along to the end — Engel is a natural entertainer." — *In Dublin* on *A Victim Must Be Found*

"Benny is likeable and resourceful, and Mr. Engel has conceived a classic (revenge and retribution) Ross MacDonald plot, and a good one." — *The New Yorker* on *The Suicide Murders*

"Mr. Engel has the tough, cynical private-eye novel, as developed by Chandler and Hammett, down pat ... This is a smoothly written, well-plotted book much superior to most of its genre. Let's hope Benny comes back soon." — *The New York Times* Book Review on *The Suicide Murders*

"Howard Engel ranks among the big three of Canadian mystery writers. This is the Canadian murder mystery at its enjoyable best." — *London Free Press* on *Dead and Buried*

"Private eye fans won't want to miss this one." — *Publishers Weekly* on *A City Called July*

"*Murder on Location* is Howard Engel's third Cooperman novel, and his wit and ingenuity of plot show no signs of flagging." — Margaret Cannon, *Macleans*

"Skeleton-rattling good entertainment. With in-depth portraits of loquacious film director, Bard-quoting veteran actor, cheery young female star and that wayward found missus. Chase finale entails, irresistibly, dying Falls." — *The Sunday Times* (London) on *Murder on Location*

"Howard Engel is in danger of becoming a national treasure." — *The Gazette* (Montreal)

"Shooting of a more lethal kind occurs, but the overall impression is of good writing, pleasant characters and an unusual background." — *Daily Telegraph* on *Murder on Location*

# CITY OF
# FALLEN
# ANGELS

HOWARD ENGEL

# CITY OF FALLEN ANGELS

*Cormorant Books*

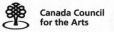 

The publisher gratefully acknowledges the support of the Canada Council for the Arts and
the Ontario Arts Council for its publishing program. We acknowledge the financial support
of the Government of Canada through the Canada Book Fund (CBF) for our publishing activities, and the Government of Ontario through the Ontario Media Development
Corporation, an agency of the Ontario Ministry of Culture, and the Ontario Book
Publishing Tax Credit Program.

Library and Archives Canada Cataloguing in Publication

Engel, Howard, 1931–, author
City of fallen angels / Howard Engel.

Issued in print and electronic formats.
ISBN 978-1-77086-379-8 (pbk.). — ISBN 978-1-77086-380-4 (epub). —
ISBN 978-1-77086-381-1 (mobi)

I. Title.

PS8559.N49C58 2014       C813'.54       C2013-907946-7
                                         C2013-907947-5

Cover photo and design: angeljohnguerra.com
Interior text design: Tannice Goddard, Soul Oasis Networking
Printer: Trigraphik LBF

Printed and bound in Canada.

The interior of this book is printed on 30% post-consumer waste recycled paper.

CORMORANT BOOKS INC.
10 St. Mary Street, Suite 615, Toronto, Ontario, M4Y 1P9
www.cormorantbooks.com

*In memory of friends who loved words:*
*Fran Baker, Anne Barnette, Lyal Brown, John Bruce,*
*Val Cleary, Des Conacher, Kildare Dobbs, Barbara Butler Gossen,*
*Gail Noble, Conor Cruise O'Brien, David Pierce-Jones, Tony Thomas,*
*Archy Thornton, Robert Weaver, and Sheldon Zitner.*

In trying to recapture the flavour of the date of this story, I have made use of expressions and sentiments that are no longer acceptable. I do this for reasons of verisimilitude, and ask for the reader's pardon in advance. Familiar names of the period are also used to this end.

# Los Angeles
# Autumn

### 1940

# CHAPTER ONE

*A*fter Paris, all my postings were a letdown. London, Moscow, and Berlin wore like cardboard half-soles on my old, hand-lasted London shoes. The Kremlin itself loomed like a marzipan castle on a dusty promenade. The political intrigues I had been sent to cover seemed like scenes from a comic opera. The truth of the matter is simple: Paris was my first posting and the best. I'd served hard time in those other places, sending stories, hard news and features, back to Toronto. I worked to find a Canadian angle on Lenin, Hitler, and Munich. My piece on the Anschluss ended up on the hook to make way for late-breaking hockey results.

"You're not appreciated, Mike Ward," the nagging voice in my head whined at me. "You're the best field man they have — even if they don't know it."

Waiting around in Paris for my boat train invited that unproductive voice, especially when I was trying to fall asleep, but often while I was working, and once when I had company. Still, roaming the once-familiar streets of the Sixth Arrondissement gave me some peace, even though it turned my whole expatriate life into the past tense. Seeing the shops along Boulevard Saint-Germain brought back memories of my younger self, who only needed to shave twice a week, and who, without knowing it, occupied a time and space that would become the envy of later generations. I was far too young to appreciate my luck. It took a much later reading of Hemingway's *The Sun Also Rises* to put me straight.

With the German armies gathering east of the Maginot Line, and my own low opinion of its ability to prevent the overrunning of France, I roamed the streets of the quarter as though there was nothing to worry about and nothing to avoid. When I occasionally ran into an old friend, I told him to cut his losses and get out of town. The French have a better stomach for soldiering than they have for war — the army was still struggling with the 1906 reversal of Dreyfus's sentence.

I learned my journalism on the job. I even had the nerve to publish a book of short stories about life in the Latin Quarter. *Seven Tales of the Quarter* won no prizes, but was well received in the pages of the *New York Times*, the *Toronto Star*, and *The New Yorker*. I got a letter from a film studio in Los Angeles, but the hopes of economic independence it raised petered out when they discovered that at that time I had no plans to come anywhere near Los Angeles. I used to see copies of the book on remainder shelves when I came home on leave. My mother kept her copy on the coffee table.

Paris, I knew now — as I roamed the once-familiar streets, looking for vanished cafés, and seeing strangers sitting at the café tables of Montparnasse — had outlived my tenancy of some years ago. It had lost most of its gaiety; the street lamps burned dimmer. As usual, the outside tables at the Dôme and the Select were crowded around the kerosene fires. Faces I recognized had aged, had become long-haired characters. They sat in a nest of younger faces, fresh from Stanford and Yale, all eager to hear about Hemingway,

Fitzgerald, and the rest of them. "Did you actually know Man Ray, Foujita, Derain, Vlaminck, and Picasso?" These imagined questions confirmed my belief that Paris was for the young. Maybe it was, maybe it always would be; but the young are, almost always, too young. Paris had spoiled me for sure, probably because I had been in my early twenties and on my first foreign adventure. Perhaps I'd made myself too much at home.

Since then I'd become my news service's reliable man in Europe. And now, just as the world was jumping into uniform, fixing adhesive tape on its windows, and sending fire-watchers up to the rooftops, I'd been posted to Los Angeles to cover the coming war from Hollywood, California. From there I could try to ignore the rumble of distant artillery, bury myself in the intrigues and excesses of movie stars. My beat was to become the gilded, pampered doings of our celluloid heroes and heroines. I'd been sent to "dig the dirt," as Cole Porter says, at beachside barbecues around private swimming pools. The lad who'd interviewed Mussolini and Stalin had a growing paunch and a bad liver, and arrived in Los Angeles to chronicle the life and times of Mae West, Clark Gable, and other employees of that company town. Maybe I could make something out of the competition of a European war to topple Bob Hope and Dorothy Lamour and their colleagues from their enchanted lives.

The prospect, from the very first, I found humiliating and degrading.

It didn't help knowing the reason why I had been so rudely uprooted.

It was 1940 and Europe was at war already. Roosevelt's America held tight to a fragile neutrality, while it maintained business relations with all the belligerents. It was beginning to look like a renewed war was going to become the fashion for the next five or ten years. America was holding its breath. Still, you couldn't see it on the streets of the city: the colour khaki was not seen on Sunset Boulevard, nor had there been an interruption in the sales of Oldsmobile, Studebaker, Ford, and Nash automobiles. Skirts were getting shorter, but I hadn't been in California long enough to read that particular barometer of the economic health of the nation. From Paris, Rome, and Moscow I'd seen one peace conference after another come and dissolve into a paper record of failure. They all left me with a taste of cordite in my mouth. I'd done my best to make my editors back home understand, but what was news was dictated from head office. I'd been covering different European postings for too long — this was the reading I was forced to give to the silence and unanswered cables. I hated to admit it, but I was overripe for a dull desk job.

I remember how hard it was leaving Berlin for Moscow: almost as hard as giving up my flat in Saint-Germain-des-Prés a few years earlier. I was a homebody at heart, which is a disadvantage in a foreign correspondent. But, like any good soldier, I could make a shelter, a home, in a flooded trench if necessary. I had set up a household in four foreign capitals for as many years each. They'd been close to everything. I hated giving them up. Stuart Winters was a fine fellow and a good reporter back in the twenties, but I didn't like surrendering to him my job, my bed, and the café where I'd breakfasted for the past forty-eight months. He'd promised to guard my books, my Tiffany lamp, and treat my beloved Quarter with the respect it deserved.

The Hollywood flat I'd rented in the Belvedere Arms was decorated with plaster trim, which gave it a golden glow under a blistering sun: a faint echo of a Spanish villa in the worst taste imaginable. But, until my money came, it was home, or as close to home as I would see for the next three months. And there were advantages of plumbing, electricity, and gas that gave it five stars. In less than a month, I'd be due for leave back to Toronto. Funny! I still called it "home," though I scarcely knew anyone there anymore. Even my old boss at the *Star* had gone off to raise goats on a farm on Georgian Bay. I hadn't met the new man; we'd only exchanged cables when necessary. News services and the papers they serve lead an elephant-and-mouse existence.

There was a car line running along the road leading out to one of the film studios. It ran past thousands of acres of real estate, all flourishing FOR SALE signs, only occasionally one that attested to a sale. It was semi-desert; improvements, such as plumbing and electricity, were still only promises.

The bureau in the Los Angeles Examiner Building was on the third floor. The elevator and the man operating it, in spite of his uniform, looked as if they had known hard times. The name of the wire service was written in gold leaf on the frosted glass door. The office itself was small, old, and run-down. It was exactly what I expected. Harold Olmstead, my employer in Toronto, had ordered my transfer. London, he had discovered, was a prize posting; he sent his nephew to learn how to run the British desk after me. And, as for me, Olmstead sent me on a junket to Poland and Czechoslovakia, then back to London to pick up the still-unexploited pieces of the crisis in coal. I got in a little fishing in Scotland after sending a dozen cables covering Gertrude Ederle's successful Channel swim. On spec, I sent a piece about Frederick Ashton's ballet *A Tragedy of Fashion*, but no one in Toronto wanted to hear about that.

I ARRIVED IN LA ANGRY. Alone on the Twentieth Century Limited, I had tasted, as my eyes tried to accommodate to all that light, my first breath of stifling, dry-roasted air. What happened next must be chalked up to culture shock. I couldn't have been angrier if I'd been sent to Timbuktu, or Anaheim, Azusa, or Cucamonga. I took a room at an ungraded hotel and lost myself in a barroom for the better part of a week before appearing in a recently sponged and ironed suit at the bureau. I had started the day early. I wanted to discover the office in motion when I got off the elevator and opened the frosted glass door. All heads were down. The editor on the rim was wearing a green eyeshade and black sleeves over the blue-and-white stripe in his Arrow shirt. His collar was shiny with use. He jumped up and strode toward me with a wide grin pasted on his face.

"Well, welcome! I mean welcome, Mr. Ward. I declare, we thought you were lost! I'm Endicott. Lawrence B. I guess you've seen my stuff."

"Sure, Endicott, I've been reading you for years. Always enjoy your copy."

"It's an honour to have a Pulitzer Prize winner on the floor."

"A story is a story." When the Pulitzer came, I was more embarrassed than surprised. I appreciated the honour of the thing, of course, but the persona of me as a crusader was a funhouse-mirror distortion. That picture stuck in my craw. I blushed at the congratulations and the slaps on the back from my colleagues. They knew as well as I did that my celebrity was built upon sand, but they looked to me as though in my place they would have embraced it and enjoyed it. The office threw a party for me. I kept a straight face through most of it, and passed out as quickly as possible.

"Are you quite recovered from your trip?"

"The Twentieth Century has taken years off my life. I can't sleep on trains."

With an arm around my shoulder he introduced me generally, as though to say: "Mr. Ward, this is your staff; staff, this is Mr. Ward." Naturally, I caught none of their names the first time around. How I ever became a newspaperman, I'll never know. I have such a slim hold on anything beginning with a capital letter. I guess it comes with my growing baldness. I've already made a down payment on my dotage, if I survive that long.

"Tell me, Mr. Endicott, where did the last head of chambers hang his hat?"

"'Head of chambers?' Oh! I see! Gee, it'll be good getting to know you. It's really swell having you here. We heard that you were coming weeks ago, but I guess you had to clean things up in Paris."

"London. Moscow before that."

"Russia! I mean, the Soviet Union. That must have been terrific! Russia before the Bolsheviks!"

"Not quite. I'm younger than I look. I missed Catherine the Great by a year or two."

"But it's really grand that you got here. I intended to meet your train, but ... You know how it is."

Endicott was a survivor, according to a briefing by Bob Judd over a pint of beer in the French pub in Soho. This session was in fond remembrance of a similar night behind the Leningrad station four years earlier. I first knew Judd in London. Then we followed one another around the merry-go-round ending up in London again at the same Soho bar. It seemed more than a slim month ago.

"Endicott's a family man," he said, staring down at the rings his glass had made on the top of the bar. "He'll invite you to meet the little woman and offer to lend you his lawnmower. Domesticity's contagious, Mike. Homes and gardens are the death of real news-papermen. Endicott never went after foreign postings. He would have missed his raspberry canes and they would have missed him."

Bob and I cut up all of our former and present employers, while the abundantly moustached bartender kept our beakers full. I admit we put away a memorable amount of ale before the night evapo-rated into the cold, sunless London dawn. Bob's now helping out the new boy at my old desk.

All of this was running through my mind as Endicott walked me through the main room, thundering with Remingtons and Smith-Coronas, to the back office behind a glass partition. "I hope you like your little corner back here. Two windows! View of Wilshire Boulevard."

The man showing me around didn't look like an Endicott. The fashionable part of my family, most of whom I've never met, knew a lot of Endicotts. Lawrence B. didn't look like any of them. He was less substantial than the name promises. He stood, slightly stooped, but moderately tall. He looked fit. I could picture him doing setting-up exercises. He continued to lead me through the office, pointing out the morgue files and the nearest bathroom. His zeal almost made me taste the envy behind his courtesy. There lurked a Uriah Heepishness about his manner.

"Is there anything I can get for you, Mr. Ward?" He was not rubbing his hands together, but I could imagine him doing so.

"'Mike' will do, Mr. Endicott. Forget the 'mister.' 'Lawrence B.' — is that what they call you?"

"Call me 'Larry.' Here, let me help you with your stuff."

He encumbered me with help, as Dr. Johnson says, and I soon had made a habitation of the office, an oasis in the desert.

"I wanna tell you how much I admire the stuff you put on the wire from Berlin and the Soviet Union."

"Thanks. I just keep my eyes open."

"Too bad about that piece you sent from London. Appeasement. That didn't go down well in Ottawa. You didn't pull any punches. I mean, you started it. Now everybody's using the word 'appease-ment.' I guess that's why you're here and not over there. Seems a pity, though; I mean, you know the territory."

"Let's shut up about that, Larry. I don't want tear stains on this new blotter."

"Oh, yeah. Sure. Sorry."

"Forget it. As Hemingway used to say, 'We don't talk about casualties.'"

With Lawrence B. Endicott looking on, I put my special good-luck items into the desk drawer. My predecessor hadn't left me a paper clip or a rubber band. While I did this, Endicott filled me in on the daily and weekly routines. It was a smaller shop than my last posting. I told Endicott how I liked to run things, and what I expected of him. I was sweating in my old Moscow-bought suit. I hadn't had the time to buy one in London. I could see that I was going to have to invest in a new wardrobe.

"Sure glad you've come aboard, Mike. This is a busy time. Interesting stuff coming up." He held out a pack of Old Gold cigarettes and waved them at me. "Something for me, I hope?"

I shook my head.

"Maud Morgan's getting married again. This time it's on Thomas S. Clifford's yacht, down in San Diego. Billy Harcourt, the polo player, is the groom."

"I'm sorry. I don't get it. What's so special about that?"

"Everybody's going to be there. It'll be the social event of the season. The vice president's coming. Edsel Ford, Walt Disney, Asa Zavitz —"

I'd heard most of the names before. Clifford owned most of the newspapers not controlled by Hearst. The polo player had shot his father in a hunting accident and made four lawyers wealthy men. The bride was right out of Evelyn Waugh and loving it. "Who's Asa Zavitz?" I asked. "The name sounds familiar."

"He's top honcho at A-Z-P, the biggest film studio in town."

"Who do we have covering big social events?"

"Mrs. Dobson plans on going. She'll cover the social and fashion angles. Simpson's planning news. And Price. Gord Price'll be there with his Speed Graphic camera. That's all, unless ..."

"No thanks. I haven't written up a wedding since I was a copy boy masquerading as a junior reporter. I'd rather beard Herr Hitler again in his mountain hunting retreat than intrude on ..."

"This might be just the thing! You'll meet a cast of thousands. See Hollywood at its most outrageous. Ten rounds with bare knuckles. Something to get your feet wet, get the temper of the town, get the feel of this part of the West."

"I've scarcely unpacked ..."

"Come on! Be a sport! We all take our turn in the barrel. Oh, by the way, in answer to your earlier question, we all use the same hat stand by the door."

I lost that round, and spent the next few minutes getting things organized for a trip close to the Mexican border, where the yacht was waiting.

I WAS SICK ON THE tender crossing to the mooring, and felt like an extra sardine being stuffed into the yacht without enough oil. There I was up to my neck in white lace and pastel-coloured chiffon wedding attire. Confetti filled the air and corks were popping off to one side. Everything aboard was lavish and, to my eyes — my jaundiced, unforgiving eyes — vulgar beyond belief. When I got the confetti out of my eyes, I attempted to make a few notes, then retreated to where the champagne was flowing. When I got close to the source of the imported liquor, I was bumped from the rear. Angry, I turned, ready to bop the person responsible and blame him for all my troubles. For everything. And suddenly my jaw dropped open. There was Errol Flynn. I mean, the real Errol Flynn. He said, "Excuse me, old boy; there's a man dying of thirst," and got between me and the bar. Then he stopped and turned. "I say, you're crying, chum. What's the matter? Lose your girlfriend? She dump you for that polo player? Friend of the bride?"

"No. Just some damned confetti."

"Maybe only a confettus. Look on the bright side," he said, coming up with a clean handkerchief. "Let's have a peek."

He held on to my arm, and turned me into the light.

"Steady on, I'll have the bugger out in no time."

He took his handkerchief from an inside pocket and carefully folded it before dabbing at my eye.

"There!" With a courtly bow, he showed me his handkerchief to prove that all was well. The tearing continued, unfortunately. I couldn't help it. Flynn was grinning as though he had just run Basil Rathbone through with his cutlass or struck a big marlin off Catalina. In spite of the wide grin, my eye didn't feel cured. It stung like Billy-O.

I took the handkerchief from him and dabbed both my eyes.

Flynn was examining me. "Where on earth did you get that suit? Moscow? Waukegan? Hobart?"

"Right the first time. I just arrived and it's all I've got; everything else needs pressing."

"Don't apologize. You've probably started a new trend. What's your name?"

We shouldered our way through the multitude and were soon toasting my Moscow tailor. Then we drank one another's health. And we did that again. After that things get blurry. I know for a certainty that I took no more notes. I recall people splashing about in their finery in the yacht's pool. About the rest of the evening and the manner of my return to LA, I remember nothing at all. But I still have Flynn's handkerchief somewhere.

## CHAPTER TWO

*T*he next day it was back to business. None of my colleagues peached on me to Endicott, or at least I never heard about it. But there were conspiratorial grins from across the floor from my wedding party yachting colleagues.

There was another assignment pinned to my typewriter when I got to my desk. Another major story. As closely as I remember, it was a society polo game. I'd seen a little polo in Lahore a year or so back, so I knew which end of the horses to watch. There was a crowded bar, and some news about the war: something I didn't hear about at the office. I tried to disengage another rerun of my old resentments. What do you do when you become bored with your internal monologue?

I caught sight of Spencer Tracy and that actress with a New England accent. Rhett Butler himself eating a frankfurter as Carole Lombard looked on. I didn't try to crash their party. I was still figuring out the difference between celluloid reality and the home-and-garden variety.

Two days later, Endicott had another story that was bothering him. I hoped it wasn't another romp in high society.

"It's Mark Norman," he said, as though he was announcing the sudden outbreak of war.

"Who?"

"Mark Norman — "

"Once again, who? Remember, I'm new around here. Just off the boat."

"Mark Norman! Barbara Lorrison's husband! Mark Norman is dead by his own hand. It looks like suicide, but the cops are keeping mum about it. I've been up with it most of the night. It's the biggest story to come out of here since talking pictures."

Although I'd never heard of Mark Norman, I had heard of Barbara Lorrison, a name that drew people to moving picture theatres across North America. European moviemakers tried to copy her; in India and Australia she was the subject of a cult. Her "all singing, all dancing" musicals were the weekend entertainment of millions. Her lively private life was the stuff of scandal sheets. Even newspapers that usually avoided the ripe excesses of celebrities bent the rules for Lorrison. She was the unchallenged queen of Technicolor. Her platinum blonde hair sold tickets from Glendale in the west to Sag Harbor in the east. Italian noblemen and wealthy tycoons stood ready to pull her chariot through the streets, except that her twelve-cylinder touring car required more than muscles and enthusiasm when it ran out of fuel. I didn't know anything about her husband. In fact, I was surprised to hear that she had one.

"Who do you have covering it?" I asked.

"Sinclair and I have been on it since the news came over the wire. The police are keeping the details bottled up. Even my usual spies haven't any idea about how it happened."

"I see. With a bride like his, he had everything to live for."

"Any way you look at it, it's international news."

"If you say so. Remember, Larry, I'm still retooling. I'm still a couple of drinks below par."

"Check the morgue. All you need to know's in there."

In a news service or in a regular newspaper office, the morgue is not where they store burned-out reporters and assassinated city editors, but a handy reference library of important or continuing stories. They are never up-to-date, but are invaluable nevertheless.

"I'll take a squint at it."

Endicott nodded dubiously while trying on a grin to cover his misgivings. "Sure thing. That'll be hunky-dory," he said.

"Who was her husband, again?" I asked from behind my desk with my back to the light.

"What? Whose husband?"

"Lorrison's."

"Oh, he was a big shot at A-Z-P. That's the biggest studio in town. He worked directly under the top man, Asa Zavitz himself."

I was going to ask him to tell me about Zavitz, but on second thought decided to burden the morgue. I didn't want to wear out Endicott's patience with me. We all have our limit, and when one is taking the much-coveted job of an old hand like Endicott, one should be careful. Otherwise he'll send off a note to Toronto asking if they were serious about sending me to LA. As I might have guessed, he followed me to the double-doored cabinet which acted as our collective memory.

Larry peered over my shoulder. "Norman wasn't a name, just a studio executive. Try to remember: his name is, or was, Mark Norman."

"I'll remember. Mark Norman. He's the guy who just committed suicide." Under my breath I was cursing both Endicott and myself. I should have treated myself to an early liquid lunch before facing my nemesis.

"The afternoon papers will make his name a household word. After a couple of weeks, he'll disappear and be anonymous again."

"Even the best obituaries end up wrapping fish, Larry. *Sic transit gloria mundi.*"

"You can say that again! This story won't crawl away and die, Mike. You won't write '30' to it for weeks."

Endicott's use of that newspaper term for "the end" made me melt a little in favour of the man breathing down the collar of my shirt.

I remembered the name Asa Zavitz from a few days ago — something to do with the wedding down the coast aboard that yacht with Errol Flynn and the confetti. I bit off some time and poked into the morgue. We had a fat file on the man. Zavitz had come from the Canadian maritime provinces, after learning the trade of a furrier in Montreal's garment district. He went to New York, where he learned the infant film business. When the production of commercial films moved to the coast, Zavitz followed. Through a series of partnerships, and a knack for buying up the contracts of promising players, he advanced himself to the point where he could boast that he controlled more heavenly bodies than the universe could provide. He bought real estate, thoroughbred horses, as well as the options of actors and actresses. A note in the file said that he was a hard-headed businessman with a sentimental streak a mile wide. It gave his address, which I noted, and listed the clubs he belonged to and the charities he supported. I read about how he once walked on to the set of a Billy Bubbles movie and lectured the director about how real kids cry when their father loses his job in the factory. Then he went on to work Billy past midnight and into the early dawn. At the time, the Screen Actors Guild was still shedding its baby teeth. Zavitz had prospered in the teens and twenties, and had become a major figure in America in the 1920s and '30s.

That set me off daydreaming. I had done well in the '20s and '30s as well. I tried not to let these memories of my early years in the business get me down. Think of today; think of the present.

Hemingway published *For Whom the Bell Tolls* in 1940. The *New York Times'* chief book critics praised it until attention was snatched away, deflected by the appearance of Arthur Koestler's *Darkness at Noon*. It was the year Churchill moved into Downing Street, and Thurber and Nugent's play *The Male Animal* was a Broadway success. It was also the year that *The Corn Is Green*, by Emlyn Williams, scored a triumph for Ethel Barrymore. Funny, when I think of that; nothing seemed further off from me at that moment than Broadway and the legendary Barrymore family.

That day, Endicott let me buy him lunch at Chasen's. He said that Chasen's was one of a very few public haunts from which the public could glimpse bona fide movie stars wining, dining, and often misbehaving. Gary Cooper, James Stewart, and Groucho Marx were regulars. When hard liquor was hard to come by, Dave Chasen, an ex-vaudevillian and a pal of Frank Capra's, got his Scotch through the influence of his silent partner, Harold Ross of *The New Yorker* and Ambassador Joe Kennedy. Endicott enjoyed telling me this, while I, just off the boat as it were, was frankly shocked that the peccadilloes of actors and actresses, politicians, and magazine editors should warrant the attention of a reputable news service. After Paris, Moscow, and London, it was obvious that I had a lot to learn about what constituted news in California.

That night Endicott took the boss home to dinner. His Welsh wife, Dympna, and their two youngsters, Torrin and Gwen, had dressed up for the occasion, and greeted me from the steps of their small house. We had a good bland meal, with nothing particularly Celtic about it, and spent the rest of the evening looking through maps of the area. I'd managed to skip Los Angeles in my travels; my ignorance of the area was unblemished. When the Pacific was at my back, I could point north, except that Endicott says it's east. Once I make it inland, my compass spins out of control like a Maxwell roadster on a sand beach. The maps jogged my memory; I'd heard these streets named on the radio. Jack Benny's program had made all of America familiar with names like Beverly Hills, Sunset Boulevard, Laguna Beach, Laurel Canyon, Wilshire Boulevard, Hollywood and Vine. "Lux presents Hollywood!" Cecil B. DeMille announces weekly on the radio to all of North America. And the whole of the continent rejoiced in the misadventures of Fibber McGee on a street in radio-land called Wistful Vista.

From the conversation over dinner, I absorbed as much of this as I could master, then begged to be taken to my flat. I blamed a series of sleepless nights on the Twentieth Century Limited, but it was really a sign of fatigue and creeping middle age. I wasn't as spry, or as resilient, as I was when I'd first arrived in Paris, twenty years earlier. I needed time. I needed a starting point. Was I this much at sea when I first arrived in Paris or London? I didn't think so.

# CHAPTER THREE

*D*uring the two weeks that followed, I bothered the public relations departments of several studios for all the free information I could get on the dear departed Mark Norman and his celebrated bride, Barbara Lorrison. I made myself a particular pest, as you might expect, at A-Z-P, Norman's own studio. Here I encountered the public relations man, Stanley Loomis, head of their department of misinformation. I could feel him writing down my name and pencilling circles around it as we spoke. If he'd had my wax image, he'd be sticking it with pins. On the phone, he sounded as though he was a dedicated employee — and the remaining span of my days might just depend on the degree of that dedication.

A day after my initial contacts, just after I arrived, I got a call from a detective lieutenant named Randall Swarbrick, who, in polite terms warned me off his turf. Twenty minutes later, Loomis was back again to nail down my coffin lid.

"The police have our full co-operation in this unfortunate matter, and we are obliged to discourage anything that might compromise their investigation. Thank you for your interest, Mr. Ward, but we must of course respect the wishes of the authorities. I wish you a safe and speedy return to Canada."

When I asked him, Endicott told me that Swarbrick was a cop to stay clear of. I'd suspected that from his telephone manner — even before Loomis called to write '30' to my story. I decided to involve myself in more immediate things. After a few days, I had mastered the basics, which were simple variations of what I had been doing for years. I had been a quick study as far as the office routines went. I learned about train schedules, plane times, and all the regular office hell. Endicott said, almost leering, that I was a fast learner. Why not, the job was the same as always; only the details had changed. He also liked to drop, heavily, a few references to my early branding of Chamberlain as an appeaser. I wore that label until the advance of the German armies cued others to claim the title.

I knew I was a good journalist; that never gave me sleepless nights, but the city was a different matter. I got lost whenever I forgot to carry my map with me — and even then once or twice. The sprawl of LA was a thorn in my rear, a worm in my liver.

Whenever I could, I was glad to get out of the office. It had begun to close in on me. I often needed a breath of air and the air on Wilshire Boulevard suited me better. It wasn't like anything else, not as warm as the first blast of it I felt when I got off the train. It was a cousin of the hot, dry blast I got looking up at the Sphinx in Giza.

One afternoon, in a small diner off Wilshire, I ordered a sandwich and coffee. While it was in the making, I went through my notebook. Endicott had given me the name of the police contact he used: Bill Alton, a sergeant of detectives, working out of the seventh precinct. When I got him on the phone, he tried to stall. "What's the matter? Endicott break a leg? Sinclair off to Reno? Who the hell are you, anyway?"

"They work for me, Sergeant Alton, that's who they are. My name's Mike Ward and I want to see you as soon as possible."

"With all due respect to the working press, Ward, we gotta three-ring circus going on here, not a peep show! If you need a chalk talk, play football. Our PR people keep you boys informed. Then it's up to you to twist things."

"Look, I'm no Hearst stooge. I'm not grinding any axes. I just got here from Canada and I need all the help I can get."

"Oh yeah? You're from up there where the Mounties get their man. Can you carry a tune like Nelson Eddy?"

"I usually get other people to do the singing. Especially when I smell dead fish."

"Where do you drink your lunch?"

"I told you, I just got off the train. You name it. I'll find you."

"One-thirty at The Colony bar. The taxis know it."

It was still early enough for me to take a walk down the boulevard. I stopped at Bullock's Wilshire department store long enough to renew my supply of razor blades, find a tooth powder, and buy a couple of maps of the city and environs. Over a cup of coffee in the art deco tea room, I found that the maps were printed a pica or two too small for my eyes; even with a lens it would be hard to find my way home. In the end, I trusted the taxi driver to track down The Colony bar.

What is it about cops that tip off the ordinary citizen that the fellow at the bar, not wearing a uniform, not noticeably carrying a weapon, not writing out a citation for illegal parking, is a cop? In LA, as in other places, cops are recruited from the general population. By rights they should look like the general population. But they don't. This guy, for instance. Bob Alton was twenty pounds overweight, six foot three, badly shaven, and looked like his face had been stepped on not once but over and over. He was at the bar sipping a Schlitz out of the bottle. When I sat down next to him he didn't look over at me right away, but poked a fancy pack of Sobranie gold-tipped cigarettes at me.

"No thanks," I said. "Things are looking up for the hard-working upholders of the law, I see."

"Don't ask me where I picked them up. I pocket things and forget where they came from. I don't have it in me to make a big score, but in this petty stuff, I don't know. I can't help it. You're Mike Ward?"

"You were expecting maybe Mrs. Nussbaum?" The cop blinked and grinned. "Thanks for meeting me."

A waitress wearing an apron over a lot of bosom stationed herself across the counter, breathing deeply in case we were talent scouts. "I'm Margot. What can I get you boys?" She giggled; it was a lot of fun being Margot.

I ordered a beer to catch up with Alton, while he shook his head instead of a further response. I watched her open the bottle and put it before me, filling the glass with no spillage. Alton and I sipped in silence for a minute. The girl walked away, wagging a large saucy bow that held her apron.

"I'm not a public relations officer, Ward. I keep these stripes by keeping clear of guys like you. If you weren't from up north, I wouldn't give you diddly."

"I may still need it before I'm through. Why does your heart warm up at the mention of Canada?"

"Eunice, my sister, lives in Winnipeg. She says nobody she's ever met there gives her much grief. I keep meaning to visit her up where the winters are long and cold."

"What can you tell me about this so-called suicide? I need some background to bring me up to speed. And, Bill, I'll not be rushing into print with what you tell me. That's Endicott's department."

"The guy was shot through the head. A single shot. The gun wasn't registered to him. The note that was found by Jeffrey Swift was handed over to the investigating detectives. They said it was next to the body. I've seen it. To me, it looked like it was written some time ago. The thing had been lying around in a drawer for a couple of weeks at least. Dust on the paper. Poor attempt to brush it clean. You know."

"You can't have been the only detective to notice that. Weren't there forensic people aboard by this time?"

He didn't respond.

"That was a question, Sergeant."

"It was expedient to hide evidence that conflicted with the first assessment. The department is comfortable with suicide. Murder makes waves."

"If it was suicide, fine; but if it wasn't, who might have done it?"

"These movie people are not the salt of the earth, Ward. They'll tell an actor his performance was wonderful, that it made them cry, and then blacken his name in every studio in town. They're not like us. You ask a question and they whistle *Aily-aily* or *My Yiddishe Mamma* in your ear. They wear hats in church, make a big expensive fuss when a son gets to be thirteen. They don't eat oat cakes with marmalade for breakfast. Like I said, they're not like us. You know what I mean? Take Zavitz: he don't like the sound of 'no'; but when he has to say 'no,' he means 'no.'"

"Just like Henry Ford."

"I think Zavitz's a secret New Dealer at heart, but he don't let it show."

"Closer to home?"

"Barbara Lorrison, Mark Norman's wife, was conveniently out of town with her mother. He had an ex-wife, too, but she's in San Francisco."

"Usually? Or at the significant moment?"

"We're not checking on her. The story we got from the studio brass dwelt on the fact that this studio boss was singularly ill endowed to satisfy his blonde Venus of a wife. Mother Nature overlooked giving him a mature set of crown jewels."

"You're pulling my leg!"

"We have information that they were both upset about the arrangements, that she chided him about his shortcomings, and took off with her mother up the coast to Big Sur. In a mad fit of remorse and frustration, he took his own life."

"Sounds like a fairy tale to me, Bill."

"It may sound like sheep dip, but it's what we got as a working hypothesis."

"'Hypothesis?' Where does a suicide take you? It's a dead end."

"The department buys suicide. So, suicide is what we got."

"Is that what the note says?"

"Obliquely, not directly."

"The maid reported the death?"

"She found him and called the studio. That's the way it is here: the studios hear things first. Both Zavitz and Swift came running. I don't have the maid's name handy."

The waitress was hovering again. I ordered a salmon salad sandwich with the crusts on. Alton relented and ordered a burger. Together, we watched the bow sashay out of sight.

"Zavitz is the studio head. Who's the other guy — Swift — who found the smoking gun?"

"That's the boy wonder, Ward. He's Zavitz's personal discovery. He's a genius at matching stars and scripts, and making it work at the box office. Works directly under Zavitz."

"When I tried to talk to the studio, they sicced Swarbrick on me."

"Yeah, it's not easy getting through to him."

"Is Swift easier to talk to? What's he like?"

"He's not so much a good fellow as he is a failed pariah."

"You didn't just make that up, Bill. You're into my line of country."

"I picked it up. You know how actors like to sound off?"

"They were on the scene early! Before your gang. Do they usually take such a paternal interest in the help?"

"Zavitz governs every aspect of their lives. Everybody who takes his money. On top of that, Barbara Lorrison's a big star. She means a lot to the studio. She's a bankable asset. And she knows how to throw her weight around. Her agent, Myer Grimpen, plays the heavy. He makes the waves, while she cries, 'Poor little me!' That's what he does for his piece of that asset. And the old lady, her mother, is always sounding off."

"But neither of the women was at home. Why were they so responsive to, what's his name, Norman's death?"

"The studio, Ward, the studio. They're as skittish about bad publicity as J. Edgar Hoover, and will call out the Marines to put the lid on any bad smell."

"I begin to see. And how much pressure do the studios put on you guys? They rattle your chains much?"

"Hell, Ward, this is a company town. Same as Detroit, same as Washington. They let us collect traffic violations, hand out citations for spitting in the street, and chase bank robbers. The studios have their own cops. And their territory isn't limited to the sound stages and the back lots. That's forbidden territory, Ward. We keep out of it. Just the way the Frisco cops stay clear of Chinatown."

"Why's that?"

"It's a foreign country. They make their own rules. They do things differently there. Just like in the movies."

"Are you going to eat anything else?"

"I emptied a lunch pail an hour ago. I shouldn't have had this. I should have my head examined. I'd better get back to my desk."

I picked up the cheque. The cop's hands were already in his pockets.

# CHAPTER FOUR

*I* was forty years old, approaching my middle age. I'd become a newspaperman when I was scarcely out of my teens and I was sick of it, burned out. I'd run out of things to say. I told myself that what I needed was a good long rest. Friends agreed with me, but, in my heart, I didn't believe it. I was that cliché of the washed up journalist: I knew what was happening to me, and, with an illogical talent for holding two contradictory ideas at the same time, I fought against the change. Literally. I knocked my senior editor down in Harry's Bar, in Paris, and later he knocked me down outside the Ritz. Together we rolled down from the square, passed the big, Greek-looking church of the Madeleine to the river, where we ended the evening with a friend of his who lived on a barge. He had a wind-up gramophone and a girlfriend with a toothache. That's about all I remember.

I came to Paris after the war, the one they call 'Great.' It was my first and best posting. In my five years, I wrote my own personal version of Herr Baedeker's guide to Paris. Mine began after dark. Now, with another war looming — I couldn't see how the States could ignore it for long — I might be able to make history repeat itself. But for this one, I'd have a ringside seat at the Brown Derby.

I'm not usually one to give in to the dubious delights of looking back at one's better days. I had enjoyed them at the time, sometimes even aware that these were likely going to turn out to be the best of my days. My prime. My golden time. Usually, I keep nostalgia away with a solid dedication to the present. I took the past out with the empty bottles and trash. But Endicott had collected a few letters for me, and I'd been foolish enough to read them all at a sitting. They were from colleagues in Europe: Shirer, Trout, Halton, and Murrow. They were pals from the good years. Now they were telling me about the good war I was missing. Bill Shirer in Berlin told me how the English were being encircled in Flanders by the greatest army to ever take the field against the British Tommies. Matt Halton told me how they were able to record sound in a small van on soft discs, getting as close to the battle lines as possible, and then ship the feeds back through London. Matt's engineer was an old drinking pal. I wished both of them well. Shirer had written to me of how he could read dignity and even nobility on the faces of hordes of evacuees along the roads of western France. I used to carry that letter around with me. I don't remember what happened to it.

As a group, they shared their war with me. I had no war to share with them. I tried writing about how divided the States was on the subject of war. Sure, they would help out, but on a lend-lease basis. And it was business as usual with the Nazis, in spite of all the attempts to muffle news of that. If the States ever went to war with the Empire of Japan, it would get back most of the Third Avenue El in the shape of bombs and bullets. I needed to find a way to clear my head of all this. I put the letters together in my desk drawer, way at the back, and tried to put them, and my friends, out of my mind. To hold on to my sanity, I needed a distraction. A feature on the La Brea Tar Pits? The zoo? A profile of Martha Raye? Gary Cooper?

I was still intrigued by the suicide of that film executive. It wasn't a peace conference or a meeting of heads of state, but it was big news here in LA, and that's where I was, and where I was likely to be until the war wrapped us up in its own confusions. In my mind, Mark Norman's death resembled a fresh shooting script, unattached in any way to the real world of Sunday breakfasts and mowing the lawn. And, to be sure, I didn't much like being told by the studio and the cops to stay off their grass.

I spent a couple of hours watching Mark Norman's widow, Barbara Lorrison, charming the safari jacket off actor Clark Gable's back. I viewed the movie at the Tivoli Theatre on Vine. The movie was *Dust Storm*. I put watching it in the afternoon down to research. I thought that she would do an imitation of one of Anita Loos's dizzy blondes, but she was better than that. I'd given her credit for being little more than an animated body, but there was more to her than the mop of platinum blonde hair you see in the rotogravures. She had poise, wit, and star quality. When she was on the screen, you couldn't look at anybody else. I could see why a man might shoot himself on her account.

I had a drink in a little hole-in-the-wall bar around the corner from the theatre. The movie had impressed me. It wasn't something you'd line up with the Russians or the French on a good day, but it was honest, contemporary American hokum, and she made all the wheels turn. I toasted the widow, and toasted her again. Sharing the bar with me and three gloomy men was a small woman wearing a close-fitting hat and veil. The little black suit, I'll bet, had New York labels. It made me think of all the goddamned funerals I have known. She was half-singing, half-humming a song to herself:

*Honey, have a* (sniff),
*Have a* (sniff) *on me.*
*Honey, have a* (sniff) *on me.*

She was looking into her empty glass. It was a casual look at first, then it took on a serious, almost desperate urgency as she lifted the glass from the bar. "I'm looking for my husbands," she said to no one in particular. Then she swivelled her bent head, knocking the cloche hat to the top of the bar and revealing dark bangs. She said, "Hello, you. Have you seen a Mr. Benchley? I'm missing one."

"Sorry?"

"They're all in here someplace." Her eyes went back to her glass.

I shifted over one stool. She didn't move until I tried conversation, then she looked me in the face and said, "What fresh hell is this?"

There were salted peanuts on the bar. I ate a bowl of them before I took myself home to sleep it off.

At the office the next day, I got the name of the servant who had found Mark Norman's body. When I rang the late movie producer's house, I was told that Violet Bowden was on holiday, and not expected back for several weeks. I left my name and number with the wire service. There was little more I could do, but, on a hunch, I looked up her name in the directory and dialled it.

"Hello?" The voice was deep. It sounded sleepy.

"Is this the home of Violet Bowden?"

"Tha's right. Who wants her?"

I filled in my name and particulars. Every time I paused, I heard "uh-huh" on the other end. "Listen, Mr. Ward, my mother's gone off to Paris, France. She's not expected back here for maybe a month or more."

"Is she working there?"

"Nah, sir, she's on holiday. We gotta telegram yesterday. She's having a real good time, but she misses the family."

"Didn't she take any of you with her?"

"Nah, sir, she's all on her lonesome. She's been to the big art gallery there, but she hasn't seen the Changing of the Guard yet."

"She'll have a long wait. That happens in London."

"I 'spec she knows that by now. She's found a good hotel where they take coloured and white folks without batting an eye. She says she might be movin' on soon, because they got a war goin' on over there."

"The Germans will be in Paris late spring or early summer. I hope she's got a return ticket? Had she been planning this trip for some time?"

"A trip to Paris? Don't make me laugh! It was a present from Mr. Asa Zavitz himself. He's the boss at the studio. Said he thought she needed a holiday after all what happened. The shock and all, you know."

"Do you have a number for her in Paris?"

"Nah, sir. I wouldn't have no call to telephone that far away. But I can tell you the name of her hotel."

"Wonderful!"

"I got it right here. Hotel de Loire, 16 rue du Petit-Pont, Paris. There's a Roman number after that: 'V I.' I guess that's a six."

"Thanks a lot. What's your name? I can give her your regards when I talk to her."

"Just say Ambrose. She'll know who it is. Tell her I got an audition comin' up in a week. If I get the part, I'll have lines. I never had lines before."

"Good for you! Tell me, Ambrose, did she tell you anything about what happened two weeks ago at the Norman house?"

"She did. But it wasn't for spreadin' around. It was private."

"Did she hear the shot fired?"

"She says she heard shootin'. Tha's all I know. One shot or more, I do' know."

After disconnecting, I called the overseas operator, who got me all the way to Paris without more than a three minute delay. The number BALzac 0182 got me the right hotel, but there was no Violet Bowden registered. I was able to bridge a terrible connection to discover that she had been joined by her husband and that they had left the hotel without leaving a forwarding address.

"When did this happen?" I asked, in a voice not used since telephones needed cranking.

"Why, only this morning, monsieur."

"Have you any idea where they might have gone?"

"But no. He was a well-dressed gentleman who called for her."

"White or black?"

"The gentleman was white. But how does that signify?"

"Did she ever mention the name Zavitz in your hearing? It's important."

"I'm sorry, monsieur, but I must go."

"Are you able to hear the German guns yet?"

"Not yet, monsieur, but I am told we will not be disappointed."

"Will you stay in Paris?"

"I am unable to elongate the conversation further." Between my somewhat rusty French and her English we must have entertained anyone listening in. I thanked the woman in her Paris hotel, half-heaving a sigh for my lost youth spent in those streets close to the river.

A return call to the Bowden house confirmed my guess that there was no obvious white man who might reasonably call upon Violet Bowden in Paris. I tried to picture the woman, with less French than I had, in the company of some studio flunky. I could see her, walking past the show windows of the Grands Boulevards, only to be pushed off the Vert-Galant of the Île de la Cité into the Seine. That thought put me in mind of my old friend and one-time partner in detection: Commissaire Léon Zamaron of the Paris police. Fifteen years ago — was it fifteen? — we worked a case together. The connection took about four or five minutes after

I had the right department. The conversation took place in both English and French.

"I would like to speak with the commissaire, please."

"But I am the commissaire, monsieur."

"Léon? Mon ami? C'est Mike Ward qui te parle. Le Canadien."

"Alas, monsieur, Léon has gone on to retire. He is growing canes for English cricket bats in his country house south of Bergerac. He is well. I see him. We meet. He remains a good friend as well as a former colleague. His wife has opened a little restaurant with one star in Michelin in Castillon. Vaut le voyage, monsieur. When he comes to Montparnasse on a visit to the galleries, it is impossible for him to pay for a drink along the boulevard. He is as much a part of the Quartier as the Dôme or the Closerie des Lilas. I take it you know him well?"

"What I know about police work, I learned from Léon. Does he still have his pictures?"

There was a pause at the other end. Then we continued in English.

"He could hardly have parted with them. Oh, of course, he had to pawn some of them when he was — how do you say, 'fauché'?"

"'Fauché'? Broke, I guess."

"Yes, yes. He was several times broke. His son helps him. He has a good eye like his father, and loves them as much as Léon. The little house in Castellane has walls bright with Utrillo, Soutine, Zadkine, Kisling, and Chagall. But, monsieur, to whom am I speaking?"

I told him about myself, about my professional and personal connection with the retired commissaire, and added some of the details of my present concerns. He took in what I was saying. "Oui, oui. You are the Canadian. Léon spoke of you to me many times. I may have seen you with him in Montparnasse." He told me his name was Gabriel Fournier, and promised to get in touch with me should any facts about the American woman's disappearance come to light. Before I hung up, I warned him that the larger-than-life movie mogul Asa Zavitz might be involved.

"Ah, yes! I know your Asa Zavitz. We met two years ago in connection with the affair of Lady Margaret Reynolds. Yes, I know the man well."

Lady Margaret, a well-heeled English socialite, had been pursuing Blake Foster, the tall, lean star of *An Innocent Abroad* and *Klondike Pursuit*, through the gossip columns of six American and several Continental papers. Pictures of them in a gondola in Venice and boarding a *bateau mouche* were still current. I supposed that Zavitz had flown over to put his three-oh mark on it. As far as I knew, the lady was back in her garden, keeping a velvet rope between herself and her public of sightseers. Poor Blake Foster had been demoted, and was now stuck in a serial at Republic or Monogram.

"Are you there, monsieur?"

"Sorry, Commissaire. What is the French for 'wool-gathering'? I was just reminding myself about Lady Margaret. Asa Zavitz is also an interest of mine, though I haven't met him yet. I am interested in what brought him to your city."

"It is a rigmarole, monsieur. A wealthy widow, a young, inexperienced actor, and his employer who tried to untie the knotted tangles in order for the film to continue shooting."

"I'm listening."

"When the actor became infatuated with the charming Lady Margaret, he left off attending to the film which was being made in Boulogne-Billancourt. There he was bothered by an Italian actress who would not appear on camera unless the temperature on the set was only a few degrees above freezing. There were many days in which no work was done. The young actor met and had a liaison with the recently widowed Lady Margaret. He was a good-looking boy of little experience. Who could blame him? Unfortunately for him the backers of the movie were of a different opinion.

M. Zavitz was sent for, and caught the *Queen Mary* in New York."

"A man of action!"

"Perpend. Do you say that? No matter. I will continue. In order to disengage the young couple, M. Zavitz interposed himself, offering himself as a competitor for the lady's affections. The charms of the handsome but callow young actor did not sustain themselves against the more practical attractions of a highly placed film producer whose attributes included an annual salary of several hundreds of thousand dollars. The lady, never a creature of sentiment, transferred her affections, the boy went back to the chilly sound stages of Boulogne-Billancourt, and all was satisfactorily arranged."

"But how did you come into it?"

"Ah, but that involves confidences I am not free to discuss. For your purposes it may be enough to know that the police, when summoned, put matters back where they had originally rested, with no serious consequences to anyone. Except that it exposed the principal players to the greedy machinations of a blackmailer in London: the infamous Emma Schneller. Emma Schneller, happily, is now in Holloway Prison, where she will remain long enough that the charms, on which she depended, will have somewhat wilted. It's a pity to think of her: diminished."

"A blackmailer!"

"One of the most charming of my acquaintance."

"She sounds like a character out of Sherlock Holmes."

"The talented Mr. Doyle would have found her difficult to imprison in the pages of a short story or a novel. Emma Schneller is in a class by herself. But I ramble on!"

"You intrigue me, my friend."

"And you must sustain yourself in that state until I will be free to take you off — how do you say? — tenterhooks."

"I'll hold my breath. And thanks. Now I must prepare to beard Asa Zavitz someday soon."

"He is a serious man, my friend. Trust him as you would trust a viper. But he is not without humour or courtesy when it works to his advantage."

"What are you doing about the German advance?"

"I do my job by day, and burn papers by night. The Bosch, they give me a nasty rash. I hope they will not stay long. You know, Daladier's government has fallen. And Reynaud is in bed with Marshal Pétain already. We anticipate hearing the sound of German 88s in the east before long. What can I say?"

# CHAPTER FIVE

*I*t was a busy time at the office. I had by now settled in to the rhythm of the routines. The streets still appeared unnaturally sun-drenched and confusing, but I could manoeuvre within the few blocks nearest the agency. I shopped for clothes that wouldn't give me away as a newcomer. Light fabrics, bright colours, and, to top it off, a straw Panama hat. It looked better at Hollywood and Vine than my old fedora. In some ways I was still living out of a suitcase. But things were coming together.

I hadn't taken hold at the office well enough to suit me. Oh, I had the routines fixed in my head, but I was still walking in new shoes. It wasn't that my new broom had cobwebs on it. I was noting the changes I would introduce when I felt more at home. Besides, Endicott liked running things, and I've never been one to come between a man and his pleasures.

"Oh, by the way, Mike," Endicott announced one afternoon, "I haven't had any luck in the Norman story."

"How so?"

"Something fishy. I don't like it. I'm not getting straight answers."

"From the usual sources?"

"Not a word. Plenty on everything else, but nothing touching Norman."

"I thought I was working this story? Who else, besides you, is assigned?" I was surprised to discover that I had a proprietary interest in this routine story.

"I just thought you might — "

"You want me back writing up celebrity polo matches?"

"Mike! Shut up and listen! I've had instructions to lay off the file. It's no longer of interest. Nobody else is still on it. Middle pages, Mike, with the obits and funeral notices. It's yesterday's blister. Forget it."

"You think it was murder?"

"That's a serious leap in the dark. We're not here playing guessing games."

"Forget the wire service for a minute! What do you think? Off the record."

"It's not very likely, but you're not the first to suggest something. Whenever the cops stop talking to us, suspicion begins to itch."

"I'll try to scratch it; see what I can dig up."

"Just as long as it's on your own head. Leave the service out of it. Leave me out of it."

I TOOK A FEW WEEKS to feel out my colleagues. Endicott was my chief worry; the others, Sinclair, Talbot, and the rest, did their jobs and stayed out of my way. I prevailed on a rewrite man named Eric Olson to pull all of our files on the suicide of Mark Norman and place them on my desk. When it came, it was a thick file held together by a green rubber band. Right off the top, I discovered that Mark Norman was born in Kobylka, Poland, in 1901. When I looked it up in the office atlas, I found it just north of Warsaw. The town would be awash with German occupiers today. He began as a puppeteer in the capital, then came to the New World with a troupe from Poland. They bombed in New York. Norman skipped the return voyage, living for a time on the streets of Manhattan, winning eating money at chess in Union Square. Later, he scalped tickets to Broadway shows, living off the proceeds. Soon he was running tins of film around Broadway, and, from Penn Station, to all the movie houses on the Lower East Side. That was his re-introduction to show business. This time, there were no strings attached. Norman was invited off the street by a man who took him into his office and mentored him. Here he learned what there was to be learned about film distribution. At night school he improved his English and picked up accounting. After a year or so, his name began to be known by the people in Hollywood. As a former puppeteer and small-time show business huckster, he loaned a sympathetic ear to the problems of A-Z-P, the studio he knew best.

In 1920 he married for the first time: Norma Fisher. She was a stenographer in the New York office of A-Z-P. Where the New York money people were blind and indifferent to the problems of production in LA, Norman showed some sympathy. For two years, Norman was the go-between between the East Coast and the West. In the end, the people in charge realized that he would be more at home, and less of a threat to New York, if he went west to join his colleagues on the coast. After that, his career was off and running. At home, things went from bad to worse. Norma and Mark had had a daughter who died of infantile paralysis six months before the marriage succumbed to another sort of paralysis.

Skipping to the most recent clippings, I found that a lavish pre-nuptial party for the marriage to Barbara Lorrison had been given by Buddy Whistler, the comedian, at his home. I made a note of the name and searched in Endicott's files for his number. When I called, I got no reply. When I called again later in the day, a servant informed me that Mr. Whistler was golfing and not expected until later in the evening.

I made a note of the name of Norman's first wife, Norma Fisher, and got Olson to see if he could find out what she'd been up to since the marriage broke up. I wondered if she used her married name: Norma Norman. It sounded peculiar. Norman had come a long way from running cans of film on the island of Manhattan. Had his first wife done well for herself? I wanted to know.

The rest of my day was taken up with office matters: a clique of younger people was down on their supervisor. I kept my eye on him over the course of the day to see if there were grounds for their complaints. The supervisor was a good friend of Endicott. I had to watch my step.

In the meantime, there were files to prepare, edit, and transmit. There were letters to write, and a payroll to prepare, because the comptroller was having her appendix removed.

Days went by, diluted by work. I tried to make friends with the city, discovered the complexity of the relationships between the City of Los Angeles proper and the various boroughs that surrounded it. The slow encroachment of the growing city eroded the physical differences. The borders between one jurisdiction and the next were only lines on a map. Each jurisdiction was jealous of its own special independence from the rest of the fiction known as Greater Los Angeles.

I made a few visits, covered some of the tourist sights: art galleries and museums. I explored a little, discovering as I went that there wasn't a good French or Italian restaurant in reach. Since I was eating out rather more than I was dining at home, I got to know the restaurants along Wilshire near the office. In most places, the portions were large, but the fare simple: steak, roast chicken, meatloaf with mashed potatoes and tinned peas. The choice of vegetables was slim, but the soups showed a little more imagination.

One Sunday, I took Endicott's two kids to Laguna Beach, where we wrestled with the surf, watched surfers tackle the big waves farther along, and feasted on toffee apples, Cracker Jack, and ice cream. On the way back, after dropping them off at their house, I started back to my place. The driver was a talkative fellow. He told me about Watts, where he lived.

"You'll have had your fill of the local restaurants, I spec, you comin' from up north. You should try the food where I live. It'll change your mine about this town. You never heard tell o' Watts, I'll bet? Watts is different, like it wasn't part of the USA."

He told me about a place that was reputed to be superior and unique to the area. I wondered whether he was getting a rake-off for every customer he delivered. But I took a chance. He dropped me at a place called The Soul Room, which was the dining room of an all-black hotel. Despite my colour, I was treated to one of the best meals I have ever eaten in public. The next day I returned to the area with a notebook. I saw ragged children sitting in front yards of baked clay. They'd never seen grass. The houses — some of them half-covered with torn tarpaper and held together with rope — looked gaunt and defeated.

I talked to dozens of the locals, who were quite open with me about conditions there: the meagre public services such as trash collection and schooling for the youngsters. I walked through one of the houses; it was as crowded as New York tenements were fifty years ago. When I got back home, I wrote a piece full of my horror and indignation and put it on the wire the next morning.

The result of this prowling around Watts and the casual piece I filed surprised me long after I had forgotten about it. The *Manchester Guardian* gave it space in England. It was reprinted in New York. As a follow-up, *TIME* magazine sent their own man to follow in my footsteps, quoting me in every paragraph. An old mug shot of me stared out of the magazine so that I could hardly face reading what their reporter had said. As a result of this coverage, with my name being bandied about, I became in a short time something of a celebrity in this little world of journalism. My name didn't reach the status of a film star, but head waiters now recognized me; some even called me by name. That was a novelty: not being invisible to waiters. And, although I knew it wouldn't last, that it was a fragile bubble, I was enjoying this fillip of worldly fame. But, as far as I know, no roofers or plumbers were dispatched to Watts; no fresh allotment of teachers or public nurses went forth.

Meanwhile, the regular routine of getting copy on the wire continued. Deadlines plagued us, train and airline schedules kept us hopping. Endicott and I were getting to know one another's working styles. I filed another Watts story. This brought letters to the papers carrying my stuff. I was becoming known as more than a man who announced prematurely that the prime minister was wearing no clothes. I could feel myself, manipulated by the papers and radio news into something we all knew was less than true. I wasn't a crusading journalist, and they all knew it.

WHEN I FORCED MY EYES open the next day, it was the old routine once more, with Endicott beaming a teetotal smile at me. "Here's something for you: a British policeman on holiday fell off the Twentieth Century coming through the mountains. Interested?"

"I'll keep my eye on it. What was his name?"

"Let me see." He rummaged through the papers he'd put on his desk. "Macdonald. Evan Macdonald. I suppose that makes him a Scot."

"So he's not a dead kipper but a dead haggis. Wait a minute! Evan Macdonald! I know him!" And it was true. There can't be two Evan Macdonalds in the London CID. Mine was a tall, lean card player and all-round good sport, who saw me back to number 64 West End Lane whenever I had a drop taken, which was at least once a week.

"What's the matter? Stomach ache? You've gone pale."

"I'll be all right. Let me handle it. Poor bugger."

"Macdonald?"

"Yeah. I'll look it over."

No sooner were the words out than I was suddenly back in my high-school classroom. Miss Ennis was looking down on me with her good eye fixing me to my seat.

"You didn't look it over," she hisses with some delight. "You overlooked it!" And the class howled with delight. Strange, the things news of a sudden death will bring to the surface.

I crossed the street to the diner where Endicott and I had both eaten a dozen lunches. The good restaurants were a couple of blocks away. You could put away a few beers here and still not overstay the normal time.

The waitress gave me a smile of recognition. I looked around the café. The room looked as bleak as a Hopper painting: two salesmen conferring over tuna sandwiches, a skinny woman sitting by herself at the short end of the counter, an old man in a patched tweed jacket counting out silver beside his empty saucer. The old man dropped a coin and got down from his stool to look for it. He didn't find it. The woman smiled at me watching the old man. Next to me I heard: "They shouldn't allow — "

"You said it!" This from a heavyset fellow in a straw hat.

The woman was reading a paperback novel; one of Ellery Queen's mysteries. My second examination of her improved on the first. I liked her smile. True, she was thin, but very well put together.

I ate my poached egg and toast, and worked on the cherry pie with my fork. The bum was still sipping cold coffee, and would probably go on doing so until it was time to retire to an overnight hostel. The fan, high above the counter, kept things cool inside, but it wasn't what they call air-conditioning. It was too cool for the woman at the end. She had wrapped a cardigan sweater around her. The salesmen had been displaced by three young men dressed almost identically, and all talking at once.

"Look, she goes into the store with the cop still chasing her — "

"No! I gotta better idea: she sees the cop, and absently picks up a leather bag — "

"Hey! I've got it! She goes right up to the cop, and tells him that a guy's been chasing her. She points to Cooper, and the cop starts questioning him, still holding on to the girl."

"Great! Coop is innocent, but sees that the girl's in trouble and counting on his help." They went on in this vein, paying no attention to the rest of us.

I paid the tab and began thinking of going back to work. I was in no doubt that Coop and the girl would work it all out at the end of the last reel. I saw Barbara Stanwyck as the girl, but I didn't mention it. Three writers were already too many.

While I'd been watching the writers, the number of diners was reduced by one: the woman left the counter. Shortly afterwards, I heard the door behind me swing shut. Too bad, I thought. It might have been interesting to get to know her better.

Almost at the same moment, as I was taking a last cold sip from my cup, I heard a screech of brakes outside. We all turned to look. I got up and peered through the plate glass. The woman I had been looking at was stretched out in the gutter.

"My God!" the waitress screamed.

With two of the writers, I helped pull her back to the sidewalk.

"I'm all right!" she shouted. "Leave me alone! I'm not hurt."

"She jumped right out in front of me! In the middle of the block, yet!" The driver was sweating and wiping his neck and face with a bandana. His face was colourless. His victim's face was similar, but brushed with dirt as well. She was trying to get up.

"Stay still!" I shouted. "Don't move!" She tried to find my face in the crowd that circled her. She was resting on her elbows.

"She just walked into me. I wasn't speeding. I swear it! She didn't look."

"I'm sorry if I frightened you," she said, looking at the shaken driver. "I'm fine. No bones broken."

"I'm a witness," someone in the crowd called. "I saw it all. I'm a witness."

"Guy like that's a menace!" shouted another.

The skirt of the girl's outfit had been rucked up, showing a bruised knee and a torn stocking. Again she tried to get to her feet.

"Should I call an ambulance?" said a witness wistfully, then repeated the offer in a lower voice. She got no clear response except from the victim herself.

"Don't be silly. I'm all right, I say." She got to her feet, and dusted herself off. There was a tear in the elbow of her cardigan. There was an oil smudge as well.

The crowd, seeing that there was no blood, began to fade away, hopeful that the next unscheduled event would hold their attention a little longer, leaving me, the waitress, and two of the writers in charge of the victim. The expressions on their faces could have inspired wartime sketches by Goya. I picked up a book that was lying beside the woman and then I lent her a hand and arm as she followed me out of the gutter to the curb. She was unsteady and clung to me.

I led her back into the café, where room was made at the counter. "Thanks a lot for your help," she said in an unsteady voice. "But I'm really okay, now." The vocabulary was pure West Coast American, but the voice and accent contradicted this and suggested a wider, richer background. From behind the counter, the waitress put a glass of water in front of the shaking woman. I put the book I had rescued next to it.

"Here's the novel you dropped."

"Thanks."

"I'm afraid it got wet in the street."

"Doesn't matter. It's not as heavy to carry around as *Anthony Adverse*."

"At over twelve hundred pages, I should say not!"

"You've been very, very kind. Thank you." The words were welcome, but her reading of them said: "Shove along now, please. I want to be alone." Everybody today echoes Garbo. I moved a stool away. When she was unable to find a tissue in her handbag to wipe her face with, I offered a clean handkerchief from my breast pocket. She used it, then looked me over once again. "I don't mean to be rude, but I meant it when I said I was all right now." I took the hint, and moved back to my original stool, to drink off the last cold swallow of coffee. The waitress gave me a tentative smile as she refilled my cup.

When at last I got up to go, and the door squeaked shut behind me, I felt a hand on my shoulder. It was the girl in the cardigan. "I didn't mean to be rude back there," she said. "I was upset and feeling vulnerable. I didn't want company just then; not even from a Good Samaritan. I didn't intend to be unkind."

"That's okay," I said. "I'm glad you're feeling better."

"Better than all those other times I've been run over?" We both laughed at that. "I'm still a little shaken. Do you know if there's a good bar around here? I think I need a stiff drink to get me going again." When I looked back where we had just come from, she shook her head. "No, no. I don't want to go back in there. Not today, anyway."

"This town isn't home turf for me, but I haven't found a bar I haven't liked yet. Let's try across the street. Or do you want to stay on this side?"

"I'm up to trying the street again, if you'll lend an arm again. I've seen enough of the gutter for one day. I have one good crossing left in me."

We had a drink. We exchanged names, and forgot them at once, the way one does at a party. Hers might have been Vivien. I gave her my card, with its scribbled recent emendations. She went off down the street in search of new nylons. I returned to the office next door.

That day, I tried to write a piece about what had just happened: how we both shrink from and are attracted to the difficulties of others. Then I turned my exploration of local restaurants to good account by writing up the best of them. It seemed that nobody had thought of turning good eating into an art form before. Not in Los Angeles, at least. First, I filed a piece about my experience as a newcomer. I wrote a few more. The reception of them was good. My former boss in Toronto sent me a wire. It seemed that I was to be forgiven. That alone was enough for a minor celebration. Unfortunately, once begun, it is hard to rein in a celebration.

After the fuss, after the ice packs, my breath smelling of raw egg and Tabasco, I tried to return to a simple honest day's labour. I tried to find the bookmark I had inserted into my career, and go back to work. I looked up the note I'd made about the comic actor who'd given a party for Mark Norman a day or two before his death. I called Whistler's number again.

"Look, April, I told you a million times —"

"Mr. Whistler?"

"Yeah, that's who I am, and thanks. But who are you? That is the question. I was expecting a call, and this ain't it."

I provided the details about my profession, nationality, and, when asked, my gender, to which he replied that he hated talking to secretaries and flunkies. I told him I was interested in whatever light he could shed on Mark Norman's state of mind on the night of the big party.

"Hell, fellah, I was flat on my back most of the night. They only got me out of my bed when the place was running dry." Again I told him.

"Look, my friend, Mark was his usual bilious self all night. He took no prisoners, and, for once, dispensed with the usual stories about Errol Flynn's after-dark romps in my lady's chamber. You should talk to Jack. He and Jack had their heads together most of the night. As long as either of them was standing. Talk to Jack. He'll tell you. If he remembers."

"Jack? Which Jack?"

"Jack, you know. The face. The profile. Jack, you know? I mean Jack Barrymore. He's the fellow. Talk to him."

I thanked Whistler and wondered how deeply I intended to crawl into Wonderland. Was there a light at the nearest exit? Was I going to get out of this day without changing into fancy dress? John Barrymore, indeed! How can you talk to a legend?

## CHAPTER SIX

*I* found myself in a taxi, driving through the still-unfamiliar landscapes of Los Angeles. Whether it was Hollywood proper, Bel Air, or some other suburb, I never did discover. All I can report is that the houses were large, extravagant, and nestled into the rising hillside. They aped every age and architectural style known to man: a Georgian villa was nestled cheek-by-jowl next door to an Elizabethan half-timbered mansion, and stood across the street from a wild Bauhaus concoction. There may have been some Persian villas and Etruscan tombs as well. All were built on a large scale, and showed off garages for two or more cars. I counted a Rolls and two Duesenbergs, but no Dodges, Fords, or Chevrolets.

"Here it is!" the driver announced, as he made out a chit for me. "The house of the celebrated John Barrymore, the Great Profile. It's a huge palace of a place, used to belong to King Vidor, you know, the movie director. Remember *The Big Parade*, *Stella Dallas*, and *Our Daily Bread*?"

"You know your movies."

"We're in a movie town. There's nothing going on here but pictures, mister."

"It looks like King Vidor lived well."

"Drove him home lots of times. He always gave me a swell tip. But he sold the spread to that New Yorker, Barrymore. You know, the Great — "

"Profile. I know."

"He's a regular on the Rudy Vallee program, Thursday nights."

I opened the back door of the car, and began to get out. "Hey! Where do you think you're going?"

"To see Barrymore. Where else?"

"What kind of sightseer are you? It's not open house, you know. They have tours for things like that, but this place ain't on the list."

"I'm not a tourist, driver. I have business and an appointment."

"Look, if you really want to see him, you gotta go see John Decker, the painter, down the hill."

"You mean I need a visa to get in?"

The driver shook his head as though I were purposely misunderstanding him. "The actor doesn't live here anymore. He ain't been in Tower Road for ages. But everybody wants to see his house, the three swimming pools and all the imported trees. Some people even steal the trees."

"I see. I see." I felt like Jack Benny, in one of his dimmer moments.

"You wanna see him, like I said, you gotta go down the hill to Decker's studio. Bundy Drive. That's where he spends his time these last few months."

"Are you writing his biography?"

"Look, a hack driver learns a lot in a week of driving in this town. Me? I'm from Hackensack, but my wife, she — you don't want to hear this. You wanna see Gloria Swanson's place? Well, she isn't living there either. Trust me."

I got back into the taxi and we drove for ten minutes more. "Here we are!" announced the driver. I thanked him for this background, and gave him a tip that probably didn't compare to any King Vidor ever left him.

Hobart, the man who answered the door in his shirt sleeves, told me that the "Monster" was in the studio. I wasn't used to houses with studios. I once interviewed a politician in his bathtub, and a ballerina in her bathtub, but I had managed to escape studio encounters with both sexes. I followed Hobart through several dim corridors. The woodwork was darkly stained, the walls were off-white and studded with unframed canvases.

The Monster sat in a large, regal chair with a high, leather-covered back. It had served as a throne in one ill-fated production of Macbeth back in the thirties, Hobart informed me. The chair was raised on a dais, where the painter of his portrait could get a better look at him. Below stood the biggest easel I'd ever seen outside of a movie. Instead of a pallet of colours, the artist was using the whole of a tabletop next to his easel for his pigments. All of the paint tubes looked to be uncapped, and were oozing.

It was with Henry Hobart that I'd made the appointment to interview the former matinee idol. Hobart poured me a drink before I'd adjusted to the light in this dim, cavernous chamber. A canvas curtain monitored what light seeped through the big north window. All the room needed was a court jester and a few suits of armour to make me believe that I'd been transported back in time to the Middle Ages. There were enough swords and spears hanging on the wall to arm a regiment.

"Jack likes this place," he said, watching my eyes travel along the walls. "It reminds him of home. I mean Tower Road, the place he had to give up."

"I don't think I can see well enough in here to make notes."

"Decker likes it this way when he's not working. What can I say? He even likes to cook in semi-darkness. When he's not throwing a fit, he's a lot of fun," Hobart said, watching me probe the gloom. "There's something half-medieval about both of them. It took me a long time to catch on to it. Here."

I took the drink, and sipped it with my eyes divided between the body on the throne and the hammer-beam, pre-Elizabethan look of the studio: high ceilings, dark wooden beams, yellowing plaster, with light cane chairs, discards from a down-at-the-heel Nairobi safari outfitter, no doubt. In the gloom hung a half-finished portrait of Barrymore, begun in happier times.

"The place up on Tower Road used to belong to the director, King Vidor. You remember his movie, *The Crowd*," Hobart said.

"Did he do *The Citadel* a year or two ago?"

"Is that the one about doctors? I forget. Anyway, that's where he lived. Garbo came there. So did most of the foreign crowd — Peter Lorre, Victor Seastrom, Brecht."

"Are you a writer, by any chance?"

"I've gotta script in my trunk. Are you anybody?"

"No. I just got here."

"I heard that when Barrymore had Tower Road decorated, he stopped the workmen from using T-squares, rulers, spirit levels and so forth. He tried to eliminate the right angles. He should have been a monk. He'd have liked that."

"You know him pretty well."

"Oh, I've been with him over a year. I came to do his books. Now I do the lot!" Hobart smiled as he sipped from his own glass.

"*Macbeth* was a few seasons ago, wasn't it? Nineteen-thirty-one or -two?"

"He never played it. He wanted to, thought about it a lot, even worked out his makeup. But, he didn't get around to it. Even made a putty nose modelled after Sam Harris's distinctive beak. Harris was not amused. You've heard of Harris? The big Broadway producer?" I shook my head. "Maybe you're thinking of his *Richard III*?

That was one of his triumphs. A bit before my time, but people in the theatre still talk about it."

"But that was earlier, wasn't it?"

"*Richard* opened in 1920. That's the sword he used in it on the wall over there. I can hardly lift it. *Hamlet* was in 1922. *Hamlet* made him and it ruined him. He could never get away from the role. Whatever he played, people saw him staring down at poor Yorick's skull and fencing with what's-his-name: Laertes. Jack's always asked to do 'To be, or not to be' in the movies or on radio. He did it for the Shriners a couple of weeks ago."

"How long will he stay like that? In the chair, sleeping?"

"You never can tell with him. He might stay like that until the sun goes down, or, again, he might be listening to everything we're saying." That gave me a start. But his eyes remained closed. A collapsed, heavyset man of middle age, he could have been made of wax, except for the occasional raspy intake of air. I think I saw a rash of some kind on his chest. Eczema? I tried to balance the picture of Barrymore, healthy, athletic, and riveting, with the wreck snorting in his sleep in front of me. "Would you join me in another drink? You might be in for a long wait."

"Sure," I said. "Rye this time, if you have it."

"Coming right up." Hobart went to a chest of drawers with Chinese decorations and removed two bottles. He poured generously and shut the drawer carefully after him, locking it.

Hobart was a stocky man, with a barrel chest. His smile had a professional look to it, but he wasn't stingy with his boss's booze. "Here's mud!" he said, waving his glass at me. I tilted mine as well, first to him and then at the body in the chair.

Sometime later — I'm not exactly sure what time it was, I seemed to have forgotten I was wearing a wristwatch — I looked up at the Monster. "He's drooling," I said.

Hobart looked over at Barrymore.

"Does that mean anything?"

"With Jack, it's hard to tell. He might be off in dodo land and he might start quoting Milton or Spenser. He's only been home a couple of days, and he didn't sleep much on the Twentieth Century. *My Dear Children* closed just over a week ago in New York. He's tired out."

"Can't find my cigarettes." The voice filled the room. I think I'd dozed off. I probed my pockets for cigarettes, but when I looked up Hobart was out of sight. "What time is it?" The voice rattled the china. "It's time to burn some sack!" This came from the chair with the actor in it. The eyes were still closed and the body had not moved. I looked over at the suddenly returned figure of Hobart, discovered standing in the doorway. He shrugged. A sudden inspiration turned my eye to my wrist.

"It's ten!" I said, and added: "At night."

"It usually is," said Hobart, with a wry grin.

"How long have you been here? I asked you that already. Sorry."

"Not long. The job's added years. I started out to be a theatrical agent, but I got sidetracked. I think I arrived as a barber, but I've become a general factotum. I empty slops, lug the Monster up the stairs, write letters, pay bills, and answer the telephone. I'm a part-time barber as well. Call me Figaro."

"Don't you find this place a little creepy? It's so dark in here. Hasn't Mr. Decker heard about Thomas A. Edison's incandescent light bulb?"

"It's his house. He likes it this way. That's the humour of it. As a painter, he's married to natural light, but he doesn't want to waste his sensitivity. He rations light."

"Angels and ministers of grace defend me!" bellowed the Monster. I dropped my glass. "As Bernard Shaw always says, with his usual happy perspicacity, 'You never can tell.' Now, pray, who the devil are you?" The eyes were closed. The velvet voice lingered. I looked around me: there were only the three of us.

"Jack!" Hobart called. "Jack, we have company!"

"Send it packing! I'm not at home. We are not receiving."

Hobart looked at me with some embarrassment, and tried again. The same dialogue was repeated, more or less. The body on the chair was not at all vague. It resounded with the full diapason of the language of Shakespeare, Marlowe, and Byron, with a little Hawthorne, Whitman, and Poe thrown in. I held my ground. I needed to talk to the Monster. An eye opened. A round, dark eye that pinned me to the wall. The second eye, when it joined its fellow, sent a harpoon through my vitals. The rest of the actor hadn't budged. "Who in the name of Milton's Hell are you?" Hobart made the introduction, reminding the actor that he had agreed to give me an interview.

"Hoist am I with my own petard. And they don't make petards like they used to."

The body shifted in the chair. He grasped the ornate arms, transforming himself into a displeased monarch whose throne I was threatening. "What's your name once more? My memory has developed a slow leak. At times, it gushes out into the stratosphere all the proper nouns I used to know. I dwell here below with the lower case."

I repeated my name, and told him the name of the wire service. He repeated it and, at last, blinked his eyes. He darted a glance at Hobart, then fixed me again to the wall. Hobart winked at me, grinned, and quietly left us alone.

John, the baby of the Barrymore family, was a mess. His face had lost its sharp outlines. He was fat, blotchy, unhealthy, and unwashed. Only his eyes burned. "Damn it all to hell, I shouldn't be talking to you," he barked. He sounded like his brother, Lionel.

"Why not?"

"One way and another, I've had a bellyful of bad press. Whatever your honourable intentions, I always end up slaughtered and flayed. Hanged, drawn, and quartered for the delectation of

Mr. and Mrs. America and all those ships at sea. I'm garbage wrap to the general public. Garlic and cheap, imitation sapphires."

"We're not all like that. But your offstage shenanigans didn't help. Some of us, Mr. Barrymore, have even read T.S. Eliot. I haven't flayed anybody in days. And, for your information, I haven't yet started eating my young."

"Very good! Very state-of-the-art! On your dignity, 'Damn the torpedoes!' and 'It is a far, far better thing I do —' You'll learn about eating your young. If they don't eat you first. Stand in profile next time with your head turned to the light. Lots of room for growth. There's a process of oxidation going around: it's the rust of cynicism, the corruption of boredom. If you're free of it now, it'll catch up with you. Oh, yes."

"That's sheep dip, and you know it!"

"I beg your pardon." He lowered his head in a courtly bow. "You're a weigher of words, I see. Words are the false coinage of ideas. Merely guidelines to direct the mind to better precision."

"It still ends up with words. In both of our professions, we live by them."

"Who the hell are you? Who let you in? Not an interviewer, I pray? Do you always abridge a man's siestas? Most members of the fourth estate are charlatans. Are you of their number? If so, quit this ground."

Although he scarcely moved a muscle, he seemed to be strutting. Was he trying to scare me off?

"Void the field, sirrah! You do offend our sight! Scarper! Scram!"

"The butcher at home in Toronto serves up better ham at the end of a busy Saturday!"

Although his face seemed to be melting before my eyes, his speech was clear and well under control. The rest of his body hadn't moved; it was slack, but not relaxed. There was still a trace of the poised panther about him, a somewhat rusty spring. I told him that, although I was new to the West, I had climbed out of my rompers some time ago. A little angrier than I expected, I told the actor that I'd made good friends over the years in London, Moscow, and Paris without compromising either my profession or my friendships.

As I turned to go, already somewhat chagrined at the vehemence of my explosion, he called me back.

"Peace! Peace! Smooth your wrinkled brow. Stand down! Desist! Put up your arms! Pardon, sir, my sore distraction."

"I want to talk to you about Mark Norman."

"Get it right! 'The late Mark Norman.' May flights of sugar plum fairies waft him to his rest. Hotchener!" he shouted offstage. "Let's have a drink. Where the hell did you come from? Your manners are not calculated to win friends and influence people."

"Go to hell! My manners!"

"That's a start. I take it, then, that you are not native to this ground?"

His brief quotations were electric. There was a stinging rasp to them. Although he had hardly moved a muscle, I had the ghost of the thrill that used to electrify audiences in New York and London.

While Barrymore was more famed for dishing out words, he proved to be a credible listener. I told him about Toronto, Ontario, Canada, about my time in Paris and points east. He liked the Paris part best. When I tried to introduce Mark Norman's name again, he waved me to silence.

Holding me with an arm around my shoulders and a finger to his lips, he whispered: "Not a word! Shhhh! Make no noise. Make no noise. Not a word! Draw the curtains. We are mutes and acolytes, sages and druids. Peace!"

We were suddenly in the storm scene from *King Lear*, sheltering from the storm. Then, suddenly, he straightened up, throwing a curious look at my kneeling figure, and said brightly:

"So you know Hemingway! Amazing! He invited me to go to

Africa with him. But I never could tell the kudu from the Kikuyu. I never shot anything all my life, save a friendly game of pool in a good cause. I knew all of his wives; liked the first best. Ah, had I but time, I could a tale unfold. I'll bet you never saw him pay for a drink?"

"Nowadays his wife holds on to his money."

"Which wife is that? I can't keep up. I think I set him a bad example. I'm the original of Peck's Bad Boy."

"From what I read about you in our morgue files, your marriages were never social-climbing excursions. His always are. Still, you can't help liking that lopsided grin of his."

"I used that smile on Lady Anne, when I was wooing her in *Richard III*. Can you remember where Hotchener hid the rye?" He rolled his eyes, probing the corners of the room.

"Who's Hotchener?"

"My man Friday. Old family retainer. Makes my dinner, wipes my chin, and drinks my liquor, the frugal swain."

"Says his name's Hobart."

"That's what I said: Hobart. Hotchener was years ago. He held me together whenever I suffered a bus accident."

"You've had a few?"

"My disastrous marriages were all bus accidents. I'm a quasi-recovering victim."

He took a deep breath and scratched his chest through his sweaty shirt. Then he pinned me again with his eye as though he'd learned the trick from Coleridge's ancient mariner.

"So, you were a pal of Hemingway? His stories still hold up. They're swell. Knock the spots off the writers in this den of thieves. At Metro, they pay a fellow to vet scripts of fine writing or high art. Hemingway used to be a decent sort of scribbler. When young, he was a good listener. I don't suppose he is nowadays. Sam Hammett says he never stops talking. He likes a captive audience. They call him 'Papa.'"

"I haven't seen him in twenty years."

"He's a swell guy when he wants to be. Smart enough to stay clear of this place."

"Last year was a great year for the movies: *Stagecoach, The Wizard of Oz, Gone with the Wind.*"

"I heard that Selznick had publicly broken wind. He suffers from gas, you know."

"Very profitably."

"The big premiere in Atlanta excluded all the coloured players. And Selznick went along with that. Not a whisper of protest."

"Los Angeles is a Southern town, I guess."

"On the set, they tried to mark the bathrooms 'white' and 'coloured,' but the cast and crew made them take the signs down. Selznick's monumental amateurism united the crew solidly against whatever he threw at them next. There never was a final shooting script, you know; just loose pages of various colours. Sometimes the lines were changed. Big speeches, after the cast was on the set."

"You seem to know a lot about it."

"I'm cursed with a good memory, except when I'm near a sound stage. I keep informed, Mr. Ward. I'm an encyclopedia of train times and tide tables. I read the modern poets, as you've observed. Tom Mitchell, good chap, gave me notes almost daily about Selznick's public fart. My daily gazette. Under those great eyebrows, he keeps his eyes open. The confusion among the cast was so dramatic, it broke down the colour bar. Did I tell you that?"

"And I thought you were a recluse," I said.

"I'm only a semi-recluse. I see the New York and London papers. I can also reel off the names of the English kings from William the Conqueror on down to the present. But don't quiz me about the binomial theorem. Are you, by any chance, pouring libations?" He looked at me with hope and managed, with a little help from me, to climb down from the rostrum he'd been perched upon. He sat down in another throne-like armchair.

I freshened both our drinks. The actor's eyes were rolling around the walls again. "I like this place, Decker's studio. Except for the sunlight coming through that damned north window. I was an artist once. Couldn't stick the poverty. Succumbed at last to the family trade. These walls remind me of home. Up the hill, I mean, old fellow, not Baltimore. I think about Mum Mum a lot these days."

"Mum Mum?" The actor was drifting off again. I could feel him losing contact with me. I repeated the question.

"My grandmother, Louisa Lane Drew. She played *Hamlet* in Baltimore and New York before I was hatched. Used to call me Greengoose. My sister still does." He found a secret reverie and lost himself in it for a minute; at the same time, he was rubbing his buttocks back and forth across his throne, like a two-year-old.

"Are you all right?" I asked.

"If you must know, old fellow, the petals of my fundament are in disarray. I thank you for your solicitude." I thought it best to change the subject.

"I heard that you know some of the characters involved in the death of Mark Norman?"

"I know them. I've been out here a long time. No remission for bad behaviour. I knew them all. From Adolf to Zukor. The Brown Derby was modelled on A.I. Smith's hat. What's on your fiendish mind? I smell a device!"

"I'm looking into the story, heard you were at a party with Norman just before it happened. His death, I mean."

"Wedding reception. The fresh-baked nuptial sweetmeats of the wedding buffet did coldly furnish forth the funeral buffet. I fell asleep on a couch. I do that. In fact I'm a well-known couch tester. I've won cups and plaques at it."

"You were asleep then?"

"So it is given out."

"You heard something?"

At this moment, Barrymore's man Hobart broke in. "We have visitors, Jack! Are you finished here?"

Jack looked Hobart in the eye with that barbed stare of his, took a breath, and shouted: "Shall we prepare to repel the boarders or should we have them in? They may know more about this matter than either of us."

I took in a deep breath, counted to ten, and acquiesced to what I was in no position to alter. Barrymore leaned across the gap separating us, grinned at me, and then replenished my glass.

# CHAPTER SEVEN

*E*ight or nine men crowded into the room. They supported so much animation that I quite inaccurately exaggerated their numbers. Barrymore raised his arms in a gesture of welcome. "Stand not upon the order of coming, but come in at once!" he cried. The first to burst free of the scrum was introduced as John Decker. This was his dark-beamed studio.

"Jack, sorry I wasn't here when you woke up. Are you feeling any better? We did a lot of damage to my cellar last night." He said this last with a glance at me.

"You, as usual, exaggerate, old fellow. Think of all those poor lobsters; they never had a chance. I wish I had a photo of you chasing the big one with your rolling pin. I'll brain Laertes with a rolling pin in Hollywood Bowl, or even better, the D.W. Griffith Amphitheatre, next summer." He mimed a preview to the event before adding: "Want you to meet an Australian member of the working press: Wilfred Bumstead."

"How do you do, Mr. Bumstead? I follow your adventures in the funny papers. You would have enjoyed the lobsters. There might still be one of them around here somewhere."

"Actually, my name's Ward. Mike Ward, and I'm not Australian, only Canadian."

"Why aren't you in the army? Aren't you at war up there?"

"They say I'm too old. All I can do is knit socks for our boys overseas."

Looking at the door — I almost said "laying siege to it," as that's how it felt — I saw the second figure push through the crowd. I recognized his face. It belonged to the father of Scarlett O'Hara. He was Gerald O'Hara. I couldn't at that moment recall his real name. In the movie, he kept reminding his daughter that nothing on earth mattered more than land, the "red earth of Tara." I heard the line echo in my head in an Irish voice. The actor was carrying a newspaper and a bag with two bottles inside. I could hear the unmistakable rattle of glass on glass. He held the bag aloft, looking at Barrymore through his shaggy eyebrows. There were two or three others, but I didn't get their names until later in the evening.

"What ho!" the actor cried. Barrymore nodded sagely, while the newcomer stooped to kiss the hand of the Monster reverently.

"You come from the halls of Montezuma?" Barrymore asked. "Or perhaps from the shores of Tripoli? This, Larkin, is Tommy Mitchell, a bloody fine thespian."

"You lie, sir! I'm a happily married man!"

"We arrived on a thunderbolt from beyond Jupiter," added another voice slowly approaching the rostrum. I didn't recognize him. But the face, just behind him, with a lantern jaw distorted in a grin, was an actor I recognized but whose name I couldn't find in my head. Hobart, who was standing alee of my shoulder, whispered: "John Carradine," and at once I recognized the itinerant lay preacher from *The Grapes of Wrath*. Casy! That was his name.

"And the other fellow?"

"Gene Fowler. Jack's biographer."

"Salaam, O great one!" Fowler said with a deep bow to Barrymore.

"And peace be unto you too, O Prophet, who brings banned books from small Paris presses. Girodias was our saviour and you are his prophet."

"And loss: you haven't paid me for *Ulysses*! Damn it all, Jack, your copy went through customs in a lady's drawers. But it wasn't Girodias this time. The publisher was a sweet bookseller on the Rue de l'Odéon named Sylvia Beach. Runs a wonderfully dusty little shop on the Left Bank."

"You are all welcome to this godawful mess I call home. If that's Jake with you, landlord? And you, my long Lazarean friend, what's ailing you?"

He was looking at Carradine, who shot back at him, "Have you never heard of the Saarland? Czechoslovakia? Poland? There won't be any naughty books from Paris for a while. They're bleeding over there! Hitler's only miles from Paris! Damnation!"

"Steady on, John. The Brits and French should have had more guns and less butter. The Maginot Line closed on opening night. But the US Cavalry will save them in the last reel. You'll see."

"I'd give my shirt to be over there right now," I heard myself saying. Some of the others nodded.

Barrymore again fixed his eye on his host. Decker grinned, then went to a cupboard to retrieve several bottles, which he placed within easy reach of the multitude. And the multitude now ringed the former toast of Broadway.

"I bear Canada no malice," said Scarlett's father: "I have been devoted to rye whisky for most of a lifetime."

"I make none of it myself, you understand," I confessed, wryly, I hoped. "But I'll pass the word up the pike."

"You are forgiven, my friend. Think nothing of it." Now he turned to Barrymore. "Jack, are you okay? I heard whispers at MGM."

Gene Fowler uttered the muffled cough of a mid-list writer.

"I defy augury, old fellow. I am prepared to donate my living organs, my very liver and lights, to anyone with a four-quart basket and transportation. The sun found me today in fine fettle." Here Barrymore touched the top of Decker's head, for luck. "I know not fettles of any other sort. And I say fit to spite Fowler, here. As long as I'm on this side of the grass, Fowler can't publish his magnum opus."

John Carradine sat down on the floor at Barrymore's feet, wrapped one long leg around the other, a court jester, the Fool at the foot of Lear. And there he stayed, face turned up, while I lost track of the conversation. The shy other visitors now moved forward to touch the hem of the great man, while I went to find a bathroom. On my return, the group began to get to its feet and talk of foraging abroad for food.

"I've had too much to drink," said Decker. "And the sweetbreads won't stretch to feed this lot. We'll have to go out. I'll burn the studio down if I have to cook tonight."

"He refuses to repeat his trick with the loaves and fishes. Well, we know when to leave." This, from Fowler, with a sigh.

Twenty minutes later, eight of us voided two taxis and made our way into a small Italian restaurant, with a sheet of cardboard covering a smashed front window. Shattered glass covered the steps leading down to the front door. Inside, things were dim, but cheerful: Chianti bottles with candles and a chubby waitress holding the gigantic menus. "Signor Barrymore! Oh, signor, I'm so glad to see you. Here! Take this table. The best in the house. For you and your friends. I will tell my husband you are here. He will be so happy."

"My dear Maria, I hope we've not come too late?"

"For you, signor, we stay open all night. You bring much honour to our little ristorante."

Barrymore spoke to her in Italian for a moment before we were all seated.

"I didn't know you spoke Italian, Jack," said Mitchell, looking up at Barrymore through his heavy eyebrows.

"Calabrian, Tom. A southern cousin of Italian. She says that vandals broke her window tonight. Graziano called the cops, but they still haven't arrived. The war, my friends, is creeping closer."

"Marching in big polished boots, you mean."

"Are you saying the broken window is some kind of war protest?"

"Look at her face. It happened because she's Italian and Italy's in Hitler's pocket."

"But the war's over there!"

"Wars aren't over there anymore. We'll have to get used to that," Jack said in a low voice.

The sawdust-covered floor was scattered with plain wooden tables, over which were draped red-and-white-checkered tablecloths. The Chianti bottles, doubling as candle holders, made it perfect. The room was not crowded: only a handful of late diners were scattered through the two-level room. As soon as we were seated, I made another attempt to catch the names of the still-unidentified members of our happy throng. They turned out to be Frank Craven and Jimmy Flagg. Much later on, I learned that the latter was the well-known painter James Montgomery Flagg. But, at the table, he hardly opened his mouth. Craven was a well-known Broadway actor. I saw him play the Stage Manager in Thornton Wilder's *Our Town* when I came through New York.

Soon a straw-wrapped bottle of Chianti was on the table while a much-needed second was being uncorked. When another party of six or eight came down the stairs into the candlelit room, Barrymore pulled a putty nose out of his pocket and covered his well-known proboscis, making him look more like Cyrano de Bergerac than the Great Profile. The others looked at one another, smiling. They had seen this trick of his before.

"This, Mr. Balentine," he said in a whisper, looking me in the eye, "is my way of sidestepping autograph hunters. This nose of mine, which once belonged to Coquelin, has saved me from autograph collectors and their greasy notebooks and pieces of cardboard since my Uncle Jack Drew showed me the good of it. As my friend Amanda Prynne always says: 'Autograph hunters never see a play, they're not indoors long enough.'"

But, in spite of his disguise, a woman separated herself from her friends and walked to our table. It wasn't a long walk, but I enjoyed watching her approach with a keen appreciation of this lovely piece of Eve's flesh. She leaned over to plant a big kiss on the undefended cheek of Tom Mitchell. The actor blushed.

"Hello, there, Tommy. Don't get up. Remember me? Virginia Hill."

The men at our table all got to their feet at the cue "Don't get up." And there we stood sharing an embarrassment that included me. Virginia Hill's voice had a musical hint of the South in it.

"We met at a party at my place in the spring. Before the fire engines came. What were we celebrating?"

Virginia Hill was an extremely attractive woman. To call her beautiful sells her short. She might have been in her early thirties. She held herself in a way that made it plainly clear that she was fully aware of the effect she had on men. Her smile was not that of a coquette, but it was not altogether without suggestion. The fur on her shoulders looked like mink.

As he was sitting down again, Tom Mitchell introduced us all, but called Jack Barrymore "my friend Stanislaus Pretorius." Barrymore took her hand and replied in a heavy Eastern European accent: "Charming! So glad."

"You can't fool me, Jack. It didn't work the last time, either. I know you too well."

Barrymore bowed. "As Mr. Interlocutor in the minstrel show always says, 'Gentlemen, be seated.'"

"A failure to convince deserves a bad notice. She's nailed me, dead to rights. I feel as caught out as an unpaid madam at the door counting Confederate bills. You've netted a half-pickled herring. My beloved last duchess, please join us," he said, with a good deal of expression in his reading of the line.

"I can only stay a minute. Benny doesn't like me to stray too far or too long."

"You require a longer rein, my dear. Can't Bugsy afford one?"

"I can pay for my own neckwear; I get it at Cartier."

As she was speaking, a good-looking man in need of a shave crossed the floor to stand by her elbow. "Everything all right over here, Toots?"

"Sure, Benny, sure. These are old friends."

"Charmed, I'm sure," Benny said without looking at any of us. "C'mon, kid, we gotta get moving." Without acknowledging us, he returned from whence he came. He wasn't being rude on purpose. He was either preoccupied or shy.

"Don't mind Benny. He's got a lot on his mind."

From across the floor Benny shouted, "Toots. Come on!"

"You're not the sort of woman to be ordered like a second cup of coffee. Sit down."

"Sorry, fellows, but I've got Murder, Incorporated, over there. It might not be smart to dump them just at present." She showed an attractive smile taking in all of our faces, before returning to her table.

"Who do you think she was calling 'Murder, Incorporated'?" I asked naively.

"She wasn't making a joke. That is Murder, Incorporated. There's Bugsy Siegel, Meyer Lansky, Joe Adonis, Kid Twist, and Joe Epstein sitting there. I don't recognize the heavyset guy at the far end of the table. Sometimes they get called the Syndicate, because they approach crime as a business. We are privileged to witness a meeting of the board of directors." All our heads swivelled around to see.

"I've read about some of them. Which one is Epstein?"

"The one with the thick glasses and big nose. Losing his hair."

"Bugsy is better-looking, but has all the social graces of a chamber pot. He's the best of them," Tom said.

"I wouldn't give him my old truss," Barrymore added.

"If that's Murder, Incorporated, what's Virginia Hill doing with them?"

"She's Siegel's special friend, Muldoon," replied Barrymore. "But she's more than a pretty face. She has more little grey cells in her head than all the rest of them put together."

"And the guy who came to collect her? Was that Bugsy Siegel?" I turned in my seat again to test the reality of the scene in front of me.

"He's Lansky's protégé, Toogood," Jack — I now thought of him as Jack — fired back at me. "Don't call him Bugsy to his face. He might be forced to chastise you for it."

"Virginia's the mob's favourite bag-doll. She takes cash to Mexico City and brings back drugs. She's very clever."

"Beauty plus utility: a rare combination," contributed the long-jawed John Carradine, glancing back at Virginia Hill. "Looking at her brings out the missionary in me."

"You've played that role."

"I wonder what they know about the death of Mark Norman?" I was thinking out loud.

"That might be the only crime they could talk about without compromising themselves," said Mitchell with just a trace of the Irish in his voice. "What's your interest in the death of a movie mogul, Ward?"

"This is a new town for me. I'm trying to break myself in. I haven't had time to find out how California feels about President Roosevelt running for another term. So, I took this case on as an easy-to-report, run-of-the-mill murder. I'm not ready to tackle the question of whether or not the US should enter the war."

"It's bad luck for our friend Sadakichi Hartmann, if we go into the war. He has the misfortune of having a German father and a Japanese mother. If the Japs line up with the Axis, Hartmann will be interned as an enemy alien. Twice an enemy alien! And he doesn't much like locks."

"I have no way of knowing whether a threat exists from the west of here."

"The on-again-off-again Russians will never take us on! But they wouldn't welcome a scrap at both front and back doors."

"The Germans gave them half of Poland. What more do they want?"

"I wasn't talking of Russia."

I was going to peep into the threat posed by Japan, but the conversation had taken a new turn by the time I was ready to make my presentation.

"His wife was more than a blonde Venus. Lorrison's not that bright, but she knows what she can do with her slim margin of talent." The others looked at Carradine.

"Since when are you the arbiter of talent?" Carradine was caught in a barrage of looks. Barrymore's familiar barbed eye had competition this time.

"Gentlemen, gentlemen, I was only trying to be precise. She's a movie actress. People come to see her. I'm not kicking at that. She was great in her last picture. But, gentlemen, Sarah Bernhardt has not been reborn in her. Nor is she Jeanne Eagels, Maude Adams, Pauline Lord, Jane Cowl, Katharine Cornell, or Lynn Fontanne."

"A pretty speech, showing off your prodigious memory again. Making fun of the fact that I can no longer remember the names of the people at this table. Out, strumpet! The thing, you pimps for Melpomene and Euterpe, is this: the movies are theatre just as much as what's happening around Shubert Alley. It doesn't begin and end when the house lights lower on 42nd Street. You purists — and you should know better — are wearing blinkers. Theatre is where you find it. Broadway and the West End have no exclusive licence. Theatre includes the big top and flea circuses, tent shows, and vaudeville. It includes 12th Street, the Congress in Chicago, the Old Vic, and, yes, it includes Hollywood. In fifty years they'll be teaching the movies in colleges all over the world, because what we're doing here is art the way *Phaedra* is art, the way *Lear* and *Hamlet* are. Don't listen to the naysayers.

"It's the same toffee-nosed crowd that begged me to close *Hamlet* at a hundred performances so I wouldn't eclipse Booth! Booth would have split his spleen laughing at the idea. Now they come begging me to return to my true home, the Great White Way. Bollocks to that! Purists make me retch. They would have had Shakespeare and Marlowe stand aside for the tumblers and fire-eaters. They all have their legitimate place in the sun, but it doesn't belong to any of them exclusively. Sure, we turn out a lot of useless rubble in a year: but so do gold mines. Give us a break, chaps. Give us a break. There: that's my rant for the evening. The next show is TBA."

The effect of the speech could be read on each of our faces. Nobody challenged Jack, who emptied his glass and went on to mine. The only comment came from Frank Craven, who had earlier not opened his mouth: "Jack and I got to know the bars around Broadway back in the Twenties. No! Before the Twenties. It was hard work then, just as it is here." That got a laugh, and Jack subsided into his chair as though he was exhausting the remaining air in his lungs.

Craven looked at the group. "Jack, you're a man after your own heart."

He spoke with the authority of Thornton Wilder's Stage Manager. Just the same, Jack looked like he was drifting off to sleep again.

By now, I was feeling restless. I get that way when I stray too far from my job. I still had Mark Norman on my mind.

"I think I'll go over and have a word with Virginia Hill," I heard myself saying.

"Don't be a moron. They'll feed you to the dogs," Tommy said, and a few of the others agreed.

"They can't kill me for trying."

"You wanna bet?" replied Carradine. To emphasize the point he was making, he drew a long finger across his Adam's apple. "They can kill you for clearing your throat."

"Be a good chap and leave your money on the table," Jack suggested with raised eyebrows and a blander-than-bland expression. "Just in case."

I got up. The squeak of my chair resounded through the restaurant. I crossed over and stood by Siegel's chair until the punchline of a joke had been fully savoured. Then I cut in: "Excuse me, gentlemen, for interrupting —"

"'Gentlemen'? Who the hell are you kidding? Take a hike, pilgrim!" I didn't know the name of the speaker, but he turned half-around in his chair, gazing up at me. It wasn't a comfortable feeling. Virginia Hill's was the only face smiling. The rest looked like a looming summer squall.

"Take it easy, Joe. We know this guy. He's a pal of Barrymore's."

"Barrymore! Which one's Barrymore?"

"Never — !"

"I'll vouch for him," Virginia Hill said. "Give him your ears, for God's sake, he's good for the loan."

"What do you want?" The figure that had glowered had now sprouted a smile of sorts. He looked up at me.

"I'm trying to get a line on the death of Mark Norman."

"Who's asking?"

"I work for a Canadian news service. My name's Mike Ward, but that won't mean anything here. I'm new in town. I just wondered if you knew anything that hasn't been in the papers yet."

"I was in Vancouver once." The fellow next to him made as if to swat the speaker on the head. "I got family there! Honest!"

"His name, for a start, isn't Mark Norman. Maishal Novitsky was good enough for him when he lived on Delancy Street in New York. He started out running cans of film from the station to the movie palaces. What else you want to know? That story about his dick is spoiled flounder, rotten fish. It stinks. I never heard a word against him in regard to that. He was hung as usual. I mean, he wouldn't have won any prizes, but he was not one of the walking wounded either. You know what I mean?"

"Thanks. But if that's true, where does the fiction come from?"

"The studio, the studio. Those public relations people can't tell you how to cross the street without twisting it a little. Look what they've done to us! We're just a bunch of businessmen discussing work over some lasagna and French fries."

"Yeah, but in the papers we're an octopus with our ten legs wrapped all the way around the planet. Look at Edward G. Robinson. Look at Humphrey Bogart. Look at Cagney."

"That's right. I didn't shoot anybody all day. I leave that to Hopalong Cassidy."

"The papers get things wrong all the time, Mr. Ward," Virginia said. "If you've ever been in a news story, you know that already. On the radio, they got John Dillinger's name wrong. A hard 'g,' soft 'g' mix-up. But he went along with it. That's how accommodating we can be."

"You wanna look up the 1924 death of Thomas Harper Ince. William Randolph Hearst bottled up the truth about what happened on his yacht. And there was another case, even earlier: William Desmond Taylor in 1922. A movie director was murdered in his house and it was treated as though he was killed trying to prevent a burglary. Believe that and I'll tell you about Santy Claus." Virginia Hill was jotting down something on her menu.

"With the stories they've been giving out so bizarre, the studios may think most of the conservative papers will drop it."

"Yeah, in this town a murder lives in the papers three days at the most. Then you can clean windows with it. A black murder's in the second section and is gone in the next edition."

"In gathering the facts about a case like this, we usually ask, 'Who benefits?' Who does in this case?"

"The lady, that movie star, Barbara Lorrison: she's free to marry again. There are no scars on her reputation. Wasn't there a first wife somewhere?"

"Yeah. What's her name? Norma Fisher."

I'd run across the name before in the office morgue.

"She's in Frisco. But that's a short run. You can get a plane to fly you back and forth."

"She was a script reader at Paramount, then switched to A-Z-P. That's when he met her," said Virginia Hill. She tore away a piece of her menu and passed it to me. Everybody at the table saw her do it.

"I don't know what she's doing in Frisco, but Phoebe Wheeler should know. They've been friends for donkey's years."

"Thanks, I'll look into that." As I turned to go, I heard:

"I hear they want Barrymore for the Monty Woolley part in the movie Warners is making of *The Man Who Came to Dinner*."

"Come on! He couldn't stay awake for lunch let alone dinner."

The rest of the evening ended in the early dawn. Four of us carried Jack from a taxi into Decker's house on Bundy Drive and delivered him into the custody of a newly awakened Hobart, who seemed to know what to do with the Monster in his present condition.

When I got back to my flat that night, there was a message to call the overseas operator. I did that. It was a call from the French policeman I'd talked to a few days ago. I tried to figure out the time on the River Seine, but gave it up. I'd had too much to drink.

"Hello?"

"M. Ward?"

"To you, Gabriel, I'm Mike. How's April in Paris?"

"Ah, Mike, Vernon Duke missed so much! But, I have news for you. The servant woman has been located."

"Violet Bowden?"

"The same. We are keeping an eye on her."

"Wonderful!"

"Before you take the bonnet from the Veuve Clicquot, you'd better hear the rest of my news. The woman, Emma Schneller, the blackmailer, was released from Holloway Prison. She is on her way to you."

"What? Isn't she on parole? She can't leave the jurisdiction. How can she skip out of the jurisdiction?"

"Did I not tell you she was a clever little thing? She is most extraordinary. She was being watched, naturally, but she managed to slip away in one of your famous London fogs."

"Don't forget, Gabriel, I'm Canadian, not English."

"From here, on the Quai des Orfèvres, it is all one."

"You're pulling my leg. You're a better *flic* than that."

"I will ignore that remark. The ship will have reached New York after six-and-a-half days at sea. Emma Schneller is now in your soup, not mine. And there is a CID man, who didn't get lost in the London fog, also booked on her ship. Do you know Evan Macdonald? He is one of their best men. Over to you, *mon ami*, and good hunting!"

# CHAPTER EIGHT

When I got up in the morning — though I call it "morning" it was pushing well into the afternoon — I pulled my very hungover self through a shower, then out under the scalding light, into a sandwich shop where I made a sad figure at a very late breakfast. Coffee and fresh orange juice were all I could manage. Optimistically, I had ordered eggs, but when they arrived at my table I was in no way up to dealing with them. I didn't want to look at them. I came very close to covering the fresh plate with a paper napkin so that I didn't have to look at it. The smell was bad enough. Another time, when I was feeling a little more hardy, I might venture some ham and eggs, but not that morning. The food here in California, I had to admit in spite of my tender innards and raging headache, was first-class. I never saw a sandwich with crusts or curdled cream. Everything offered was at its peak of perfection. The trouble was, although that was not the best morning to remember it, the freshness and crispness were both the outer limits. The cooking was all right, but it didn't fly. It didn't take off the way my little café in the Rue Campagne Première did. There an omelette was a Rubens, a Botticelli. Here we had to settle for fashion spreads by Condé Nast and Coco Chanel. But all of these imperfections were bathed in golden sunshine. I might have been going soft in the head, but I was beginning to see some of the virtues of Los Angeles.

The morgue at the office was not extensive. Nor was it balanced. There were only three clippings about Dollfuss, two about Mackenzie King, one concerning the British Labour Party, and a dozen about the child star Shirley Temple — with glossies for reproduction, dating from six years earlier. She was twice six years old now. I was looking into the deaths of two film directors, as suggested by my talk with Virginia Hill last night. There was nothing useful in the files, just the usual glamour-puss bumph about hairdressers, young female movie hopefuls, and couturiers. I had to fall back on the note Virginia Hill had given to me the night before. It stated:

> *For gen on Norma Fisher, phone Phoebe Wheeler at MA 6038.*
> *Good luck.*

V

I read the note twice, at first not remembering who the names belonged to. Then it came back with a wallop. It was Norman's first wife and the friend who knew where to find her. I dialled the number, in hope, but I got no answer. She was probably at work. I'd try again later.

The business of running a wire service occupied the rest of my day. I was learning the local system better and better. The equipment here was better than what I was used to. In Moscow, my typewriter ribbon looked as though it had been used to make confetti for a Russian wedding. When the machines broke down, we had a mechanic who could create parts: Soviet parts for heavy-duty Remingtons, L. C. Smiths, and Underwoods. Here, the ribbons were in ample supply in a cabinet referred to as "the coffin," which smelled of rancid oil.

Staring into "the coffin," my mind went back to schooldays: the wonderful smell of all those packages of chalk, pencils, erasers, and notebooks. Suddenly I thought of a teacher named Macdonald. Then I remembered the name of the British CID man following Emma Schneller. A card-playing friend from London days. I call him "a friend" now that he's dead. Would I say that if he was still alive? I wonder. He was the man who fell from the Twentieth Century. Fell or was pushed? By now, Emma Schneller was here in LA. How does one go about finding a needle in a haystack as big as LA with all of its suburbs? I didn't know where to begin.

I called up my only friend at the LAPD, Sergeant Bob Alton. When I got through to him, he was too busy to talk. I left my number. When he called back, half an hour later, it sounded like he was no longer in his office: the busy office noise had been replaced by the dead sound of a public telephone booth. I asked if he had anything new that he cared to share about the dead man's first wife in San Francisco, or his movie-star second wife and her mother.

"Do you always get other people to do your research for you, Ward?"

"Naturally. Why not? In my place, wouldn't you?"

"What do you want this time?"

"Where were the women in Norman's life on the day of his death?"

"You don't want much for nothing, do you?"

"I'm not proud, Bob. I suspect that your brothers in blue are going to come after me before I can file any of this. For some reason, the studio has set the dogs on me."

"Easy to tell you're just off the boat. Business in LA is movies.

This is a company town. They have enough trouble getting you, me, and Mr. and Mrs. America to shell out a quarter to see one of their epics. I don't blame them for being nervous about a party-crasher like you."

"Ouch! I hear you. But I bet you like being pushed around as much as I do. If you can tell me anything of use, fine; if you can't, that'll be one more splinter in my rear end. But it won't set me off writing up garden parties in Santa Monica or Beverly Hills."

"Barbara Lorrison and her mother are joined at the hip. They go everywhere together. Lorrison has no secret private life, at least not one her old lady doesn't share. They have a spot down in La Jolla; pool by the ocean and more privacy than you can find around here. They visit the zoo if they need company. Norman's wife is in Frisco, but we don't know where she's living. Hell, Mike, this is still a free country. It's no crime to disappear into the woodwork. Just the same, I know we have people trying to track her down up there. As the deceased's first wife, she's at the very least a person of interest in this case."

"Then, there is a case? Is that now the working hypothesis?"

"Depends who's asking and who's answering. The department's divided. Take your choice. The forensic people won't look you in the eye if you ask about that goddamned suicide note." I tried to arrange to meet him for a drink later in the day, but he begged off. "Hell, Ward, haven't you found a girlfriend yet?"

He was right. If I had a more stable private life, I might spend less of my time listening to the life stories of paper cup manufacturers from Duluth and trying to get excited about the Brooklyn Dodgers.

I could see no merit in further delaying my second attempt to call Phoebe Wheeler. I dialled the number and waited.

"Hello?"

"Phoebe Wheeler? This is Mike Ward of the Metropolitan News Service."

"Are you a reporter?" I was disarmed by her direct approach.

"Of a kind. I'd like to talk to you about the death of Mark Norman."

"Another one! You boys have been on the wire for a month. Some nerve, I'll say! I've got nothing more to say to you. I talked to a dozen newspaper people. And the cops. I was warned. I'm not talking to anybody now."

"I'm sorry. I understand." I was suddenly back on my first newspaper job, collecting a photograph of that morning's traffic victim. How long ago was that? But the feeling never goes away. We cover up the bad feeling with coarse inside jokes with others of the profession, but even at my age I still felt like a pariah, an unwelcome voice on the end of the wire, more often than not, beating the police with the news that Daddy won't be home for dinner tonight. Or any future night.

This time, at least, it wasn't a fresh fatality. Not another pick-up. I wanted off the line as fast as possible. "Let me leave my number, just in case you change your mind."

"I don't know — "

"Look, I'm from a Canadian wire service. All I'm looking for is background."

"Sure, sure."

"I promise I won't attribute anything you tell me. I won't nail you to your front door."

"Okay, okay. I don't need my arm twisted. I've been warned about shooting my mouth off. You promise people the moon, but you forget your promises when you get back to your papers."

"Look, Phoebe, I'm not just trying to peddle my papers. And it's not a paper, but a Canadian news service, a foreign wire service." I could hear her breathing through a long silence. I added: "Virginia said that you might want to talk to me."

"She said I should?"

"No. She said you might. To the right person."

"I hear you talking. I got a pencil handy." I gave her my name again and a number where she could reach me at the service and the number where I was living. It was hard to make her out. She didn't sound like a lot of people I've talked to who legitimately didn't want to be bothered. Phoebe sounded more like she was following orders that didn't start with her.

"Miss Wheeler, you sound like you're under a lot of pressure. Can you tell me where it's coming from?"

"From all over. Ever since it happened. Reporters want to hear what I know, and the cops and the studios want to shut me down. The *Times* offered good money, but I couldn't take it. What are you offering?"

"We'll talk about that when you're free to talk."

"I should live so long!"

"Nevertheless!"

"Two weeks ago nobody ever heard of me. Isn't that a laugh?"

"It's funny, all right. Could we meet someplace? Some spot handy to you? Is your place being watched?"

"You think it might be? I never thought of that. I don't like the feeling that gives me. Not at all."

Before I disconnected, I'd talked her into meeting me in a bar she knew. It was a place called The Annex, next door to Ciro's, a big restaurant on North Evergreen between Winter and Malabar. She named the time: half-past six. I hung up the phone feeling as though I was finally getting somewhere with this story. I suspected that the tale of the death of this movie mogul was a long and twisted skein of yarn. But at least I thought I had hold of one of the ends.

Later, just as I was about to find a new place to have lunch, Eric Olson came to my desk. "Mr. Ward, I've been busy looking up material about that first wife. Mark Norman's first wife."

"Great! What have you got?"

"It's too complicated to go into right now. There's a lot of background and a few surprises. May I bring it in tomorrow? You'll want to see this."

Olson made me feel like a teacher trying to decide on a pupil's request to leave the room. He was a fairly good reporter, a fine researcher, but somewhat subdued and obsequious, stemming from contact with Endicott, I supposed. While he could only be in his thirties, he looked more like me: as though he'd seen action in the European wars. As a matter of fact, he told me once at lunch, rather shyly, that he had been taken for me at one of the places where I drank my lunch.

"Why don't you drop it around to my flat after dinner tonight? We can go over it then when there isn't all this hanging over our heads." My "all this" referred to the various messes waiting to go out on the wire tonight.

"Sure thing. I'm not far from you. I looked it up yesterday."

"Good man. I'll see you tonight."

Just after a coffee break, when I grabbed some lunch — a curly cheese sandwich and an orange the size of a grapefruit, washed down with beer — I was sorting out a story about a hit-and-run file brief involving a US senator and a cyclist. It wasn't looking good for the politician. When I glanced up from the L. C. Smith typewriter, I saw four blue-clad upholders of the law waiting to have my full attention. "Gentlemen! To what do I owe this visit?"

"You're Michael Ward?"

"That's right."

"I'm Corporal Whithers and this is Patrolman Brownlow. This is official business. We're not collecting for the Veterans of Foreign Wars. Can I see your passport?"

"What's this all about?" I found the document in a pocket of my jacket on the back of my chair. One of the officers took it without answering my question. The first cop looked at it, examining every page, even the blank ones, then passed the document to his partner, who went through the same motions.

"You're not a citizen of the United States?"

"That's right; I'm Canadian."

"You're not a tourist, not here on holiday?"

"That's right. I work here. I have a work permit and a visa, as you can see, with the passport."

"We've got orders to take you in for questioning. Downtown."

"In regard to what? I've only been here a few weeks. My papers are in order and were checked when I crossed the border."

"We'll get it cleared up at the precinct. Get your hat."

"Let me have a quick word with my colleague. He'll have to take charge while I'm out."

"You can do it later. Come on."

"Hold on a second! This is a wire service, remember."

The hand on my elbow eased off long enough for me to have a quick word with Endicott. He nodded as I spoke. The shock would hit him later.

"Tell Olson about this, Larry. Don't forget."

"There's a car outside," Whithers said, re-establishing his grip on my arm.

# CHAPTER NINE

*T*he interior decorator of the Twenty-First Precinct would never win a prize or get much credit for renovating a former insurance office into a working environment for this representative of the Los Angeles Police Department. For one thing, the place looked as though it wasn't quite finished. It was more than the drab industrial paint or the worn floors and shabby filing cabinets and desks: the walls looked as though someone, many years ago, had tried to smooth them with an axe. The place looked tired, as if no one really believed in it or gave a damn. If furniture can look tired, if floors can look defeated, if ceilings can throw in the towel, this cop shop won the top award for failure.

The men at those desks too seemed as though the rasping routines had worn them away, as a pounding surf beats its way into a retreating landscape. They moved around the space without noticing the people sitting in chairs waiting to be relieved in some way from whatever burden brought them there.

I took my turn sitting, waiting, and observing the punks in thread-bare trousers, the pimps in their gaudy finery, and the bewildered first offenders. They all had the same look; looks that gave them away: "I'm here by accident! There must be a mistake!" "I just have to sit it out. My mouthpiece will have me back on the street in an hour." "Don't tell my mother about this. Please! I'll do anything!" I'd seen the cages in the Commissariat near the Pantheon in Paris, the Tombs in New York, the jail behind St. Paul's in London, and the lock-up in Moscow. Now I was doing my own share of sitting and experiencing part of the ritual: "Let them sweat it out."

I saw the time for my appointment to meet Phoebe Wheeler come and go. The only telephones in view were on the desks of the cops on the other side of the wooden bar that separated the waiting detainees from the processed detainees. I was sure that Endicott would send me legal assistance as soon as he could arrange it. Reporters are lucky that way: there's always somebody on a retainer to get a newsman out of a tough corner. As a working member of the press for nearly a quarter of a century, I'd been there before.

Eventually, I was given the preliminary treatment. I was printed and searched, had my full face and right profile fed into their records. My personal possessions were placed in a foolscap-sized envelope and I signed for them. The attendant behind the desk never looked at me once, but continued typing with two stubby fingers.

A telephone was ringing on one desk or another all the time, with a teletype machine spewing out paper down its front, lending bell sounds to the general racket, adding an uncheery percussive obbligato.

One of the plainclothes officers came over to me. "Your name Ward? Michael Ward?"

"That's right."

"That was your boss, Mr. Endicott. Says your lawyer is in court and won't be able to get to you for at least another hour or two. Just what you needed to hear, right?"

"Thanks." I didn't bother pointing out that I was Endicott's boss, not the other way around. Funny thing about Endicott: he likes the title, I like the work. The thought didn't help the waiting any. What I wouldn't have given for one of the old magazines in my dentist's office back home. I guess that meant Toronto. Home is where you get your teeth fixed. I was at last dozing in my chair, sitting up, when: "This way, Mr. Ward." The invitation came from a carbuncular youth in blue, a newcomer to the division, I guessed. He led me past the doors of tiny cubicles on both sides. There was an electric fan in good working condition trying to keep things cool. "In here," he said, when we had reached the last door at the end of the corridor. He held the door open for me as I walked past him into a room with natural light coming from windows on two sides. Funny how petty bureaucrats the world over measure themselves in small ways.

Detective Lieutenant Swarbrick was seated behind a desk that was smaller than the one I'd been expecting. It was made of metal and rust stains marked the floor where it had stood in some earlier regime. It was a bare linoleum floor. Swarbrick didn't fuss with the papers in his hand when I came in. He dropped them to the desk blotter, and indicated the chair facing him. I took it.

Swarbrick was a big man. His shoulders told me that he had worked his way through the ranks, that he knew the job, and that he knew where the edges and the fissures were. He could walk the line, or deviate from it, as he chose. His forehead was high, above a long, thin face, with bright blue eyes that reflected little of the light in the room. What hair he retained was lank, a dusty brown. Swarbrick's lips were thin. His smile, which he showed on occasion, had no warmth in it. I preferred his serious look, a half snarl, which he aimed at me.

"I once had a peeper in here who you remind me of," he said, after giving me the sort of once-over I'd just given him. He was playing with his Waterman pen and examining papers, an act I was certain he did for effect. The emptier the bureaucrat, the longer he dallies with irrelevant papers. "He tried to stir up the ashes of a dead case in our files, one that involved some serious people. Sure, he was just doing his job. He was a family man with a wife, two kids, and one on the way. Personable, but unreasonable. I talked to him. I'm the father of two kids myself. But he wouldn't listen. I pointed out that the public was not in any way being served in his dragging through all those dead files. He peeved a few of the wrong people, out there and in here as well. Some of the cops involved had been pensioned off, some were dead, some had caught a bullet in the execution of their duty."

He shook a Lucky from a nearly empty pack, and waved it at me. He wasn't offering it to me, but I shook my head anyway.

"Your parable is almost Biblical, Sergeant. What am I supposed to make of it?"

"The obvious. You want me to spell it out? What right have you, a foreigner, to come down here and stir up what's none of your business?"

"I suppose you know I'm not a 'peeper,' as you say. I'm a journalist and licensed to ply my trade in this state. You want to see documents?"

"We have trouble enough with the foreign press as it is, without you coming down here to sour our wine. We don't need peepers, and we don't need amateur Dick Tracys or Sam Spades dancing on our streets. You follow me?"

"Spade's up in Frisco. You mean Marlowe."

"We don't need any more lip from you, and that's a fact."

"Maybe you need a stenographer to record this conversation. Or is your language too colourful to preserve?"

"I want to know what you're doing here in my town. You're going to tell me why you're trying to upset my wagon. I want you off these streets and out of print. That's a bookish term you should know."

"I heard that same message from the head man at Gestapo Headquarters in Berlin just a year ago. In Moscow it was the OGPU. It changes its name every decade or two. But the same fellows run it. No little parable that time, but his meaning was clear: 'Stop doing my job.' I've had colleagues of mine — pals, drinking friends — vanish altogether, or wash ashore to be identified by their rings. Even their scars had disappeared. I thought you did things differently over here."

"You're damned right we do! And we don't hold with foreigners showing us how to do things their way. I'm going to hold on to your passport. I'm suspending your work permit. You now have no business in Los Angeles except behaving like a tourist. As a tourist, it's hunky-dory with me wherever you go."

"It was a cop who invented that word. You have all the words on your side."

"Get out of here, Ward! Pull up your socks! Go see the sights, visit the studios, find a bus to show you the homes of the stars, get postcards at the La Brea Tar Pits, eat a bellyful of prime citrus, then get the hell back to where you come from. You'll get your papers back when I see your ticket out of here."

Fear, which had been holding me together, stood me on my legs, and saw me to the door. "At least you stifled the parables. Where are the tar pits?"

"Try Hancock Park. Now get the hell out of here!"

I got the hell out of there. As though I needed an invitation. But not before I retrieved my wallet and checked it, counting my money, and making sure I had all the important papers and cards. Among the latter, I found a membership to The Little Club in Soho. Why was I still carrying an expired membership to a club that offered drinks after afternoon closing time in London? I'll be saving orphaned shoelaces next. I was pondering this when I heard my name called.

"Mike! Damn it. I don't believe it!" I looked back at the tall doors leading into the police station. There were two men, both well dressed, but one looking as though he had been sleeping rough: his clothes were rumpled and unpressed, his hair uncombed, and he was in need of a barber. His vest hung open, where it might have hidden a wine stain. The right pocket of his jacket was torn. The other fellow, a heavier man, was tidy enough, but looked out of sorts, much the way I was feeling. I scanned both faces without recognizing either one of them.

"Mike, don't deny me in my hour of need!"

It was the rumpled one who was speaking. I turned and began climbing back up the steps toward them.

"Christ, Mike. Am I that different?" Then I recognized him. It was the writer, Scott Fitzgerald, whom I'd known in Paris twenty years ago.

"Scott! How the hell are you?"

"The lock-up here's a lot worse than the one in the Fifth Arrondissement in Paris, but better than the one in New York." I laughed to be polite, and grabbed his hand. He looked terrible. He had held on to his hair over the years, but his face looked bloated and unhealthy. He still had the same electric smile.

"Let me introduce you to my collaborator, a companion in revisiting my naughty college days. One of Walter Wanger's dimmer ideas. This is Budd Schulberg, of the Hollywood Schulbergs, Mike. Budd, this is Mike Ward. We knew each other in Paris. Damned good newspaperman."

"Glad t'meet chah, Ward. You're not going to file this, are you? Just forget you ran into us."

"C'mon, Budd, it's hard enough for me to get ink these days. Don't spoil my chances."

"I wasn't sent here, Mr. Schulberg. This is a chance meeting, completely off the record."

"I owe you the money for crashing me out of there, Budd. I'll not likely forget this. I'm damned sorry about your golf game."

Scott Fitzgerald and his wife, Zelda, were the toast of the Right and Left Banks in Paris when I first lived there. He wrote novels about flaming youth and living the life that the papers and magazines lapped up. Zelda kept him supplied with antics to stuff into his novels. Life among the well-off expatriates, just after the Armistice. Here he stood: a veteran of the café wars and too much foie gras, no longer the popular young novelist he had been. Scribner's continued to publish him, even though his debtors collected most of his advances and royalties. Back in the Twenties, Scott Fitzgerald's name was associated with the Jazz Age as surely as Hemingway was with the Lost Generation. Fitzgerald kept turning out books although the age had changed and he hadn't. The last short story of his I read was in *Esquire,* on the boat from Cherbourg.

"I like your stories, Fitzgerald. I used to buy *Esquire* just for the Vargas girls, now I have a better reason."

"Gingrich is part boy scout, Mike. He hates to see one of his writers vanish down the toilet like the contents of an overflowing ashtray."

"No, Fitzgerald, they're good stories."

"Don't believe it, Mike. I'm all washed up."

"You'll have to excuse us, Ward, I've got to return Scott to his place. There still are people who worry about him."

"Of course. Sure. Great bumping into you, Scott, and meeting you, Mr. Schulberg."

"Sure thing. So long."

"Mike, I'm in the book as 'S. Graham.' We need to meet, old sport."

"I'll ring you tomorrow, if I can."

The two of them continued down the steps of the police station to a waiting taxi. The driver was in a dispute with a traffic cop. I made my way on foot out of that neighbourhood as quickly as possible.

## CHAPTER TEN

*I* walked about ten blocks after that without looking up, except to make out the colour of the stoplight. I put away thoughts of Fitzgerald from the front of my brain, after recollecting what a bad drinker he was. He was always below par with a glass in his hand. Scott, and thoughts about those days, would keep. My mind felt like a blank, except that it was full of all the unexpressed things I had failed to say to Swarbrick. By the time I reached vaguely familiar territory, I'd become an eloquent fellow in my own estimation. No courtroom lawyer defended a client more brilliantly than I parried all of Swarbrick's thrusts at me. Or so I thought at the time.

That night, I let Endicott's family talk me into accompanying them to hear the Los Angeles Philharmonic at the D.W. Griffith Theatre. I'm glad I went along. The Rimsky-Korsakov selections from *Scheherazade* had a good effect on my nerves. So relaxed was I upon leaving the amphitheatre that I have forgotten the name of the conductor. I do recall that the orchestra filled up the punch bowl-shaped outdoor shell to the brim. It was a smaller place, built on the same principle as the Hollywood Bowl, which I visited later in the month for a fair comparison — and for Mozart. I won't break up that sensation into what little I know about the science of comparative acoustics. The effect was greater than the science. You might blame it on my time at the Twenty-First Precinct, but I'll give the amphitheatre and the orchestra top marks. By the time Endicott dropped me at my door, I was in a better mood, no longer tilting at windmills or policemen.

I may have set out on the evening excursion with an idea of improving morale at the office, my head full of *It is a far, far better thing I do this day ...*, but I lived to enjoy myself and the taste of family life of which I saw so little. An LAPD cruiser was pulling away from the front of my address as we parked.

The landlady met me just inside the front door. Her face was ashen. I'd used the expression before in news stories, but I had rarely seen it up close. In another moment, it had gone even paler. "Oh no!" She dropped the cup of coffee she was carrying. "You!" she shouted. "I don't believe it! I don't understand! You're dead!" She repeated this several times, each time louder than the time before. The coffee pooled around her felt slippers. She took no notice.

By now, with all her screaming, her husband was in the hallway as well, dressed in an old bathrobe. His white face matched his wife's.

"What happened?" I asked as calmly as I could.

"It's you! They came to get you and took you away."

"Who took me away? I just got here. Take a big breath and tell me what's happened." The two of them exchanged glances. At last Mr. Granovsky spoke.

"We heard the front door open, then we heard loud noises, like a car backfiring. When I came out to look, there you were on the tiles in the front hall. Lying on your face, you were. On the floor with blood everywhere."

"Your blood," his wife added. The floor in the hall was damp; there was a wet mop leaning on the hall table.

"The door was open, and you were just inside. Where you're standing now!" She stepped back, as though I was still lying there.

"But I just got here! When did this happen?"

"Mr. Ward, I'd just finished in the upstairs hall when I heard it."

"You usually leave the front door locked. Was it open tonight?"

"We needed the air. The fan's broken again."

"It's on my workbench. I was planning to fix it," Mr. Granovsky added.

"You called an ambulance and the police?"

They both nodded.

"They were here in fifteen minutes and took you away in an ambulance," he said, nodding.

"But first, it was the police!" Mrs. Granovsky added.

"It was only fifteen minutes ago. The last of the policemen just left. They gave my wife a card with a number on it. Do you still have it, *liebchen?*"

"I gave it to you. It's in your pocket." Mr. Granovsky patted all of his pockets, then handed me a card. In all this excitement, all I could read were the initials LAPD. I thanked my landlords and saw them back into their ground-floor apartment. While they were pondering how I could be both lying on a slab in the morgue and at the same time standing at the threshold of their flat, I put their kettle on the stove and lit the burner. I was having a little trouble with the problem myself. Mr. Granovsky handed me a cup; his wife began to slice a sweet loaf without looking at me. Time passed. Soon, I sat nursing an empty cup, while the Granovskys went through the details once again.

I couldn't take hearing the story again. I made a lame excuse and left the house. I walked three or four blocks, then flagged down a cab.

The driver took me to a cheap hotel out near Watts. It had a torn, ruffled awning outside to frighten away prospective guests. I booked in under an assumed name — that of my high school principal, Stanley Martin — and carried my bag up to the third floor. From there I called Endicott at home. I was no longer sure of the time, but I was certain that he'd be back by now.

"Hello?"

"Larry? It's me, Ward."

"You left your umbrella in the car. I told you that you'd forget it. I'll bring it in the morning."

"Listen, Larry, did you tell Eric that I had been picked up by the police? Remember, he was supposed to drop by my place tonight."

"Yeah, sure. I remember your telling me, but I didn't get around to it. I forgot."

"Damn!" I didn't have the stomach to tell him what had happened until he started reminding me how much I owed him for our evening excursion. That angered me enough to overcome my reluctance. "Damn it all to hell!"

"Christ, Mike, have I committed an indictable offence?"

"Olson is dead, you idiot, because you forgot to warn him. He's been shot at my place."

Here Larry made a confusing confession of disbelief.

"Do you hear me? He's dead. Does he have a wife, children, parents? Can you pass along the news? He was shot in the doorway at my place."

I got off the phone as quickly as I could. I had been shouting at Endicott, not listening.

"Poor Olson!" I thought out loud. "Why would anyone want to kill him?" Then it hit me how slowly my brain was working. It wasn't Olson. Poor innocent Olson. I had been the intended victim.

I called Endicott back. I apologized, explaining that I was upset, and that I thought that Olson had been shot by mistake. I was the man they had planned to kill. I tried to explain this to Endicott.

"Somebody thought Olson was me. I'm going to have to lay low for a while. Was there a Mrs. Olson?"

"Jesus, Mike! What's going on?"

"I'll fill you in later. You know the coffee shop you took me to when I first came to town? We'll meet there. I don't think it'll be safe for me to come to the bureau until this breaks in the papers. It's your story. Run with it any way you like, but I would appreciate some slack. Let it sit overnight. Until it's known that the body at my place was poor Olson and not me, it's unlikely that they'll try again. Did he have a family?"

"Sure he did. Wife, kids, mother-in-law, the works. Christ, Mike, don't drag me through this. We'll both go crazy." He added this in another voice. "Your old pal, the London cop, Macdonald?"

"Yeah? What about him?"

"He was on a case, not on holiday."

"He was following Emma Schneller, right?"

"Right. Give that man a box of Snickers! Where are you staying?"

"I'll tell you when I see you. Noon tomorrow."

"Sure, yeah, sure. Take it easy."

My hands were shaking when I got off the phone. The place I'd picked had no bar of its own, but there was one at the corner.

WHEN I ARRIVED AT THE coffee shop across from the office the following morning, unshaven and wretched, I ordered my eggs and coffee without much appetite for either. Endicott came in a few minutes later. I moved the eggs across the table, out of my sight. I laid the situation out for him in more detail than I had the night before. As a coda to that, I reminded him of the fact that I had very likely been the intended victim, and added that Swarbrick would not be unhappy if that had been the news. His first reaction was to lecture me on how, since the founding of this bureau, they had prided themselves on keeping on friendly terms with the LAPD. I listened until I could sit still no longer.

"Listen, you poor sap, this isn't the world the New Deal promised. This isn't Moscow. It's more like Berlin. If you play possum, the Swarbricks will have us all locked up. There is still a presumption of innocence and the rule of law. Remember the old maxim from Edward G. Robinson's radio program, *Big Town*: 'The freedom of the press/Is a flaming sword./Use it justly, hold it high,/Guard it well.'"

"Of course, of course. Yes, in theory! But, Mike, in practice we have to live within our means. It's easier to kill a story than to fight for the freedom of the press in the courts. Our bosses? The owners? And with the reporters bound over to keep the peace, who's going to keep sending cables back home? Save your speeches for a movie scenario." He was trying to smile at me, to show me that things were not as dark as they seemed. "In Berlin, the Nazis keep you under surveillance. Ditto in Russia. As press we have a lot of privileges, but there's a limit."

"Go to hell! This isn't a police state. Or at least it wasn't."

"Calm down, Mike. You're overexcited."

"I'm not overexcited. This is indignant rage. A colleague of ours has been murdered. I've been turned into a target in a shooting gallery. I refuse to be treated this way and remain passive! Hell, I yell when I stub my big toe; why not now?"

"Then you'd better report back to Toronto. You've been turning all the wrong dials since you got here. You're supposed to be a journalist, not a crusading private police force. We owe Toronto the right to call the tune. Nobody in Canada's interested in reading more about the untimely death of the late, lamented Mark Norman. Damn it! I'd almost forgotten his name. Why are you burying yourself in a barrel of dead herring? You can't carry on like this and work out of here for long."

"Are you passing on the word from Toronto?"

"They think it would be best for all concerned — "

"Sure. I catch on. They'll send a wreath to my funeral, but don't count on them for anything else. Thanks a million."

"Mike! What did you expect? They're not in a mood to ship you back across the Atlantic. Not these days."

"You mean the war? The States isn't in it yet."

"Sure, and there are plenty of people and interests who like it that way. Families can't spare their sons in a distant, foreign squabble. There's no market for it. You can't sell it. Ask the President. Roosevelt'll tell you. He's found out it won't fly."

This Endicott was no stranger to me. I'd been running into him and his sort all my life. There usually was a way around such people, the hand-wringers and do-nothings. At the American embassy in London I ran into a newspaper owner who thought that the States was becoming cozy with the wrong side. He thought we should join the Germans and carry the war into Soviet Russia. I spilled a cocktail on him.

When I left the coffee shop, I was a free man. There would be paperwork to follow, but I could consider myself one of the unemployed. I walked for several blocks before becoming aware that I was being followed. In the normal course of my work, I had shadowed people often enough. And I have been followed, too. Once, in London, an MI5 fellow dogged my footsteps for a week before we settled matters amicably enough in East Ham, in the smallest pub on the north bank of the Thames. Billy Chalice! He used to send me a Christmas card. With that name, I figured he must have been brought up by the diocese. I wondered whether the man a block behind me would end up telling me how hard it was to get along with the rival Special Branch chaps. Here, I guess it would be the FBI.

But this fellow must be a policeman: nothing very secret, nothing very sensitive about me. Just a journalist who didn't know how to take a hint. No doubt the Americans had a federal secret police.

Wild Bill Donovan was setting something up. But they would hardly be bothering me. My fellow was local. I was pretty sure of that. Dispatched by Swarbrick to keep an eye on me, to see if I left town.

That warmed my heart a little. It told me that he didn't know I was dead, that he hadn't set me up last night.

I hailed a taxi. He took another, and stayed behind me until we entered Watts. I paid the driver, and scooted out the door across from where the other car was pulling to a stop. Keeping to the dark patches without proper street lighting, I walked back towards my place, keeping my shadow behind me at a good distance. My last sight of him was of a man standing in the middle of the road, scratching his head.

Once I was in my room, I took a shower. Dry again, from my window I spotted my dedicated watcher under a lamppost across the street, half a block away. I was thinking of him as a "him," when I should have thought in terms of "them." With cops, it's always them. Three men in three shifts, and a paper report to file, probably on their own time. But with freelancers, you never can tell. I thought about having him up. I also thought of giving him the slip, but I didn't really have a clear enough destination. I'd save that trick for later on, when I might need it more. Besides, I had an advantage in knowing that he was shadowing me, while he remained unsure about whether I was on to him or not. If he thought that I was blandly unaware of his presence in my life, he would keep me in view where I could find him when I wanted to. Once he discovered I had smoked him, he'd have to get clever. He might be replaced by a cleverer operative. It's funny how, when you run into rough terrain, you find advantages in adversity.

When I checked my window half an hour later, he was still there. Twenty minutes after that there were two of them: the changing of the guard. While they were in conference, I slipped out the back way, managing not to upset any of the trash cans I encountered on the back stairs.

I hadn't been clear-headed enough to bring my map of the city. I tried to keep track of the backyards I'd gone through and relate my progress away from my keepers by what I could recall of the main streets of the neighbourhood. When an alley ended at a main street, I looked for someplace with a telephone.

I found one in a corner Rexall drugstore: a standard phone booth in back, where the whereabouts of the lavatories was easily detected. The rattle and jangle of my nickel in the coin box exploded noisily. For the past few minutes, the loudest thing I'd heard was the sound of my own breathing.

"Hello?"

"Phoebe Wheeler?" I was still out of breath. "It's Mike Ward. I was supposed to meet you yesterday."

"I waited over an hour!"

"Sorry. The LAPD interrupted me before I could get to you. They've put a tail on me, but I've got free of them. They're still watching my apartment, and now my rented room."

"You better not come here. They may still be following you."

"I don't think so, but you're probably right. I'll stay away from you until things cool down. Can you tell me how you know Norma Fisher?"

"We were friends in the typing pool eight years ago. We both got promoted. I was a script reader. I made notes and synopses and passed the word to Mr. Norman."

"And your friend?"

"Norma was popular. First she worked for Mr. Zavitz in the New York office. Handled all the hush-hush stuff. Then she became Mr. Norman's confidential secretary, his girl Friday. Then they got hitched. She never asked me round to see her place. Lots of pictures of it in the papers. Snazzy layout."

"Do you have a number or address where I can reach her?"

"Sure. But she's not local anymore. She's up in Frisco."

"All the same, I'd like whatever you've got."

"Sure." There was another delay, but when it was over, I had both a street address and a phone number.

"Tell me about the last time you talked to her."

"She made me promise — "

"Phoebe, her ex is dead. The cops say it was suicide because that's the way the studio looks at it. If Norma was anywhere near her former home, I'd like to know about it."

"Okay, she went to see him. She was crazy, out of control. I don't know what happened at her house. She told me there was a strange car in the drive when she arrived in a cab, and drinks for two on the coffee table. She fired off a shot at Mark, and ran. I gave her a sedative, but she wouldn't see my doctor. She went back up the coast to Frisco that same night."

"Thanks. You're as close to an eyewitness as we have."

"Don't lay it on. I already feel bad about talking to you."

"While I have you on the phone, do you know how I can reach your friend Virginia Hill?"

"'Friend'? She's not exactly a friend. But in a tight pinch, I guess you could call her that. Remember what that lady said about Byron?"

"Lord Byron! What lady?"

"His discarded girlfriend. She came in like a lamb and went out like a lion. Didn't you see the movie? She said he was 'mad, bad, and dangerous to know.' Now, do you get my point about Virginia?"

"Look, I'm not planning to set up housekeeping with the woman; I only need to talk to her. I'm not looking for a fight with her boyfriend."

Phoebe didn't answer right away. I could feel her weighing my words before she was with me again: "Just a minute."

She left the telephone for about thirty seconds. I could imagine her rooting about for the number. When she gave it to me, I thanked her and said that I would be in touch in a few days.

"Don't split a gut trying. I don't need any fresh excitement in my life right now."

We both laughed at that briefly, before we disconnected.

I looked the street up and down while apparently gazing at globes of coloured water in the druggist's window. My shadow was not in sight when I came back outside. The coast was clear, but I was unclear about what to do next. I was tempted to return to the pay phone and call the number I'd just been given. "Hang up if a man answers," I heard that voice inside me saying. Instead, I grabbed a taxi and gave the driver the address of Virginia Hill.

Virginia lived in Beverly Hills. That's as close as I can come to placing it. The local geography still buffaloed me. At first there was a highway and then streets that ended in knots of big houses. With salt water out of sight and the desert over the hills somewhere, I was lost without a boy scout. Happily, the taxi driver knew his city.

It was a big, well-grounded three-storey house, a lot like a house in Toronto's Forest Hill or Rosedale. I rang the bell.

A woman answered it, wiping her hands on a kitchen towel. "Yes?"

"I'm here to see Miss Hill. Tell her it's Mike Ward, from the other night. I was with John Barrymore."

Without nodding or any sign of approval or disapproval, she turned back into the house without shutting the door in my face. I took that as a hopeful sign.

In three minutes, she was back. "You're to wait in the front room," she said, adding "In there," when we were in the hallway. She ushered me to a chintz couch in a large, comfortable room, with broadloom-covered floors and a few shelves of books. I remember thinking that I hadn't seen a room with books in it since I left Europe.

"Mr. Ward, how nice!"

Virginia Hill was wearing a very plain black dress. It had the look of being French, but without any sewn-on bows or doodads. Her fine figure was decoration enough, and she knew it.

"I don't often get calls in the afternoon anymore. Benny scares them away. He's off in the desert. Do you know where that is?"

"You mentioned it the other night. But before that I've heard nothing about it."

"Benny says that in another five years everybody will have heard of it. He says it's going to become a major tourist attraction. Right now, frankly, it's a construction site in the desert. Would you like tea or coffee?"

"Either one. I'm still getting on to your ways out here."

"Coffee is normal in Santa Barbara at four, except among the English colony. Do you know C. Aubrey Smith? He's the leader of the English colony out here. He's a darling with the ladies, but endlessly boring on most subjects. Did you see *The Four Feathers*? 'Rather fancy a spot of rough shooting this morning, General? Wot?'"

It was a good imitation.

She went on. "And he's old enough to have known everybody. He knows Bernard Shaw, Gielgud, and the Thorndikes. He was the first Henry Higgins, opposite Mrs. Patrick Campbell's Eliza Doolittle. She said it was like acting with a cricket bat. Coffee, then?"

I nodded and she rang for it.

"You aren't here for information about the naughty things they are trying to pin on me, are you?"

"I want to find out what you can tell me about the so-called suicide of Mark Norman."

Virginia frowned at me, then smiled. It was a smile that repaid my taxi ride.

"From the very beginning, people put quotation marks around the word 'suicide.' Nobody believed it. The studio's version of what happened — bizarre as it was — became the official version."

"But those inverted commas remain."

"People won't swallow quite as much as you might like them to. The studio created a scandal to cover up a bigger scandal," she said, pouring the coffee.

"It was murder, then?"

"Have you ever doubted it? Sure, it was murder. He was killed by Norma Fisher, his first wife. She came down here from San Francisco and went back right away. She took a ferry ride to Sausalito and jumped over the side. It was a murder-suicide."

"Amazing! Your friend Phoebe doesn't know she's dead."

"You'll get used to being badly informed the longer you stay in Hollywood. We're like a nest of villages. We don't give a damn for the people over the horizon. We're starved for news out here. Oh, we hear about New York, and Broadway. But if you want news from Sausalito, move to Sausalito."

"But why did the studio push their own version?"

"Because Norma Fisher was one of their own. She had been a close associate of Asa Zavitz, the studio head, and her husband, of course. Zavitz was paying her to stay away from Hollywood. He didn't want the cops or reporters digging through the leftovers of her life. She knew where all the bodies were buried, well back to the beginning of the studio."

"So, he threw the papers a true headline-getter to keep the real story dark."

"Sure. They didn't know, when he first faced the cops at Norman's house, that she was planning to do away with herself. By then, every paper had printed the studio's version. Norma Fisher's suicide only made the Frisco papers."

"It wasn't big news."

Virginia nodded, and searched my face to find the missing pieces of the puzzle.

"You're fascinated by this story, Mike. Why? It's been a month. Isn't there anything else going on in the world?"

"Not in Hollywood there isn't. Hollywood is the world and the world is Hollywood. I've been here just long enough to have learned that."

"How did you get here?"

"I took the Twentieth Century, like everybody else."

"I meant to my house. Did someone drop you? Did you come by taxi?"

"Yes, by taxi. Why?"

"You'll soon go broke in Hollywood without a car, Mike. Hollywood isn't like New York. Cabs aren't out there looking for you. You need a car to get about in. And I know just the place."

I could tell that she had turned me into a project. I was a babe-in-the-woods and she was going to save me from all the lions, and tigers, and bears.

Virginia rang, and the maid who had let me in appeared from the back of the house.

"Mrs. Chambers, I'm going out. I'd better wear a coat."

The maid nodded and left us, as we gathered ourselves into the front hall.

"You've just witnessed half of a funny commentary on our times, Mike."

"What is? I'm sorry."

Virginia shot me a wide grin in the front hall mirror, while fixing a wide-brimmed picture hat in place. The reflection responded to her interest; she made a few quick adjustments, while continuing to speak.

"I call her 'Mrs. Chambers,' and she calls me 'Virginia.' A complete reversal of the social order. Isn't that a howl?"

Mrs. Chambers appeared with the mink and we were off. At least Mrs. Chambers didn't call her Virginia in the presence of company. The social order still hung together by a thread or two.

# CHAPTER ELEVEN

*I* didn't keep track of the streets we drove along. This town still had me buffaloed. And the distraction of silky legs on the clutch and gas pedal further reduced my attention to traffic. Virginia Hill drove fast and well, putting the black Cadillac through its paces, manoeuvring the car through traffic the way I would have. She was, as Bob Imill used to say, "a ballsy driver." Virginia's questions took up what remained of my concentration.

"Are you married, Mike?"

"Not now. But I was, twice. Both times, the marriages died of neglect. The life of a journalist is a broomstick in the wheel of family life. We're still on fairly good terms. The wounded have retired from the field. We exchange cards at Christmas and for birthdays. We keep our distance. When I passed through Paris on my way here, I thought of calling Solange. In the end, I didn't. I pay dearly for her freedom. Sometimes I feel I'm working for them."

"Are there children?"

"Why?"

"I'm a curious woman, Mike. I always ask rude questions on the way to buy a car. Don't you?"

"There are two. One with Solange, one with Laure. One boy, one girl. Very conventional."

"But you don't see them?"

"They have no interest in seeing me. I don't blame them. I was a rotten father. I was never home. We were always moving and changing schools. That kind of rotten. What about you?"

"Oh, we're going to talk about me, are we?"

"Turnabout's fair play."

"You're right, of course. Well, I can say that things weren't always this good: furs and Cadillacs. Under this carefully trained voice lies my original Southern drawl. But it wasn't at all picnic hampers, strawberry socials, and eligible beaux. No moonlight and magnolias by the river. No Gaylord Ravenals in my past. No duels fought over the girl who lived behind the car barns. I've gone hungry, waited on tables, worked hard, had a rough year or two. But now I'm getting even. I'm one of the lucky ones, getting my own back."

"You don't seem to me to be a typical product of LA."

"I'm learning. I'm good at it. And, it's true, I didn't always talk and dress this way. I've had help."

"Benny?"

"Sure. Why not? Under that rhinoceros hide, there's a sensitive boy. Don't ever tell him I told you, but he likes me to read to him. He keeps me on an even keel. I have a tendency to shoot my mouth off — that's a no-no in Benny's circle. They may enjoy a bright broad, but she's got to watch her mouth. Most of them haven't been over here all that long."

While she was talking, she drove the car into a lot with a string of red, white, and blue pennants and coloured lights over the shiny cars, all marked with prices on the windshields. A lot of the effect was lost with the sun bright overhead, but the lights did wink on and off prettily. The sign above read LAZY LUKE: NEW AND USED CARS. Another, less professionally painted, read LA POSSESSES ONLY ONE LAZY LUKE'S CAR LOT, AND THIS IS DAMN WELL IT. A fat man with sideburns and a coonskin cap came out of the shed in the middle of the lot.

"Hy-yah, Toots, what can I do you for?" He opened his mouth to continue this patter, then closed it abruptly. "Hey, you're Bugsy's girl!"

"I don't wear a collar, Luke. Not now, not ever. How yah been?"

She'd fallen into the car man's way of talking at once without seeming to notice it. Virginia Hill could flirt when she wanted to. Luke enjoyed her big smile and occasional deep breathing. They shot the breeze for three or four minutes and then Virginia asked, "Luke, I'm looking for a car for my friend here."

She introduced me. He shook my hand as though his life depended on it. He was sweating.

"What sort you lookin' for?" Luke asked me, squinting into the light.

"Something to get around in. Not too expensive."

"I gotta sweet little coupé I can let you have for five hundred dollars. Belonged to a Pentecostal minister who dropped dead the first time he took it on Route 66. It's been in a barn ever since. Took me a day nearly to clean off the bird droppin's. At five hundred, it's a steal!"

"Luke!" Virginia said, almost in a whisper.

"But for you, a friend of the family almost, I can let you have it for four."

"Luke!"

Luke wiped his mouth with the back of his wrist. "But if you take it just as she stands, you can drive it out of here for three hundred even. Shake hands and you gotta deal!"

"Thanks," I said, once again getting my hand crushed.

"Luke, that Studebaker's for a good friend of Benny and me. You can do better than that for a once and future customer."

Luke's face went grey, but he hung out a wan smile which seemed to please Virginia. "Okay, okay! You're whittling away at my liver, but I can see my way to letting you have it for two-fifty. She's solid and in the pink, except for that fender. You won't getta better shake than that."

"You're a prince, Luke. Benny and I appreciate it." Virginia nodded her approval.

With his instructions, I wrote a cheque for the car dealer. He didn't ask me for my bank reference. As a matter of form, because I was still too far behind these sudden events to have normal reactions, I thought I had better see what it was like to sit in the car and hold on to the steering wheel. It was like the car had bought me. I didn't even kick the tires.

"You like it?" Virginia asked through the open driver's side window.

"I guess I do. I'm a little overwhelmed, Virginia. Thanks. I really mean it."

Before getting in beside me, she said something to Lazy Luke, and flipped him her car keys. Virginia smiled a warm, triumphant smile. I opened the passenger door; she settled beside me, smoothing her skirt under her.

"Let's see how she runs. Luke's going to change my oil and have one of his boys drive it back to my place. Now, let's burn some rubber."

Virginia stretched out her long legs as she spoke, as though she were sitting behind the wheel.

I started the motor, after letting it recover from my first attempt. The smell of gasoline filled the front seat.

"Relax, Mike! We're just going to take a run down to Venice beach for a hot dog."

WITH JUST A HINT OF mustard running down my bare arm, Virginia and I were walking on the beach. The waves were rolling in. The full list of clichés was observed: a few children were playing along the shoreline with toy buckets and shovels. A sandcastle, half-eaten away by the Pacific, had no interest for them, although it would have been impressive less than half an hour earlier. Virginia had taken off her shoes and stockings, and seemed to be enjoying the outing.

"Mike, why are you digging into this Mark Norman business? What's your connection to it?"

"There's no connection. I don't know any of the people. I don't even think I'm very interested in exploding the official version of his death. I mean, who really gives a damn?"

"Then, what is it?"

"I'm an ornery, damned straitlaced Upper Canadian. I don't like being pushed around."

"What's an Upper Canadian?"

"A little like being from Boston: old-fashioned notions of propriety."

"Sorry, I interrupted."

"I didn't like it when Swarbrick told me to pull up my socks and I still don't like it. I guess he made me mad. And I don't like the fact that the studios can push the cops around. I don't like it the other way, either. I guess I'm in a muddle. Swarbrick isn't the worst of them. He's just a megaphone for Stanley Loomis, the studio's flack merchant."

"In a short time you've managed to step on the corns of Swarbrick and Loomis. Where did you get this death wish? And stop looking over your shoulder! Nobody's behind us. They don't know where you are. They don't know you're with me. What's the matter with you?"

"As a baby, I was dropped on my head. Often."

"The serious threat comes from Asa Zavitz."

"You think it was Zavitz who has called down the ten plagues on me?"

"Asa's an autocrat. He gags on the word 'competition.' With him for an enemy, don't even try to look for help in this town. Of course he'll have put the word out on you."

"And what's the bad news?"

"You've got mustard on your face."

"Why are you being so damned nice to me? I want to get this straight. I don't want to jump to any wrong conclusions."

"You're worried about Benny?"

"In my place, wouldn't you be?"

"Look, Mike, I think you're one sweet guy. I could easily fall for someone like you. My problem is that I'm stuck on Benny. I can't sleep when he's out of town. I worry about his crazy schemes. I'm frightened of his friends. The only thing I don't like about the present arrangement is that Benny keeps me corralled, shut in, watching Mrs. Chambers polishing my silver. It's not enough for me. I'm used to a richer diet than that. I hate watching clocks, Mike."

"So, you enjoy getting out of the house and being helpful to visiting firemen like me?"

"I like talking to you, Mike. You're good company."

"I'm glad to hear it. Don't forget to tell Benny that I'm just good company, a friend of the family. I wouldn't like to provoke him."

"If you knew him as well as I do, you'd know just how funny, how exaggerated — "

"I don't think I want to get to know him too well."

"Have you had enough of the ocean?"

"The Pacific has its points. For an ocean, that is. Do you have others?"

"There's one at Coney Island. And you still have mustard on your face."

# CHAPTER TWELVE

*W*hen I got Virginia back to her place, she invited me in for a drink. "Don't worry about Benny. He's up in the desert supervising the construction supervisors. He's not expected."

"That's a fair description of people who always turn up when they're not expected."

"Mike! Relax."

"Should tiny Belgium have trusted German promises? Should we turn away from Europe without watching our back? Never trust husbands."

"So, who's married? We're not married. Take it easy. This isn't an invitation to an orgy. I make a good cup of coffee. Come on. Coffee awaits."

"Okay, okay. It'll be something to tell my grandchildren."

We went inside. The chintz patterns on the couch and armchair reached out to grab me. I felt like a foolish schoolboy with an aged prophylactic in his wallet. I needed her help, I told myself. Benny is miles away. My presence here is innocence itself. Still, I felt a hackneyed cliché closing in on me.

Virginia excused herself when we came in, "to get the coffee started," she said. I picked up a copy of *Life* magazine, and scanned the photographs. Through the venetian blinds, I could see my Studebaker sitting at the curb. For a moment I stared at it. How often in a lifetime does one buy a car? Today was the day. I'd bought it with no more thought than if I were buying razor blades or tooth powder. Maybe that was a good thing. God knows I've lived all over the place. Surprise is a rare reaction to my experience of society. Still, there it was. I'd paid my money and the proof was parked across the front lawn from where I was sitting.

Virginia walked back into the room carrying a tray. She had not slipped into something more comfortable. She wasn't playing Myrna Loy to my William Powell. So, why was I still sitting on the edge of the couch?

The coffee was good. I'll give her top marks. There were cookies too.

"I can't take credit for the bickies. Thank Mrs. Chambers." Now she was peering at me with a lined forehead. "Mike, what the hell's the matter with you?"

"'What's the matter?' I'll tell you. A man was killed on my doorstep. The killer thought it was me. I can't go back to my flat without the LAPD catching up to me again. I have no job to go to. And I've managed to get both Swarbrick and Zavitz looking daggers at me. Isn't that enough?"

"Don't worry about the cops. If Zavitz can buy 'em, Benny can buy 'em. It's a matter for negotiation. As far as Zavitz is concerned, you just have to convince him that you're not out to destroy him and his precious studio."

"And how, my dear, do I manage that? Do you have an inspired scheme?"

"Don't be condescending. It doesn't suit you," she pouted, purring like Myrna Loy.

I was beginning to relax and enjoy myself, when, with the dramatic sense of a Belasco, the front door opened. "Hey, Toots! I'm back! Those sons of bitches up there don't know their — Who the hell are you?"

"I'm — I'm Mike Ward. We met the other night at the Italian restaurant. I was with — "

"Yeah, yeah: Barrymore and that crowd. You in pictures? I don't see all that many." He shrugged, looked around the room to see whether I had imposed my order on his things. Virginia's mouth was open. He grinned. "So how is it you're sitting in my living room?"

"Miss Hill's been helping me."

"Benny, you — "

"Shut up, doll." He smiled at her, then turned back to me. "'Helping you? Yeah? How?"

"I've stepped on the tail of Asa Zavitz and a cop named Swarbrick. Virginia, I mean Miss Hill, has been trying to save me from the heat."

"Swarbrick, huh? I know him. Big shoulders, small head. On the take from every studio in town. What'd you do to raise his hackles?"

"Benny, you've got to help Mike. He's been stirring up more trouble than he can handle. And he doesn't know anybody."

"John Barrymore? Since when ain't he somebody?" Benny cocked his head and winked.

"I just met him. He's going to try to help out, but — "

"So, how come he comes here looking for you, Toots?" Now he wasn't looking at me. I wasn't even in the room.

"Benny, don't turn this into one of your little scenarios. You look done-in, hun. You wanna drink?" she asked, but didn't move. I could see that she was taking a share of the tension I was feeling.

The front doorbell sounded. This was attended to by Mrs. Chambers. Then, suddenly, there were two pairs of gigantic shoulders in the hall.

"Hy-yah, Virge. I gotta horse for you. Belmont. Interested?"

Nobody attempted any introductions when they came into the living room. On any stage, they would be packing hardware. They looked like they just walked out of something by Damon Runyon. Benny saw me giving the boys a fast and furtive once-over.

"Toots here calls the boys 'George' and 'Lenny' out of some movie she saw. With Burgess What's-his-name? Hey, kid, you gotta drink around here?"

"Sure, Benny. Like a trip to the bank, it's coming right up. What about the supporting cast?"

"Count me in. Make mine Schlitz!"

"Ditto. You got any more of that corned beef that was here this morning?"

"The icebox's still in the kitchen. Take a hike, boys." They moved off like a pair of linebackers, quite pleased with themselves. That left me onstage under a big amber spot once more. Benny tried to resurrect the conversation, still standing in the middle of the room, shifting his weight from one leg to the other, like a handsome metronome.

"Those fellows give Virginia a big kick. They remind me of the sheep-headed boys in the Ringling Brothers' sideshow. They were albino blacks, and when I saw them, they were both completely bald. That's a hell of a way to disappoint a kid." He grinned at me, stopped rocking from foot to foot and sat down.

"What's your racket, Mike? You got restless loins around Toots, here? Or is there something else on your mind?"

Benny Siegel went through the same questions I'd been answering since I first lifted the telephone in search of information about the late Mark Norman. He was better at it than Swarbrick. There must be first-rate cops in LA, but Swarbrick wasn't one of them.

I tried to make my answers short, trimming away the confusing details that could be added later if needed. Virginia didn't seem to mind the repetition.

"Soooo!" he said, when I had finished. "I really gotta laugh at the hornets you've stirred up by kicking over the biggest hive in town. Do you have wheels?"

"Sure. That's my Studebaker out front. Miss Hill helped me pick one out this afternoon."

"She's a real Girl Guide when she likes somebody. Toots, me and the boyfriend are gonna take a little ride."

"Benny!"

"Toots, you surprise me. I thought you knew me better. I am sincerely surprised at you. I'm trying to help him out. If I don't, he'll sit in this stew until it goes sour and starts smelling up the place. Come on!"

This last was addressed to me. I got up, glancing at Virginia, searching for some hint about my future in her face. She wasn't telling.

# CHAPTER THIRTEEN

*I* was back in the passenger's seat in Benny's Buick heading through heavy traffic. At every stoplight, somebody waved to Siegel. He was popular. I hadn't known that. My education needed a lot of remedial work, if I only had time. I was learning on the job, and I was curious about what Bugsy was going to show me.

As he threaded the car through traffic, he took a sideways look at me. I kept my eyes forward, as though a drill sergeant were sitting on the hood of the Buick, frowning. In three blocks, he examined me three times.

"You're a reporter, right?"

"That's right. I work for a wire service. Our stuff is picked up by several newspapers in Canada, abroad, and in America."

"You go to school for that?"

"The war was my school. I lived over in Europe back then."

"You ever run into Lucky Luciano over there? Good-looking, heavyset mug?"

"Sorry. I wasn't around Italy much."

"You been to Verona?"

"Once. Just once. Good food, but my bed wasn't anything to write home about. Why?"

"That's where Romeo and Juliet came from. I hear they point out the house where one of them lived. I forget which one. But after all these years ..."

"Remarkable."

"That story's about a breakdown in the mail service. Not about people at all. You read *Julius Caesar*? You don't have to tell me. I can keep my mouth shut when it's important."

"Yes. In school. I was one of the assassins in the school play. I was Casca."

"Yeah? No kidding? They were all a bunch of Moustache Petes, if you ask me. Cassius had his head screwed on right, except that he took a big chance in having Brutus along for the ride. Brutus may have been well liked, but he went to pieces when he needed his head on straight. Know what I mean?"

"I think you're right. By the way, where are we going?"

"Mark Antony was the biggest crook of the lot. A gonif! It didn't take him long to start cutting up shares and double-crossing his partners."

"You should have a talk with Brooks Atkinson or George Jean Nathan one of these days."

"What mob are they with? And another thing: that Danish prince, Hamlet. What a mug! What was he, a faggot or what? He wouldn't have thought about killing himself if there weren't paying customers out front. And how about the lines! It was a stagey moment, so he grabbed it. Lucky ticket buyers! But he shouldn't have let that Norwegian mob move in on him."

"You're not going to tell me where we're going, are you? There are people I trust who know where I am. There's no way you can get away with this!"

"Relax! It won't be long now. It's on the other side of town. We're more than halfway there."

"You're planning to kill me, right?"

"Don't make me laugh while I'm driving. I wouldn't shoot any friend of Virginia's. She'd make my life a living hell. I'm nuts about that broad. If there's any killing going on, it's news to me. Don't get me wrong, it's not because you don't rate it, but when we whack somebody, it isn't out of pique, as they say. You're a stand-up guy, a friend of the family. Why would I whack you? She wouldn't talk to me for a week. I'll bet you haven't got more than fifty bucks in your pocket, and half of it's in American Express cheques. Am I right or am I right?"

"This is a strange bloody country, Mr. Siegel."

"Can the 'mister.' I'm Benny to my friends. But I don't like that other name you may have heard of. You get me?"

"Sure, Benny. I always liked that name. Are you now going to tell me where we're headed?"

"Warner Brothers. One of the biggest lots in town. There's a guy there for you to meet. An old pal of mine."

We drove down a long, straight stretch of road lined with tall palms on both sides. The trees looked dishevelled and molting, with discarded clumps of fronds in the street. The buildings along the way never made it above the second floor. Some had decorated fronts like the main street in a western movie: false cornice and gables. At last, after beating a streetcar across the tracks, Benny turned into Warner Brothers. There was an archway with a uniformed man at the gate. Siegel poked his head out the open window and talked to the elderly fellow, passing on a few coins to him. The old fellow touched his cap and we drove along to the sound stage that the guard had pointed out.

"Stage Eleven," he said. "That's down on the end on the left side. They're shooting something about truck drivers in there."

When the car had been parked in front of a fire plug, we got out. "This is how I support the local law, Ward. Otherwise, we'd be drivin' around for days. Come on."

There were a series of barn-like sheds with curved roofs. Barn-like doors kept us from seeing what was going on in Number Eleven. Then, a small door opened in a set of big ones and we went through the opening.

People were moving around in the semi-darkness. It took my eyes a few minutes to adjust to the light, which was mostly centred on a brightly lit set, representing the outside of a big, double-car garage with an electric-eye switch for opening and closing. Behind the garage, the rest of the scene was wrapped in black curtains. Silhouettes of lighting booms and cameras blocked the whole picture from us. It was quiet, except for the actors in front of the cameras, where movements looked frozen. Nobody seemed to notice our arrival. We stood and watched for about five minutes without attracting any attention.

One of the players was having his face brushed, leaving a fine mist of powder hanging about in the air. Then I recognized the actor. He had played Little John in Errol Flynn's *The Adventures of Robin Hood*. That came out last year or the year before, 1938. I tried to dredge up the name. It wouldn't come.

"That's Alan Hale getting brushed off. He gets killed in this one by a crazy broad." Benny was whispering, even though the cameras were still. The director was conferring with a script assistant of some sort. Two men were bending over a camera, which was hidden inside a surrounding box. The stage was at ground level, lighted brightly by huge Klieg lights. For each of the lights, a crew of four men stood by, whispering.

"Hey, Benny! You lookin' for George? I think he's taking a nap back there in his dressing room."

"Mike, this is Bud Sayre, the best stuntman in the business. What have they got you lined up for, Bud?"

"They're brewing something. I'm going to have a talk with the AD

when they take a long break. Are you a writer, Mr. Ward? Bu—
Benny likes writers. I tend to look out for stray women. How's
Virginia, Benny?"

"I'll tell you she's not goin' to get back on a horse again soon.
There must have been a burr under her saddle last time. She was
bruised all over."

"I warned her about that mare, and you was there and heard
me, Ben. Virginia can't be talked out of things like normal people."

"She's all right now." Benny said this through tight lips. He
wasn't encouraging any further conversation along these lines.
"How's the boy?"

"Hell, Ben, he's a total loss." Sayre took the cigarette butt he'd
been squeezing and extinguished it on his shoe. "Looks like Jimmy's
going into the family business. Can't talk him out of it. He's got
the movies caught in his teeth. He's working as a truck-wrangler
on this show. Mr. Walsh took him on as a favour, but he's making
out real fine."

"He's a good-looking boy, he should get work in front of the
cameras," Benny said.

"That's what his mother tells him. But you tell me if you know a
youngster who listens to good advice? No such animal."

"What's this scene all about?" I asked.

"Alan Hale's wife is setting him up to bump him off in the
garage. She walks though the electric eye, breaks the beam of light,
and it's curtains for her ball and chain. Carbon monoxide. Ida's
great as the wife. Crazy as a loon. That's how she plays it."

"You're talking about Ida Lupino?"

"Yeah. This morning we all got a lungful of that exhaust, but they
have the effect roped tight now. This is Alan's last day. Stick around,
there'll be drinks when we quit. In the meantime, help yourself
over at craft services."

"What's that?" I asked.

Benny shifted his head in the direction of a sandwich stand

against a far wall. "Don't ask me why they call it craft services. Movie people have funny names for things. When they want to get rid of a prop, they'll say 'kill it,' or more often '86 it.' Nobody knows what that means or where it came from. When they are shooting without recording sound at the same time, they say they're 'shooting MOS.'"

"And that stands for ...?"

"'Without sound.' That was to make fun of the German directors over here now who can't say their Ws."

"When are we going to see the person you want me to meet?"

"Keep your shorts on. I'm enjoying the look of you squirming with suspense. I shoulda been a shrink. I like helping people, and get a kick out of watching 'em fidget. Come on."

I followed him to a far wall, where a number of small, portable dressing rooms had been set up. The name on the door that Benny Siegel was knocking on read GEORGE RAFT.

George Raft was the name of the familiar actor who played in *Scarface*, *The Glass Key*, and *Each Dawn I Die*. He was a well-known name on theatre marquees. I could picture a stolid, unsmiling face. I remembered him always flipping a coin in one of his gangster pictures. George Raft! But why George Raft?

The door opened, and there he was, with a makeup towel wrapped around his shoulders. "Benny! For the love of Mike! I was just thinking about you." Raft backed into the dressing room to make way for us. It wasn't set up for much entertaining, but there were a few chairs as well as the big chair on casters Raft had been sitting in. The big mirror reflected the light from the naked light bulbs surrounding it. An open box of makeup authenticated the scene. I guess it had a cachet of a kind. Benny introduced me as a visiting Canadian. After some irrelevant talk about Vancouver, interest in me subsided.

"You didn't come all the way down here to redeem your marker from Thursday night? I know you're good for it. You're damned lucky you found me here. Except for a few retakes, this picture's in the can." To me, he said, "Benny and I were practically born in the same bed. My best friend, Baby Blue Eyes."

This wasn't the stiff, unsmiling face of my memory, but an open, generous, smiling one, covered with flesh-coloured makeup. He pulled the towel away from his collar and motioned us to the chairs against the wall facing the makeup table. "You son of a bitch! It's good to see you, kid!"

"Likewise, you ... you ... What the hell you got on your face?"

"Liechner five and nine. It's to get rid of my beard. You won't believe it but I shaved twice today already. Tell me, what's going on up north in Nevada? You getting a divorce settlement in Reno?" The actor spoke in a deep, flat, unaccented voice, almost a monotone.

"Where you hear that?"

"I figured it. Isn't that what Virginia wants? How is the doll? I haven't seen her since we sold that old gambling tub to three Greeks who got pinched."

"The Limassol brothers! I'd forgotten them!" They both broke out laughing and exchanged bear hugs. "Hey, Georgie, you're looking good."

"You think so? I put on a few pounds. I don't know. I should work out more, but I'm a lazy bum. I gotta trainer who knows how to make me sweat. You think I look okay?"

"You do."

"You sure?"

"What? I'm going to lie to you, my oldest friend?"

"I got this trainer who comes in. He'd have me workin' out all day. Me? I prefer a day at the races or a couple of hours by the pool. That's only civilized. Right?"

"Right."

"Now they got me readin' a script they want me to do. You ever see a play called *Everybody Comes to Rick's*? It ran on Broadway a couple of weeks."

"Musta missed it."

"I'm not crazy about it. The hero's always crying in his beer about some dame who ditched him. I think I'll pass on it."

"Don't let the studio push you around."

"They can give it to that hack Reagan. It's his speed."

Now it was Benny's turn to bring me into the conversation. George nodded as he listened. Benny had most of the facts right, but the details were somewhat embellished. In the main, as Huck Finn says about Mark Twain, he told the truth.

"So you're digging into the suicide everybody's been talking about?"

"And he's got Swarbrick and Asa Zavitz on his tail. Me and Virginia are playing Dr. Watson to his Sherlock, sort of. What do you know that might help?"

"What makes you think I know anything about that crowd, Benny? Come on! I don't see those people! They don't come over and sit around my pool."

"Don't kid a kidder, Georgie! You play pinochle with Asa twice a week. If that's a lie, I can't count up to forty-eight cards. Don't bury the Jack of Diamonds on me, sport."

"Uncle! Okay! Okay! I give up! What do you want from my life?"

"How can we get at Asa?"

I was keeping my mouth shut through all of this, only taking in how much alike the two of them looked arguing with one another. It was hard — impossible — to tell which was the movie star and which the racketeer.

"I think I gotta angle," Raft said to both of us, switching his eyes from Benny's face to mine and back again. "There's a small debt of honour that has not been discharged since a week ago last Thursday. Asa's always on the back of anybody who don't pay up. Says it's his code. Well, I guess I've got him over a barrel. Will that help you guys out, or what?"

Benny grinned, and I joined him.

At this point Alan Hale broke into the dressing room asking for a clean towel.

"It's hotter than a barbecue out there! Those brutes are murder!"

He didn't stay for introductions, but was gone again as suddenly as he'd come. It's funny how the brain works. I couldn't get over how much like Alan Hale Alan Hale looked. Why did I expect Errol Flynn or Basil Rathbone to turn up next? I'd already encountered Flynn. I still had his handkerchief in my pocket. Was that what passed for a casual meeting in this town? Next time we'd be old friends.

Wars and peace conferences I could take in my professional stride, but this ...? I was not finding it easy, this hobnobbing with the stars. I found politicians easier to swallow.

## CHAPTER FOURTEEN

*I* made the necessary phone calls from one of the booths at a drugstore on Sunset. I didn't speak directly to the great man, but maybe the secretary next to the personal and private secretary. I came away from the phone feeling as though I had just been in one of those endless royal corridors with flunkies announcing my approach to the throne as I moved through one double doorway after another. When I hung up, I had a time and an office number in the main building at A-Z-P.

I remember buying a paper at the corner of Hollywood and Gower and carrying a paper cup of coffee back to my car. That's when the lights went out. I didn't see who did it, but the glimmer of day in my head flashed silvery-white starbursts then quickly faded to black. I dimly remember seeing black clothing. This led to a dream of a Berlin rally I'd covered the year before. I'd been watching a parade of troops, then along came a brass band with the players all dressed as travesties of ugly women: striped stockings, outlandish wigs, enormous breasts, hideous masks inspired by comic strips. The crowd was laughing and pointing to the players. I began to grin, too, until I saw the dull green boots marching, *click, click, click,* under the bizarre wired skirts. A muted trumpet was playing "wah, wah, wah."

"Mr. Ward?"

"I'm not marching today."

"Mr. Ward!"

One of my eyes let in white light, which struck me as funny since I had been seeing black uniforms a moment earlier. Now they were white. I was looking into a pretty face looking down at me. There was no smile of recognition.

"Where am I?" I said unoriginally.

"Cedars of Lebanon Hospital. Head Injuries and Strokes. Fifth floor. I'm Crawford. Do you remember me?"

"Cedars? That's a hospital!"

"That's right. And you're in it. You've been here two days. Don't you remember talking to me? We've had some long talks, you and I."

"Sorry. I can't remember anything. Do I have a bump on the back of my head?"

"Yes. There's a bump with a bandage covering it. We had to shave away part of your hair to get at the wound. You've had a fairly serious insult to your brain."

"Just like Nick Carter and Philip Marlowe."

"Only this wasn't in a book or movie."

In a moment she was gone and I had an uninterrupted view of the ceiling. When I turned my head, I could see two other beds with bandaged heads in them. That was enough for one outing. I closed my eyes again and slept.

The next time I tried to open both eyes, but only the left one worked. Again I saw the nurse, looking straight down at me. "One of my eyes isn't working," I said.

"Not to worry. It's swollen shut, that's all. There's no damage. Did you enjoy your visit?"

"What visit? Who came to see me?"

"They said they were your brothers. But they gave false names. I wrote them down for you. Here: Claude Dukenfield, John Decker, and Jack Barleycorn. I think I've seen one of them before someplace."

These memory lapses bothered me, but my nurse, Miss Crawford, told me that it was to be expected. "You can't just get up and walk away with a head injury like that."

"They do it in the movies."

"But this is Cedars, not a Saturday matinee. And one more thing that I'd better warn you about. Don't drive your car. Your Ontario licence has been suspended."

"Damn it!"

"It's all part of the service. You can take your test again in six months."

That evening I tasted real food again. The boys were back to see me the following morning. After they left, Crawford helped me to get out of bed. She assisted me in having my first-ever shower in a sitting position, and with a pink rubber shower cap keeping my head dry.

The next morning, I joined my fellow sufferers in a lunch room down the hall from my own room, which I shared with G. Marchese, D. Cass, and H. Ohlendorf, according to the signs posted on the door. They made pleasant companions, although Cass was always trying to climb out of bed. He didn't seem to be able to talk lying down. Marchese kept shouting, "Everybody just calm down!"

During the week I was there, I got to know my floor. After the first few days I had earned status enough to be able to get out of bed on my own and fetch my own coffee from the ward's meeting room. As my dressings were changed regularly, and my head began to heal, I felt that I had the run of the place.

One morning there was a call for me from Asa Zavitz's office. It was a complaint that I had failed to keep an appointment. This struck me as odd. Even with scrambled wits, I could see that Zavitz must have known of my injury, since he knew where to call to leave the message.

The hospital social worker gave me a lesson in how to cope with the outside world. He furnished me with a couple of prescriptions, phone numbers, and a pamphlet on home care for head injuries. Then, somewhat to my surprise, they sprung me. Crawford showed me where my street clothes had been hidden. I walked out into the sunlight once more. It was hot. That's when I noticed that the hospital must have been cooled with air conditioning. The shaggy palms nodded as I blended into pedestrian traffic.

I RETURNED TO MY FLAT to sleep off the previous week. I heard no news on the radio, read no papers, and saw only Virginia Hill, who came over with a hamper of fruit and other edibles. We made a picnic on the floor of my flat, while I tried to remember whether the pamphlet I took away from Cedars said anything about hard liquor.

Virginia returned with Benny Siegel a couple of days later, but we had our picnic at Laguna Beach.

"I know it's a bit late now, but it was stupid of me to return to the Granovskys' place. That's where Olson was shot. I need my head examined."

"Maybe you need another place to stay. It's a big city."

By the time I felt like myself again, I sent my apologies to Zavitz's outer reach of secretaries, and made a brand new appointment.

ASA ZAVITZ WAS A SMALL man with glasses, sitting under a huge equestrian portrait of Napoleon Bonaparte. It was a copy of the one in the Louvre. Without this backdrop, there was nothing about him that would arrest one's attention. On the street you would pass him by. But I'm certain he was not prone to pedestrian travel, unless it might be for showing off his domain to visiting royalty. He appeared to need the *mise en scène* of the late French emperor to point out that he was not a walk-on or spear-carrier in this drama. The carefully combed hair and the display handkerchief in the pocket of his well-cut but simple double-breasted suit illustrated another facet of his personality. Flamboyance and simplicity working the same street. But to make everything perfectly clear, he was sitting behind the biggest desk I've seen outside a courtroom. At first I didn't see the dais on which his leather, high-backed chair stood. Mr. Zavitz was self-conscious of his height, and took advantage of the stratagems that would lend stature to his authority. It was a foolish notion, for, as head of the studio, he was the ultimate authority. He needed no props or acolytes, no visible bowing minions. This idea had either passed him by, or he had ignored the notion that enough was enough.

He didn't get up when I entered his enormous office, but at least he didn't fuss about with papers in front of him to show what a busy man it was that I was interrupting. He looked up when I was about a quarter of a mile from his desk. His baby-blue eyes followed my progress across the broadloom. As I advanced, he waved me to a chair.

"You're not a cigar smoker," he said with some deliberation. "I can always tell a cigar man, and you don't have the look."

"Isn't that like saying you can always spot a Jew? You never know when you're right or wrong. It's not good science. But, just the same, no thanks. I don't smoke anymore."

"I get these made for me in Havana. By the case. The next shipment is late. Young Stan Loomis, who has a meeting with me in fifteen minutes, always helps himself to a handful of them. He doesn't even ask. But the mirror to your right tells me things when I straighten my necktie. That's how he takes advantage. Unfortunately, somebody's always taking advantage."

I had to admire the clever way he brought introductory chat down to the point. Then, he spoiled it.

"The funny thing is, I've never seen him with one in his mouth. I think he gives them away at the golf club. Makes him a big man. On my dollar!"

He was looking me over, as I was him.

"It was good of you to see me at short notice."

He waved his left hand as an answer.

"Tell me, Mr. Ward, what can I do for you?"

I took a deep breath and tried to remember the things I'd worked out to say in the car as I drove to the studio. After filling him in on who I was and why I was sitting in his office, while he nodded regularly, absently rolling a cigar between two fingers, I told him all of what I knew and most of what I suspected. "My interest in the death of Mark Norman is not a casual one. I've long been convinced that the story is longer and deeper than we have been led to believe. The public already suspects more than it sees in the papers and hears on the radio."

Here I was interrupted. "Look, Mr. Ward, I could let you go on about this, and look over at you with big eyes full of surprise and wonder. But I'm in the business of dealing out surprise and wonder. The surprise and wonder of millions of people right across this great country and around the fucking world, I'm talking about! So, I'm something of an authority on surprise and wonder. But I'm no dealer in bullshit! It's a waste of time and an insult to the intelligence of both of us. Okay?" He used the naughty words with ease and familiarity. He could turn it on and off as the situation demanded. I nodded, but said nothing. He was already drawing breath for another oration.

"So! I could pretend I never heard of you. I could play innocent. But you've been a stitch in my side since you got off the Twentieth Century. That cop, Lieutenant What's-his-name ...?"

"Swarbrick?" I said.

"Swarbrick! He's a few charges short of an indictment, if you know what I mean. But he's useful for the usual problems we have with the public. At the studio, we have our own men. Do you think there's going to be a war, Mr. Ward?"

"Canada's already in arms. On their way overseas. Germany's been bombing London."

"Damn it all! I wish I could help out! I told Sam Goldwyn six months ago. They're making a movie over at Metro now."

"Are you going to help out? Or are we going to beat the Germans here on your back lot?" I said, trying to bring his eyes back from the ceiling to me.

"It's terrible what's happening over there: the persecutions, the overthrow of law."

"What are you doing to put a stop to it?"

"Like everything in life, my friend: it depends." He wasn't looking at the ceiling now. "Can I trust you?"

"I'm not here to make a deal, Mr. Zavitz."

"Settle down! You'll make a deal if you have to. If it's in your interest. You didn't make a deal with Mussolini or with Dollfuss. That article you wrote in London took courage. Ah! That is why you're here! Your employers were not happy with you over there. Ha! Now, you're making waves over here. What can they do with you, Mr. Ward?" It was an unkind smile, the smile of a bully, of a bad loser in a moment of triumph.

"My readers are numbered in the dozens; you reach millions."

"You pinned the appeasement label on Chamberlain."

"You've got your researchers working overtime. That's flattering."

"Flattery's the way to cut through red tape and bull. There are other ways as well. Look, Mr. Ward, we are both grown-up men with some experience of the world. Most of the people I see are like children. They can't see farther than the end of their opinions. You know what I mean?"

"No, I don't know what you mean. You say a lot of things. I

didn't come here to give you a swell time, Mr. Zavitz. What I'm after is information. You and your people have polluted the source. My job is to cut through that misinformation and get at the truth. Sure, that might not make good publicity for you and the studio, but think of the mess that will eventually come out. The longer you sit on the lid, the louder it'll pop."

"Mr. Ward, how would you like to come and work for me? I understand that you are no longer with your news service."

"That's right, thanks to you."

"I can pay you more than any news service."

"When I write this story, I won't have to look far to find a place to file it. As to your offer: thanks, but no thanks. I've got work to do. And look, Mr. Zavitz, I'm not out to blacken the name of this studio or any studio. I'm just trying to get at what happened."

"What does it matter? Who cares? This isn't Pulitzer Prize material. Your words are not going to be chipped into a monument. They're tomorrow's fish-wrap. Try to understand my situation. I got a beautiful, talented woman works for me. She's a close personal friend. More than that, she's money in the bank. You know what that woman's worth? That's why I got to protect her."

"That sensational story you gave out? Was that to protect her?"

"The boy got carried away. He's inventive. Maybe too inventive. But I can live with it. Come work for me. I got a good place for you."

"Maybe you'd like to send me on an important assignment to Paris, where I might run into other people on your payroll. And, maybe you haven't heard. Emma Schneller is no longer in an English prison. She's got a long memory for names like that of Lady Reynolds. She boarded a boat bound for the US, and took the Twentieth Century from New York. I have reason to believe she's here already."

"Stop that! I won't listen to you!"

"You can't bottle secrets, Mr. Zavitz."

"Get the hell out of here! You hear? Scram! Beat it! You've made a very dangerous enemy, young fellow! And there's no place in this town for you to hide!"

## CHAPTER FIFTEEN

"*I* could hear that all the way out here in the hall!" The voice came roaring down the corridor. It belonged to a tall, slim man with a sports jacket, an open shirt, and a smile you could drive a truck through. I needed a smile after what I'd just been through. At first I thought it was a screen actor, whose face should have been familiar to me, but I couldn't pin a name to it. The stranger followed me as I groped for the way out. My mind had suddenly gone on French leave.

"This way," the voice shouted, catching up to me.

By now, I glimpsed the sunshine coming through a big glass door. The tall fellow pushed the door open for me, and followed me back into that near-Egyptian sun.

"Poor chap, you look like you could use a drink." He punctuated the remark with a snigger that was almost a laugh.

I stopped to look my pursuer in the face. "Who the hell are you, anyway?" I can't explain the vehemence in my voice. A release, I guess. I regretted it at once.

"I'm the fellow who gets what you just got on a daily basis. Believe me, I know what it feels like. I'm supposed to be Number Two around here. Ha! Mostly I feel like I'm the office boy or the postman. I'm making my escape, trying to catch up to my sanity. Have you seen it? And, by the way, do you have transport?"

"You sound like an English public school boy. I came out here by taxi. I hope I can flag one down, or get the man at the gate to call one for me."

"Don't worry. I'm headed for a ride. It might as well be in your direction."

"Who did you say you were?"

"I didn't, but my name's Jeff Swift."

"The Wonder Boy?"

"Now don't you start! It's hard enough around here without that!" He sniggered again, and it was still incongruous with his bearing. He had the looks of a leading man, slim, well built, with a haircut that looked seasoned, broken in. His face was as smooth as George Raft's, covered with flesh tone.

We did not walk far. I could see the general car park about half a block farther down the lot, but Swift stopped before three motorcycles parked under a sheltering palm and acacia bush. "I hope you don't mind riding pillion? It's not a bad ride. You'll see."

It took me a minute to realize that I was being invited to mount one of these two-wheeled beasts.

"Which one's yours?"

"They all are. But we'll take the Crocker. She'll see you home."

"My name's Mike Ward, by the way. I've just had a set-to with your boss."

"I heard that through the door. Asa hasn't yet discovered the art of conversation. He's always giving a public address. He knows everything about the business, but has rarely heard the word 'no.'"

"I've heard that."

"It irks him something awful. Mike, you're not one of his favourite people this month."

As he exchanged his sports jacket for a leather windbreaker and a leather helmet with goggles, I tried to draw a bead on my new acquaintance. I knew he stood high in the studio's hierarchy, second only to Zavitz, himself. But I was looking at a very young man, a boy almost. His face was long and affable, although in his leather coat he had become a little daunting, almost sinister. He held out an extra helmet to me and I strapped it on. I felt a little like Buck Rogers in the twenty-fifth century.

Swift bestrode the machine in one movement, and waited for me to climb on behind him. He kicked the Crocker to life with his foot, then revved the engine with the hand throttle. A moment later, we were away. The studio buildings slid behind us; through a narrow passage we were suddenly on the back lot, which looked like a giant's playroom. We drove past cut-away submarines, the bridge of a battle cruiser, and a road of tall poplars, reminding me of rural France. Then we were driving up an alley lined with beached small craft: lifeboats, launches, yachts, and, on turning a corner, there were all sorts of horse-pulled coaches and buggies. In the next row, I saw a naked guillotine standing silhouetted against a bright sky. Nearby, I glimpsed the facade of a Southern plantation, next to it a Cape Cod cottage, across from the front of a sprawling ranch house. The next moment, the bike was roaring though the main street of a wild western town, with pieces of lath closing shut the saloon's swing doors.

While I was still catching my breath, Jeff Swift had pulled us back among the sound stages, row on row of them. He pulled up at a curb and turned to see if I was still clinging to the seat. I gave him thumbs up and he underlined his grin with another roar of the big V-shaped motor. And we were away again, this time off the lot and into traffic.

As a pedestrian in Los Angeles, I found things confusing. I had learned very little geography from the back windows of taxis. But from the pillion of a motorcycle, I could learn nothing at all. I recognized the props belonging to a city: lampposts, hydrants, intersections, and storefronts, but no map of the area was forming in my mind. It was a jumble of drugstores and haberdasheries slanting by us as we rounded a corner, then more of the same when we went around the next.

At last he pulled up across from a large nightclub, with the unlighted neon silhouette of a woman's face over the entrance. A sign by the doorway read: THROUGH THESE PORTALS PASS THE MOST BEAUTIFUL GIRLS IN THE WORLD.

"Where the hell are we?"

"This is the stony heart of Hollywood. Sunset near Vine. That's Earl Carroll's place across the street. He opened it just after Christmas a couple of years ago and runs it with Beryl Wallace. She's chief wrangler of the female staff. If you're looking for a girlfriend, this could be a starting point."

"They don't look open. The sign's dark."

"It's not a daytime spot. I thought we might have a cup of coffee across the street." He dismounted from the Crocker in a long, lazy motion, a cowboy climbing down from his saddle horse. I clambered off as well as I could, feeling the stiffness in my knees and ankles. I followed Jeff Swift into a small restaurant with a bar down one side and half-enclosed booths down the other. The all-over look of the place was a disagreeable, smoky yellow. He picked a booth partway down the narrow room with its patterned tin ceiling and mirror-studded walls. He ordered coffee for both of us.

"Tell me about yourself," he said, smiling.

I did that, skipping over birth, baptism, the measles, whooping cough, and two bad marriages, but stressed my romps in the flesh-pots of Paris, Berlin, and London. When done, I lit a cigarette, and demanded reciprocity.

"I came to A-Z-P as a bookkeeper. Before that I worked in a shoe store. I quit when my boss, Irving, told me I had a big future in selling footwear. Then I trained to be a flight attendant for an airline that went bust. At my best, in my early career, I was a very good salesman." Once again that snigger.

"You did all this here in L.A?"

"Born and bred in this brier patch. Why?"

"No special reason. How did Asa Zavitz discover you?"

"A year after I started here, my father died, and I took some time off. Asa sent a wreath to the funeral home. When I came back, he had his eye on me. He's really a soft-hearted man, Mike. Heart of gold. We get normal and Jewish holidays off. Whatever they say about his sort. Only I know how much he gives to charities every year. Asa's no Jack Benny with his money. He treats everybody at the studio like family."

"One big happy —"

"Cut that out! Asa's a wonderful man and a generous employer. He provides entertainment for millions. Don't sneer at him!"

"Okay! Okay! Sorry! I'm just trying to get my bearings."

"A.Z. treats me like his own son." He pronounced the "Z" in the American way, so that it rhymed with "tea."

"I said I was sorry. What do you do around here to amuse yourself?"

"Well, there are the girls across the street."

"Yes, you mentioned them."

"Although Beryl watches them pretty closely."

"And?"

"I do some target shooting. Howard Hill's coaching my archery. He taught Flynn for Robin Hood. I go fishing up at Tahoe and off Santa Rosa. I have a small yacht. We sail off to Catalina or down to La Jolla. I like fencing, and a few of my friends have bikes — Indians and Harleys. Last month I sold my Brough. You would have liked that."

"What's a Brough?"

"Brough Superior SS100. The bike Lawrence of Arabia was riding when he crashed. I also swim a mile every morning before breakfast."

"No wonder you look fit!"

"You should get in some swimming while you're out here."

"Yes, I should do that."

"Are you staying long?"

"Some people are trying to make it permanent."

"I heard about that from Asa."

"My fate was in the hands of my Toronto employers. I was moved here from London as a punishment for talking about appeasement before the word became fashionable. Now, I don't know what I'm going to do."

"Are you for or against the war?"

"I'm a reporter. I write about what happens. I'm essentially a man of peace in my private life. You?"

"I like the way Hitler's got Germany moving again. He knows how to handle labour. And he'll keep the Reds out of Western Europe."

"Not without cost. I've seen his Third Reich up close."

Swift scowled, then added: "I don't see how a war can help our business. They're talking of building ships out here, but I can't see how a war can help anybody. We're losing most of our European distribution. I'd just as soon stay neutral and sell to both sides. Who gives a damn whether Germany takes a bite out of the Czechs' rump? Bunch of foreigners. None of our business."

"How well did you know Mark Norman?"

"Can't you give it a rest?"

"I get paid for asking awkward questions."

"Nobody's paying you now, Mike."

"Old habits die hard."

"But why this story? There must be a million stories as interesting as this one."

"Your man Loomis whetted my interest when he sicced the cops on me."

"Loomis is a good company man, but like many guardians he gets carried away. He has a couple of LA's finest in his pocket. Like Swarbrick."

"Don't remind me."

"Swarbrick may strike you as a clown, but he has brass knuckles and his people know how to give you a hard time."

"Where did Norman fit in?"

"We were Asa's right-hand men. He handled distribution, I kept my eye on production. Asa keeps — kept — his eye on Norman and on me. He doesn't trust anyone one hundred per cent. I admired the way he tried to introduce some discipline into the people working under him. If this great country lacks anything, I think discipline would head the list."

"So you saw a lot of one another?"

"On the lot and off. We both enjoyed tennis. He liked to play cards, and did that mostly with Asa. I don't gamble much. Asa and Mark liked horses, too. Asa's a well-known breeder and sportsman."

"Tell me about the day he died."

"What is this, an inquisition? 'Turn off that light in my eyes, Sergeant! I won't rat on my pals!' 'You'll burn for this, kid!' 'No, no! You got nothin' on me.' I thought we were having a friendly conversation. They do the good-cop-bad-cop routine better at Warners."

I liked the way he acted both parts. I guess it goes with the territory.

"Sure. But, like the rest of this town, I'm interested in what happened. Write me down as a Barbara Lorrison fan. I can't get enough of her."

"Oh, Babs is okay. She's got a lot of talent and a lot of heart. We all love her dearly, and are committed to helping her through this rough spot."

"Did that include creating the suicide story?"

"Not you too!" Again the nervous snigger. "Hell, Ward, where do you get this stuff? Were you the guy who started the story about concentration camps in Germany? The English started them in South Africa. Did you know that? They're just a way to organize a crowd of people you don't want running loose. They get food and shelter, which is more than some of them deserve, more than they can get on their own."

"You're changing the subject."

"We're talking about spreading stories without proof."

"Who put the muzzle on the cops? Why try to set my tail burning? Why run the family maid off to France? Come on. I wasn't born yesterday. Why the crazy suicide story?"

"I told you a minute ago that I run the production side of this business. I don't run the studio. I'm production, not public relations. Asa's got a talent for organization. More important, he's got the job. He knows where every picture in the schedule is as of this date. I suspect he could give you a count on the number of paper clips we own and how many writers are under contract. If you want to know about production, I'm your man. If not, ask Asa."

With the timing of a great actor, Swift got to his feet and looked down at me. But, instead of enlarging the furrow along the lines he'd been hoeing, he grinned, and said, "Come on."

## CHAPTER SIXTEEN

*T*HROUGH THESE PORTALS PASS THE MOST BEAUTIFUL GIRLS IN THE WORLD, the sign read. Another read CLOSED MONDAYS. We breasted traffic in the middle of the block, and entered Earl Carroll's. The beauty crop of the world was not in evidence.

It was cool and dark inside, not the dark of a mine or of midnight, but the deep gloom you experience when you come out of the sun. It took me a minute to adjust to the normal inside light of day. The room was almost deserted. A bartender was shining glasses and stacking them behind him on the bar. Although I could see bottles, hundreds of them in all shapes and sizes, they were locked behind a steel grid beyond the bar. A grey-haired man wearing a jersey with tuxedo trousers came from the back. His expression read *I'm sorry, gentlemen, we are closed*, but upon seeing us he said, "How wonderful to see you, Mr. Swift! Is Earl expecting you? He didn't say anything to me."

"I'm not looking for Mr. Carroll, Albano. We've just come in to get out of the sun. I know you're not open."

"Make yourselves comfortable, gentlemen. I'll send some coffee right away."

Exit Albano. Enter, soon after we were seated, an extra with a tray carrying coffee cups and a brimming beaker. "I hope you can handle more java, Mike? I should have asked."

"Sure. Coffee's fine."

"I forget sometimes that there's a gate to our lot, and that the influence I wield there stops at that gate."

"Come on, Jeff, you're too modest. I think you have a good grasp of the influence you wield. We've just seen a good sample of it."

"Oh, don't pay any attention to Albano. He was born bowing and scraping. It's second nature. He's Italian."

"But if I drop in tonight, I won't get any farther than the velvet rope."

"Ha! Now who's being modest? With those pieces you've been writing about restaurants, and a Pulitzer? Every head waiter in town knows you. I've got you there, Mike."

We both laughed at that, once I allowed for my pinched vanity.

Jeff sat back and drained his cup. "Let's have a real drink. The sun's well above the yardarm and we're both of legal drinking age." He signalled the bartender, who was tending his glasses. He summoned Albano, who unlocked the liquor. I ordered a Canadian Club, Jeff ordered bourbon.

Drink on an empty stomach sometimes leads to inspired questioning. That day, whatever skills I had in that department had abandoned me. I heard myself asking questions I was sure I had already asked. "How the hell did you get into the movie business, Jeff?"

"Well, I wasn't a New England furrier, or a junk collector from New Brunswick. I was born right here in LA."

"Some of those junk pedlars call it the steel business these days. Don't condescend."

With a few reservations, I enjoyed talking to Swift. He appreciated the dance of language the way some of my newspaper and wire service friends did. Language was the nuts and bolts of communication, out of which we had made our world. In language we are at home. It is our residence, our curse. Here, if we toil not nor spin, we almost certainly eat not.

"You were telling me how you got into this racket."

"That's right, I was. 'How I came to be the Wonder Boy.' The short answer is that I was a good bookkeeper. That's my version. The papers say I worked some magic charm on the old man. That he made me into the son he never had, that I wormed my way into his sentimental heart. That's not the truth, either. Asa has a son my age, and he adores his father. Asa knows I'm a better business risk than Kevin."

"Kevin?"

"Kevin Zavitz. If we ever film his life story, we'll call him Chauncy Shapiro or Izzy McTavish."

"I wasn't wondering about the sound of his name. It's that I know him. He was at the London School of Economics when I was covering a story there last year. I knew the name Zavitz sounded familiar when I first heard it. He wasn't clinging to Papa's coattails back then."

"Sure, he's a good kid, but I'll bet he's never slept in a one-star hotel. In London, he compromises on his allowance to stop at the Dorchester."

"When's the last time you slept rough?"

"Look, Mike, there are many people in this town, to parody Handel's *Messiah*, who are acquainted with relief."

We had another round. "Do I detect a note of —?"

"Sure! Wouldn't you? When the kid gets tired of playing schoolboy, they'll take me out with the daily trash."

"Where you'll be fought over by every studio in town. You're sitting in the catbird seat any way it works out."

"We'll see what happens. We'll see."

While I never boast about my capacity for strong spirits, I have a veteran newsman's stamina. Jeff Swift was less fortunate. Midway through the third round, he began to look as though his features were settling to the lower half of his face. Under his healthy-looking Hollywood tan, he'd gone pale.

"What English king came after James II?" I forget how we got on to British royalty.

"Wasn't it Charles II? I don't remember."

"It was Willy of Orange, called the third of that name."

"Okay, genius, tell me this: Who came after Lincoln?"

"Wendell Willkie. I don't know."

Albano had been keeping an eye on us. When Jeff finally passed out, I asked him to get us a taxi and to look after the Crocker, or Brough, or whatever he called his motorcycle. He helped both of us into the taxi when it arrived.

"Do you know where Mr. Jeffrey Swift lives?"

"Maybe you want a tour bus. I just landed this hacking job from my brother-in-law less than a week ago." Flummoxed, I went back into Earl Carroll's to find Albano. Sane and sober in a crisis, he looked it up under a green lamp on an antique writing desk. I seem to be more sensitive to colours I never notice when I'm quite sober. I passed the address to the driver, and settled back into the seat, where Jeff was beginning to remind me of the Monster at Decker's house. I tried to watch where the driver was taking us, but, as usual, this city confused me. It might have been the drink, but I had been confused before in this city without the taste of stale liquor on my breath.

We stopped on a semi-circular drive in front of an impressive Palladian mansion somewhere in Beverly Hills. It possessed a centred front door with a fan light recalling New England.

The driver helped lug Jeff's body up to the door, where I paid him off without thinking of my own getaway. Now, feeling slightly naked, I rang the doorbell.

I delivered the body up to a butler, who looked like he'd come from Central Casting. His expression suggested that this was not the first time the master had come home in such a condition. Jeff was hustled upstairs and out of sight. A moment later, I found myself back on the street with no taxi waiting.

A little the worse for wear myself, I realized that I still didn't know where the hell I was. I tried walking a block, prospecting for a busier street. I needed lights, traffic, people. But one suburban street wound into another. And I had no map.

I retreated, while I still had some memory of where I had come from. Again I rang the bell to be greeted, if that's the word, by the same stony face. "Mr. Swift has retired, sir. He is not receiving visitors."

"I could guess that much. Will you call a taxi for me? I have no idea where I am."

"Certainly, sir. Would you like to wait in the library?" He showed me the way, giving a great impression of Eric Blore, the best-known movie gentleman's gentleman. "May I offer you a drink, sir?"

"Have you any Bromo-Seltzer?"

"I'll see what I can find, sir. May I ask your name, sir?"

I told him, and in a few minutes I was feeling a fine spray of exploding bubbles in my nose. Soon after, I heard what I thought might be my taxi coming to the door, but I was mistaken. It was, or it appeared to be, the lady of the house.

"Who the hell are you?"

She was a handsome woman, blonde as cornsilk, with her hair coiled high on her head. She had fine, regular features. She sloughed off her mink coat, letting it fall to the mushroom-coloured broadloom.

"My name's Mike Ward. I just came home with Jeff."

"Was he conscious?"

"I didn't notice. There's a taxi coming to see me home."

"Would you like a drink?"

"I've just had a Bromo. Thanks, anyway."

"Mike Ward. You're the fellow who likes his corn pone, chitlins, and collard greens? I've read your articles. You may have started a trend."

"I hope you're right. I assume you're Mrs. Swift. Is there another name that goes with that?"

"You mean, you don't recognize me?"

"Sorry. I'm new here, freshly imported from the Continent."

"I work under the name Martha Collier."

Immediately, I felt like an idiot. Of course the name was familiar. She had starred in umpteen top-grossing films over the last decade and a half. In Moscow, people asked me about her. In Paris, couturiers copied her clothes, and, in England, young actresses imitated her special delivery of a line of dialogue. I was impressed. I'd seen her films *Cleopatra & Co* and *Joan of Arc*.

"How do you do?" I said. "You said you work under that name. What do your friends call you?"

"Mary Tait. But I haven't used that name since I came to A-Z-P. I'm new baptized. They changed my name, my hairline, my eyebrows, and my clothes. There isn't much of 'me' anymore."

"There are thousands who wouldn't believe that."

Just then the taxi came and I have nothing to tell my grandchildren about the rest of the evening.

I gave the driver the address where I'd first met Barrymore on Bundy Drive. Even though I'd spent a good deal of the day in the company of Jeff Swift, who was closely connected to the font of all my troubles, I still didn't feel it was safe to return home. I wasn't sure that my place wasn't being watched. I knew it was a long shot, but I was feeling lucky. So, faster than I expected, I was once again at the front door of John Decker's studio. This time there was no Hobart. Decker opened the door himself. Now, I've known a few artists in my time. I was used to all sorts of shenanigans and eccentric dress among them. The painter Mondrian, who we called "the Dutchman," used to greet his guests in a dirty undershirt. In Brantford a painter I knew worked in a three-piece suit and tie. This made him look more like a banker or bond salesman than a painter. A dear old friend, who painted portraits, regularly wore his ancient Trinity College blazer at his easel. A hard-rock-miner-turned-landscape painter once greeted me wearing a frilly pink apron. Another wore a chef's striped apron: very Parisian. Decker opened his front door wearing an academic cap and gown, both so paint-smeared that it was impossible to make out the original black.

"Ah! You're the Australian." He moved back from the open door, inviting me to enter his dim, medieval dwelling. The house, throughout its shadowed corridors, thumbed its nose at light itself, until we got to the bright studio. It shimmered with light coming through a huge north window.

"I forget your name, I'm sorry to say. You're a pal of Jack's. I remember that much. Am I right? I think I still remember my own friends."

I gave him my name and reminded him of our first meeting.

"Of course, of course. My head has not quite recovered from that night. Still, I'm glad you came. Sit there on the rostrum. The other chairs have brushes soaking on them. I want to try something."

Decker went to his easel, moved it closer to the rostrum, and climbed after me to arrange me and the chair I had taken. He placed a freshly stretched canvas on the easel and clamped it down.

"Jack got up early this morning and left before I was awake. Hope you're not in a hurry? I think he's dubbing sound over at Metro. I don't know why they can't get the sound and pictures right the first time, but then I'm not in the film business. Would you like a drink? Hair of the dog?"

"Sure. When do you expect him back?"

"With Jack that's hard to say. Depends on who he runs into on the way home." Decker was now adjusting a curtain over part of the window. "He has been known to get lost searching for a carton of Philip Morris," he shouted across the studio floor.

"May I ask what you're doing?"

"Something to do with the way the light was hitting your face. I won't be long. Jack says that you lived in France a few years ago?"

"I spent a few years in Paris. I don't know much about the rest of the country. I know a few of the large cities, but mostly it's just Paris."

"Golden years!"

"I guess so. They're becoming fashionable. What with Hemingway and Fitzgerald writing about the city, my past is getting richer with every passing year. At the time, it was the stench of urine under bridges, cold rooms, and smelly plumbing."

"I wish I'd been there. I spent the war on the Isle of Man as an enemy alien. Didn't see much art on those canvas walls. Did you know any painters?"

"A few. Mondrian, Kisling, Foujita, Derain. There were a few others. Picasso made a few rare appearances on Montparnasse, but he, like Matisse, was spending more time in the South."

"Ah, Derain! What did he look like?"

"He reminded me of a wholesale dealer in truffles. A heavy man, more like a farmer than the popular idea of an artist."

"I guess, good and bad, we owe a lot to Pistachio. And it grudges me."

"'Pistachio'? Oh, I see. Well, he's not in La Coupole or the Select nowadays. But he still has a studio across from Roger la Grenouille, an old haunt of mine by the river. He has a place north of Aix."

"That's right. They say he bought the mountain down there. What's-its-name?"

"Mont-Sainte-Victoire."

"That's right. And he has his nerve. That mountain's sacred to a local boy, Cézanne. He grew up around there, a pal of Zola's, another southerner."

"May I ask you a favour?"

"Keep your head still. What?"

"I need a place to stay for a few days. Zavitz, his studio, and the cops are after me. A man, who looks a little like me, was killed entering my place."

"Not a friend, I hope?"

"Somebody doing me a favour."

"Studio cops, city cops, local cops?"

"All flavours: chocolate, strawberry, orange, lemon, and lime."

"There's a spare room at the end of the upstairs hall. I'll get Hobart to shake it down for you."

"I'm asking a lot, but —"

"I try to reduce casualties when I can. Say no more about it. But I can promise you, you won't find much peace and quiet around here. Last night we didn't see Flynn off the premises until after three-thirty. And I think Fields is still on the couch in the front room. Don't go back for your stuff. Your place will be watched. There's lots of stuff around here you can use."

"Thanks. I appreciate this."

"Keep your head still. I'm notoriously bad at noses."

# CHAPTER SEVENTEEN

*I* decided not to move my things out of the flat across to Beverly Hills. What few things I brought with me from Europe were in need of a rest. Decker kept interrupting my settling in with offers of quality drink, food, and entreaties to mount the rostrum so that he could add a dab or two to the portrait he had started. Within a week, I had become familiar with the regular visitors to the studio. Gene Fowler was a regular. He was working on an autobiography called something like "Solo for Tom-Toms." He was curious about my background. I think he doubted that electric lights and paved streets had crossed the international border at Niagara Falls. I tried putting him right: "I grew up in Toronto, with summers in Muskoka. My journalism didn't really take off until I left the *Toronto Star* and went to France." He shrugged, as though I had told him the streets of Timbuktu flashed green, yellow, and red lights at every intersection. I told him that I had enjoyed his movie *What Price Hollywood?* a year or so ago.

"Hell! There were more writers on that shoot than there were stars and extras in the cast. I don't know what I contributed; I never had the nerve to buy a ticket."

Another regular, when Jack and the rest of us gathered for cocktails before one of Decker's monumental meals, was W. C. Fields, the former juggler and present film star. Fields enjoyed conversation that matched large, gaudy theatrical fonts of type. I remember the large wooden letters that transformed simple English words into a shout. He often began a thought with the phrase: "During my peregrinations in Somerset, as a guest of the Duke of Plaza-Toro ..." It was a high-pitched, drawling, male voice, and not unfamiliar to people with the price of a matinee ticket in their pockets. Occasionally he was gathered together and carried off by a little brunette called Carlotta. Fields called her "that goddamned Chinaman," as she tried to get him out to her car parked outside. I was slowly getting used to the sudden appearance of people I knew only by repute, if at all, or from seeing them on the stage or screen. The cool logic of Ida Lupino, the fun and wit of Marion Davies, when she had temporarily escaped her master's chain, gave us many memorable evenings. Marion once confided that William Randolph Hearst was so innocent, when she first met him, that he thought a tubal ligation was a sort of foreign embassy. I'd been surprised that Gary Cooper could carry a conversation beyond "Yup" and "Nope." His analysis of the war raging in Europe was both cogent and precise. "We're goin' to be in it, one way or another. A fellow can't sit and watch while the world gets poked in the eye. We can't sit playing tiddlywinks."

The conversation of these nights has long ago altered and blended in my mind to one long continuous drunken romp. But there wasn't always drink. There was a need to keep Jack off the stuff for the good of his health. Sometimes the evenings were carried along into the wee hours by the force of good fun and good conversation.

Sadakichi Hartmann was another irregular member of these gatherings; a Japanese gardener with a German last name, he carried the reputation of a poet, but he reminded me of the part played by Mischa Auer in *You Can't Take It with You*. "You sit in the lap of luxury," he was fond of saying. "What do you know of the world. Phooey! You are children playing in a sand pile. Double phooey!"

Hartmann liked to see himself as a truth-teller. His truths were always the embarrassing ones. He hit us in our inadequate defences. A balloon-pricker by nature, he was avoided like Cassandra in the Greek dramas. The announcement of Hartmann's approach could clear a room faster than the fire alarm.

After a major evening like this, I slept late. It was a good way to get out of the office routines that had formerly bound me strongly to my work habits. Neither Jack nor Decker was an early riser, except when Jack had some chore at his studio, or a lunch with his agent. I didn't hear from my erstwhile employers in Toronto, nor from Endicott, the local man.

Sometimes Decker began a meal in his kitchen, but was too far gone in drink to get it to the table. On these occasions, I helped out. All of us enjoyed the painter's cooking, and a few times, when the guests were still conscious, I was able to fill in at the last minute. Usually, I could tell what he had on the stove; the rest of the time I had to play it by ear. They liked my version of a Spanish paella and my cassoulet, although Jack complained that cassoulet hit him in his most vulnerable place.

"When I was in India, I learned how to cook with spices," he said. "The trick in Indian cookery is to cook the spices with the early ingredients, not sprinkle them on afterwards like a tip to an agreeable madam. They deserve a deep and thorough cooking." His versatile left eyebrow underlined and gave authority to this counsel. The advice was sound enough, but never in my time there did Jack venture into the compact kitchen, unless it was to help with what the English call "the washing up."

ONE DAY, I CALLED ENDICOTT to see what was happening with my severance pay.

"These things take time, Mike," he said on the phone.

"I understand, but time's the stuff life's made from. And I'm running short. When do you think you'll have a cheque for me?"

"Mike, you've turned your name to mud in this town. Why don't you go home?"

"Will you lend me the fare?"

"Borrowing's no solution, Mike. There should be something for you in a week or two, I'm sure."

"Thanks a lot!" I told him where he could reach me when the money came. I probably shouldn't have done that. He disconnected and I listened to the buzz on the line until I got tired of it.

"Who do you know, Jack," I asked after dinner one late evening, "who knows and understands motorcycles?"

Jack stroked his chin thoughtfully, with his face backlighted by a bunch of candles burning on top of a skull. Yorick's, no doubt. "There's that producer who works with Zavitz," he said helpfully, then he shrugged, shifting his eyebrows high on the great stone face.

"Isn't there a fellow named Croft who collects antique bikes? Fred Croft? Jack brought him here one night last year."

"I've no recollection," Jack said. "I must have been out."

"You were out, all right. That was the evening you tried to fire the head waiter at that German restaurant, when he tried selling you a plate of National Socialism with your sauerbraten. We had to hustle you out of there before the police came."

"Nevertheless, I do not recall this motorcycle fellow. Why do you want him? There are cars enough around here, and you have your own quaint Studebaker."

"I'm trying to learn what I can about Zavitz's remaining senior staffer, Jeff Swift."

Decker whistled surprise. "Whatever do you want to know more about him for? He just breathes out what Zavitz breathes in. They're alike in everything but age. They're like the Smith Brothers on the cough drop box. They are the local Brothers Grimm.

"The Brothers Grimmer, you mean!" added Jack, emptying his glass.

"I think I have a number for Fred Croft. Let me see."

Decker got up with some difficulty from his deep safari chair and went back to his studio. On this rare occasion, there were just the three of us at home. It had been a relaxing evening, with all of us telling stories about the mad picture business, the madder art world, and the maddest of all, the pursuit of journalism in a naughty world.

"Here's his telephone number, Mike. He's a good fellow. He'll see you right." I thanked him and pocketed the information.

# CHAPTER EIGHTEEN

After breakfast the following day, I called Fred Croft. I told him a little about myself, pretending more of an interest in Crockers and other bikes than I actually possessed. He invited me to drop in as early as was convenient. As soon as I had done my share of the washing up and crated the used bottles from the previous night, I got into the Studebaker and, after studying my map, headed to what Croft called his studio.

I expected to find a dark, greasy workshop, smelling of oil and gasoline. Instead, I found myself in a large studio as clean as many operating rooms in the best hospitals. There was no metallic mist hanging above the workbenches. My finger came up clean when I ran it along the top of one of them. The walls were hung with whole bikes and parts of bikes. The tools were tucked away in their own cupboards, the work surfaces were uncluttered. Decker should have seen it.

"You're Ward?" The young man asking was wearing an immaculate white coverall. His hair was neatly combed and parted in the centre. The smile under it was warm and his offer of fresh coffee was not refused. I followed him from his studio — I mentally compared his workroom with Decker's, and grinned to myself — to a chair under a bamboo awning suspended from a pole that rose from the middle of a round table. It was a cool retreat, away from cutting lathes and hoists.

"Are you a collector?" he asked.

"No, I'm a former newspaperman working on a case that may get me my old job back. That is if the LAPD doesn't catch up with me first." I gave him a quick rundown of the mess I was in, and what I was trying to find out. He nodded appropriately as I moved through the tangled skein of what had happened since I'd stepped off the Twentieth Century Limited into the steam bath known as Los Angeles.

"Along the way, I met Jeff Swift at A-Z-P. He gave me a ride on his Crocker. He has three bikes at the studio."

"He's got more than that. He's got a minor fleet of them. He's a collector. He owns a Brough Superior SS100, you know."

"A what? No. Wait. He told me about the Brough and Lawrence of Arabia."

"It's a very famous bike! It was an accident near his place at Clouds Hill in England."

"Right! That was down in Dorset. You know your stuff! I remember Jeff mentioning the name. What makes it so special? Never mind. I don't think I know enough about engines to understand. What else can you tell me about Swift?"

"He's won a couple of important races on one or another of his bikes. He owns a string of polo ponies. He supports charities, and he's been instrumental in saving *The Spirit of St. Louis* from the junkyard."

"That name's familiar. Wasn't that Lindbergh's airplane?"

"That's the plane he crossed the Atlantic in. The knackers nearly got it. Swift saved it, had it restored — it had been damaged by tourists both at Le Bourget in France and then again back on this side. I think it's in a museum now."

"What's he like? He's been damned decent to me."

"Well, I guess you'd have to put him down as a conservative. He likes the old ways: families, homes, Christian values. You know. But he can be funny. He's not stuffy the way some of those well-off producers are. I've seen him in the bleachers at ball games. And he has his own seats out of the sun. I can't figure him sometimes."

"Thanks a lot for this."

"Fellow you should talk to is Harald Grumbacker. He keeps the One-Two Bar near the corner where Wilshire meets Santa Monica Boulevard. He knows his bikes, but he goes back a long way with Swift. Tell him I sent you; otherwise he'll button up when you start asking questions. You know how barkeeps are."

I left Fred in his studio workshop, looking into the bowels of a motor with a heart murmur. Back on the street, I put on a recently bought pair of sun cheaters, and studied my street map.

I found the One-Two. It was a corner bar. It looked like thousands of corner bars, only this one was decorated with motorcycles hanging from the ceiling and mounted on the walls. Harald Grumbacker was leaning his impressive torso on the elbows of his massive arms. He was hunched over the bar like an animal over his kill, wearing a bright Hawaiian short-sleeved shirt, further patterned with a dusting of cigarette ash. He didn't look up when I climbed onto a stool in front of him. When he raised an eyebrow, I ordered a Schlitz. He opened the bottle, without eye contact and without moving the saucer of nuts along the empty bar in my direction.

"Fred Croft sends regards," I tried as an opener.

"Yeah? How's he doin'?" This much got me the peanuts. He blew off the accumulated ash on his cigarette without removing it from his lips, walked to the other end of the bar. I drank the beer, which I was comparing to all the different kinds of beer I had tasted over the years. In general, American beer was lighter than German, French, or English brews. I thought of the beers of my Toronto years; after school, when the thrill was not being asked to show proof of being old enough to drink legally. What was the age when it became legal? I'd forgotten. I downed a second bottle and the peanuts. I was into my third bottle when Grumbacker — if it was Grumbacker — refilled the bowl.

"You keen on bikes?" he asked.

"Not when I'm with people like Fred, Swift, or you, I'm not. Jeff gave me a tour of the A-Z-P lot on one of his bikes the other day. He's a good man, knows his wheels."

"Yeah, he's pretty good. You one of his protégés? If you're an actor, don't come here lookin' for dessert. I like to discourage all business but drinking at this bar. You get it?"

"I hear you. But I'm not an actor, and I'm not looking for company. I'm a newspaperman on the limp end of a junket that was a lot of fun while it lasted. Now I have to gear my way back to Canada. Thought I might do a piece on Jeff, but I don't know all that much about him. After talking to Fred, I decided to see you."

"Fred don't know shit about Jeff. All he'll give you is the stuff you can get from *Fortune* or *Vanity Fair*." He blew away the cigarette ash again.

"Hell, I don't need a whole encyclopedia. I'm looking for two thousand words and I'm on my way back home."

"Where's that, again?"

"Toronto, Ontario, Canada. Where the ice worms breed in the spring."

"We get a lot o' people in here cruising, and undercover cops cruising the cruisers. This state don't hold with that sort of thing. But one night, couple o' weeks ago, two cops tried to hustle one another."

"I hope they found true happiness."

"I'll drink to that!" For the first time, he smiled, showing strong white teeth interrupted by gold ones. His mouth looked like a discarded ear of half-eaten Indian corn. "Happy days!"

"What can you tell me about Jeff that will get me out of here and won't land him in the hoosegow?"

"You know about the races he won?" This time a little of his cigarette ash landed on me. "Sorry."

"Yeah, Fred told me."

"He mention that he's a polo champ?"

"Yeah, has a stable of ponies. Yeah, I've got that in my notes."

"He's played a few games over in India and in Iran, too. I'll bet Fred told you about *The Spirit of St. Louis* too?"

"Yeah, yeah. He was quite a hero there. I guess the Smithsonian has the original?"

"Search me. Did you know that he stood by Lindbergh when his infant son was snatched?"

"Sure, everybody knows that story. I need something new. Journalism would be a lead-pipe cinch if we could print all the repeated gen we get. Maybe I should do another piece on Bogart or Flynn."

"He was with Lindy, over in Germany. Saw all the stuff Herr Hitler's throwing at the Poles and Czechs. Lindy got to fly their best fighter plane: a Messerschmitt 109. Oh, we should get a dozen or two of them. There's nothing can stop 'em." He put out the stub of his cigarette in a saucer and lit another Lucky Strike from a nearly empty pack.

"Do you think we're going to need a fleet of fighters like the ones he saw over there in Germany?"

"The busier they get over there with their war, the better it is for us over here. Like the man says, the business of America is business. Let those foreigners kill themselves and more power to them. Just as long as they keep out of my backyard. We're sitting pretty. We got deals going with both sides. Like Swift's French pal."

"Which one?"

"Bedaux. Charles Bedaux. The Duke of Windsor and Wallis Simpson got married at his place in France."

"Oh, that Bedaux. He got stuck in the mud of northwestern Canada testing Citroën half-tracks about six years ago. He took a movie crew along with him to document his triumph, but the mud and the mountains defeated him and his half-tracks. So, he's a friend of Swift?"

"Yeah, the Frenchman's now working for the Reich, busy turfing Yids out of France. We could use him around here."

"Think we should get into the war on that side?"

"How can we lose? If we don't go along with Germany, we'll all be eating borscht and blinis and brown bread. That's the best offer you'll see this year. But, still, it's harder getting parts for bikes built over there. That's not my biggest worry. I can live with that."

"Who's dragging the States into the war?"

"If you ask me, I'd say its foreigners running the movie business, the radio networks, the papers, and Washington. They need to be cleaned out, root and branch."

"What you're suggesting sounds like a big job. Who do you think is up to it?"

"Look, my friend, we wouldn't have had a country here if it wasn't for a few people who got together to toss out the English. You ever heard of the Boston Tea Party, or of Concord or Valley Forge? They didn't happen by plebiscite, but by a hard-knuckled small group of dedicated men."

"It's a history worth remembering."

"You just remember that you're a guest in the greatest country since Adam was a pup. That we got Washington and Lincoln, Jefferson and Jackson, Scott and ... You get me?"

"Yeah, and Roosevelt. What do you think of the president?"

"He's looking for a knot hole to drag us all into that war over there. Damned if he's the man the first Roosevelt was. You gonna argue with me about that?"

"Not on your life. As somebody once said: 'Except in my domestic life, I'm a man of peace.'"

EARLY THE NEXT DAY, I phoned Endicott. The LAPD were still watching the office. He reminded me about the funeral arrangements for poor Olson.

"Damn! When is it?"

"At four this afternoon. I told you last time we talked."

"Sorry, I forgot. You know I could be killed if I showed my face in public?"

"He was a colleague. It's your choice." If I didn't already dislike Endicott, I was now working at it. Before I broke the connection, I asked if there was any other news. He said that all the papers in town had dropped the story of Norman's death altogether. Endicott gave me the name of the funeral home — the same one from which Jean Harlow had been launched into eternity — and I told him I would be there if I was still at large.

When I called the bank, from which I had been estranged for over a week, I got better news. My money had come from Paris, so I was no longer one of the hundred neediest cases. I could now chip in to the household management on Bundy Drive.

When I told Decker about Olson's funeral, he nodded, and I thought better of attending. But then after a lunch I mistakenly called stew when I should have said *boeuf en daube*, he and Jack came at me with sticks of greasepaint and hair dye. Although my protests were heard, they were universally ignored.

"Did you know your head's flat back here?" Jack asked, towelling me off.

"I never look back there. How long is this going to take?"

"Relax and enjoy it. Here, dry yourself. I don't have to do everything, do I?"

"I'm gratified that you're both having fun. Will this stuff wash out? I don't want to be red-headed for the rest of my life."

"That'll be the henna," Decker said with insouciance. "Now, we'll do the makeup proper. Relax, Mike! You may get to like it."

"If you have to bury me, change it back again, and write my father and mother."

"My boy, my boy, you have two of the greatest artists of our time giving you the perfect disguise and all you can do is complain."

"I think we can make you look like King George VI. Your features are regular enough. But that might attract attention. What we want is something that is strikingly not you. Let's see ..." Jack pondered. It was worth the trip to see Barrymore pondering. "My friend, once at Universal I helped a friend to invent the makeup for Boris Karloff."

"*Frankenstein.*"

"*The Mummy.*"

"Let's calm down now, everybody. I'm getting out of here!"

Four hands held me down in the chair; I was unable to escape their inventive artistry for another half hour. When it was done, Jack held up a mirror. "There!" he said, looking me over as though I were a piece of prize porcelain. "Take a look. Decker, this is your masterpiece!" He held up a shaving mirror and turned it so that I could see a stranger's face in it. He wore his lank, red hair parted differently. The face under the red hair belonged to a stranger. Except, when I looked closely, it looked real, not like a makeup job. It was quite overwhelmingly real. I had to blink and leer at the face to establish that it really was me.

"Don't you think," Decker said, looking at me in the mirror, "that a little scar running under the left eye might improve it, Jack?"

"Not a wart or wen; no carbuncles or cicatrices. You've utterly transformed him, Decker, my friend. Maestro, I salute you! Lay your foot on my neck!"

My retreat to Decker's place was not only safe, it was a distraction from the outside world. It was a crazy, mad world with W. C. Fields curled up on a couch, Jack Barrymore making scrambled eggs while singing "O sole mio" at the top of his morning voice, and Decker and Hobart running around changing bedding and foraging for damp towels in the most unlikely places. It was paradise. But outside the front door was a malevolent city, a city of fallen angels, some of them looking for me with thoughts other than a good breakfast on their minds.

# CHAPTER NINETEEN

$\mathcal{E}$ndicott lost his smile when I spoke to him at the funeral home. When he looked at me, I felt like a plague he wished would go away and leave him alone. When he told me what had happened, I tended to sympathize with him, and wished there was an easy way to get out of town.

"What did you do to your hair?" he asked.

"I'm trying to look less conspicuous. Less like me. Is it that bad?"

"Not bad, exactly, but not you; that's certain."

The disguise had worked well. People from the office had failed to spot me. Not being recognized gave me the peculiar feeling that I was attending the wrong funeral. But there they all were. I recognized them, but they didn't recognize me. I felt like Claude Rains in *The Invisible Man*. I had to give the two Jacks full credit for a great job.

I had spotted a few characters at the graveside who looked a little like George and Lenny, the tight-suited friends of Benny Siegel and Virginia Hill. But nobody questioned me.

Endicott continued to stare at my hair. We didn't stand together at the graveside, but I followed him after the workmen began pulling away the pretend grass, and started filling in the grave. He left the cemetery by a noisy, rusty gate and walked to his car. I followed in a taxi, and paid the driver when Endicott parked behind the bureau. Instead of going back to work, he went into the coffee shop where we'd met before. I took a stool next to him. The smell of overheated cooking oil was strong on the air. The fan didn't help. We both ordered coffee.

"I've already eaten," he said, "but you order something."

I did that.

"God, I hate funerals."

Endicott told me again how the cops had come to the office with a search warrant, looking for contraband. "They took everything apart, then carried away a ton of our files going back thirty years. Margaret nearly had hysterics. We were all rattled. They wanted to know where you were." He went on to inform me about the rhubarb he'd been getting from Toronto. He defended his record by reminding head office that I had been Toronto's idea in the first place.

"Were you followed here?"

"Come on! I've been in this game long enough to spot a tail if they'd hung one on me."

I was missing some of what Endicott was saying. He'd started in again on the destructiveness of the cops' invasion. He had had to go down to the station to answer questions. "They were mostly asking about you, Mike. I tried stalling them. I don't think I said anything that might lead them to you. You know, Mike, you've got a hell of a nerve putting the service in this mess. They're still cleaning up back at the office. They took my signed copy of *Dodsworth*. Is Sinclair Lewis a Red or something?"

"You've taken on a lot of grief for me, Larry. I'm sorry."

"They had me under the lights, third-degree-style, and were about to bring out the rubber hoses when I demanded to speak to my lawyer, Bob Hohnstock. They're afraid of him. The counsellor's been defending the service for the last five years. He's got their number, and they have learned to respect him."

"Sounds like you handled it well, Larry." I felt almost sorry for the trouble I'd got him into, but I don't think that my use of his first name cut through the ambivalent feelings I had about him.

"Where are you staying, by the way, Mike?"

"Better you don't know, Larry. Then they can't make you talk. When the life preserver sinks, hang on to deniability."

"Oh, Mike, before I forget, here's your severance packet. Sorry, Mike, but that's the way it is. You know head office. You can always count on their giving in." He handed an envelope to me. I slipped it into my pocket without looking at it. Again, I thanked him and told him that I was sure that he was the right man to run the shop without me. We shook hands and he got up to leave. Nobody followed him out the door. If he had had a tail, I was now it.

"Hello, there! I didn't think I'd see you again. What happened to your hair?" It was the woman who'd narrowly missed being run over.

"Hello, yourself. Been run down recently?"

"Does it show? I must send myself out for dry cleaning. What did you do to your hair?"

"Don't ask about the madcap life of a journalist."

"I've been worried about you."

"Worried?"

"Well, wondering, I guess. I know you gave me your name, but I haven't had time to look you up. You know how it is in newspaper work."

The waitress had just handed me my bill, without her usual smile. I put my money on the table: ten cents for the coffee, a nickel for the muffin, and another for the waitress.

"I was just leaving," I said lamely. "Our timing's out of order."

"Let's start over fresh, at that place across the street."

We negotiated the street safely and ended up in a place called The Venetiana Room, the only visibly functioning part of the Evergreen Hotel. Its moth-eaten awning warned customers away from the entrance. But inside, the place seemed friendly enough. There was a cop perched at one end of the bar looking into a lonely beer, while a bald counterman polished the glass top of the bar. In California, zinc-topped bars were not the fashion.

"My name is Mike Ward," I announced once we were safely installed.

"I'm Karen Roberts. How do you do? Much thanks for past favours. And, by the way, any sudden tumbles from this stool are my own fault, nobody else's."

"Okay, you're on your own from now on. But remember to stop, look, and listen before you step off the curb. What are you doing in Los Angeles?"

"I used to work at Disney. Now I'm at Schlesinger's studio in Burbank. I'm an inker and inbetweener."

"Once again in English?"

"You could say I'm an animator. I make drawings move. As in Donald Duck and Mickey Mouse. I worked on *Fantasia* and *Dumbo* and a film still in production based on a book about a wild deer. The author's Felix somebody. I left after two years. It's dull and repetitive work, and not everybody's suited to it. I get a little more room to develop ideas at Schlesinger."

"You're an artist?"

"In a way. I used to be. I had a canvas in a show in London's West End once, and in one of those small galleries on the Rue St André des Arts in Paris. But I haven't done much since coming here — a case of bread and butter winning out over self-expression."

"I used to live in the Rue Bonaparte."

"Near Saint-Germain-des-Prés? The street with antique dealers! I know it well."

A waitress came, we ordered, and, in a few minutes, we ate not brilliantly, but well. The dim lighting made it easy to look directly at one another across the table. A candle made her face shine. I could feel myself warming to the desire to know her better, the desire to be with her, and to desire itself.

I will not describe what happened next. Iris out.

# CHAPTER TWENTY

"Is this S. Graham?"
A woman's voice responded in the affirmative.

"I'm looking for Scott Fitzgerald. It's a friend of Scott's calling, an old friend from Paris, Mike Ward. I saw him the other day when there was no time to talk."

"That's right. He mentioned that he saw you, and that started him reminiscing again about those rotten 'good old days' of his."

"Sorry to cause a commotion, S. Graham. Should I get down on my knees? I don't do that much anymore. I can't stand the noise."

"Forget it, Mr. Ward. He's sleeping now. I think it's not a good idea to wake him. You know about his heart attack?"

"I only talked to him for a minute the other day. He didn't look well."

"You can blame his damned creditors for that. I've never seen a man work so hard in all my life."

"Spoken like a fan," I said, then regretted it.

"Spoken like a mistress, Mr. Ward."

"And does she have a Christian name? I'm new to these parts."

"I have a name, but it isn't Christian. That's why he calls me his 'beloved infidel.' You may call me Sheilah, in person or on the phone or at the Brown Derby. Don't say you honestly haven't seen my byline? I don't believe it!"

"Believe it. I've just arrived from a war zone. Let me catch my breath. Wait a minute! You're not that gossip col —"

"How do you do?"

"Sorry!"

"Hold on." There was a pause. "I think the body's coming back to life. Don't hang up." Another pause. I could hear the sparrows dancing on the wire.

"Hello? Who is this?"

I told him, and after a moment I could feel him homing in on me like a four-engine plane on a radio beam. "Mike, for God's sake, how the hell are you?"

"Pretty well for a wanted man."

"It's the damned Fascists, Mike. They're over here now! Hell, Mike, I can do twenty minutes on what's wrong with this world and never get to Roosevelt. Where do you stand?"

I don't remember what I said, and I was sure that when he awakened in the morning, he wouldn't either. I arranged to meet him at the Brown Derby three days from when we were speaking. He sounded glad not to have to face a longer conversation just at present. He handed me back to Sheilah.

"Hello, you," she resumed. "I hear that you're a wanted man, Mr. Ward. You've got Swarbrick and his hounds out looking for you."

"Be a pal and spike it, Sheilah. I've already got all the sour stew on my plate."

"It's a deal, if I get it all when it's ripe to harvest."

"It's a deal, but don't try harvesting stew. Look to our friend."

She gave me the address and directions. I thought that I was as interested in meeting my old friend's mistress as I was in my reunion with Fitzgerald. "Talk to you later."

DECKER HANDED ME A SMOKED salmon sandwich when I got off the phone. It was welcome both as nourishment and as a work of art. I joined him and some of the others in the studio. Decker tried to lure me back to the rostrum, and I took my place, after removing a sticky brush from the chair. We didn't hear the phone ring in the other room. Hobart handed me an extension on a long, curling cord.

"Mr. Ward?" A familiar voice, although I'd heard it only once. Even over the telephone wire, I could feel an unwelcome frisson.

"Yes, Mr. Zavitz. I won't ask you how the devil you got this number."

"Being a powerful man has its advantages, Mr. Ward. But I want to talk to you about some of the disadvantages. When can I see you?"

"The last time we talked, you were trying to run me out of town."

"A miscalculation. I apologize."

"I'll bet you don't do that often in a week."

"The more likely, Mr. Ward, that it is sincere. I want to talk to you."

"Emma Schneller has been in touch with you!"

"You truly are an amazing man. Yes! She called me not fifteen minutes ago."

"I knew that she would have arrived with enough time to settle somewhere, and now she has got down to business. Did you meet the woman when you were in London?"

"Meet her? Sure I met her. I took her to dinner. At the Savoy, no less. I should have had my head examined."

"Tell me about it."

"Here? Now? On the telephone?"

"You can tell me on the phone or you can suggest a meeting place. Unless you are worried about being overheard, I suggest we talk now. If your phone isn't safe, it follows that you don't move about the city with any great secrecy either. Tell me what you know about Emma Schneller."

"I thought she was an actress. She has a lazy, languorous way when speaking English. She also speaks French and excellent German. Yiddish too, though I don't think she's Jewish. She's blonde, tall, well-turned out. Like a model. Of her education I'm no judge. She knows how to survive, how to get what she wants."

"How old?"

"Born around the turn of the century, I'm guessing. She had a nasty war. She'd be about forty now, but looks younger."

"She was blackmailing you because of Lady Margaret."

"I had to get her out of young Spooner's room and out of his life."

"Spooner? Who's that?"

"Blake Foster. We changed his name. Didn't help. A nothing talent, but under contract."

"So you distracted the titled lady to your own purposes."

"Don't be meshuggah! I did it strictly for business reasons. The genius of Emma Schneller shows in that she was clever enough to realize that my wife would never swallow such a story. It would be Reno for sure. Look at me. I'm a dumpy middle-aged businessman devoted to his cornflakes and Ovaltine in the morning. I have a waistline problem, I take a dozen pills with my morning cereal. I'm no Clark Gable or, God forbid, Errol Flynn. Everybody knows that. But not Donna! Not my wife!"

"What did Emma say on the phone this morning?"

"She wants to see me, of course. She talked about Lady Margaret. She was hinting. She knows exactly what cards are in her hand. Mr. Ward, I'm sick with worry."

"Have you talked to your tame policemen? Loomis, Swarbrick, and the rest of your home guard?"

"I don't want to get rid of one blackmailer in exchange for another. I'm not crazy, only desperate."

"What about your young motorcycle rider, the wunderkind?"

"He's at a sailing regatta in La Jolla. He has no head for this business. Believe me. When I hang up, I've got to fire a writer." Was he now confiding in me? I wondered.

"You've fired hundreds of writers."

"That's right. But this writer's no ordinary writer. Besides, I've fired him before. I hired him and now I'm firing him again. Who knows how many times? But when all the hundreds of writers working for me are forgotten, people will remember Scott Fitzgerald," he said.

"So, why fire him?"

"He's a drunk. What can I say?"

"You have sober writers who write better?"

"Mind your own shop, I'll look after mine! You think you can come down here and take over? Try it sometime!"

"What did you say to Emma? We were talking about Emma. Did you agree to meet her?"

"What else could I do? Of course I agreed! What else could I do?"

"Where and when?"

"She wants to meet me by the stage of the D.W. Griffith Theatre. That way she will be able to see if I've come alone, as instructed."

"When?"

"Tomorrow morning at six."

"Did she ask for money?"

"That's what we're to discuss. Look, Mr. Ward, by you I'm a rich man. By everybody in this country I'm a rich man. But my fortune is invested in pictures, in horseflesh, in contracts. I can't suddenly lift a large sum out of the bank without leaving a hole that will be discovered. I'm not a man, like you, Mr. Ward. I'm a corporation!"

"I'll keep the cheap jokes for later. How do you think you'll get in? It's easier to do in the movies than in real life. Even at that hour, there will be watchmen."

"I have some influence there. I won't have any problems."

"What about her? Is she as influential as you are?"

"I dislike the sneer in your voice, Mr. Ward. Help me or don't help me, but keep your opinions to yourself!"

"Touché. You got me on that. What do you want me to do?"

"Will you come with me?"

"Didn't she ask you to come alone?"

"Yes, but —"

"Better keep to what she says. I'll be there. You won't see me. I'll follow her from the amphitheatre and report back to you later on."

"Thank you! I won't forget this!"

"I'll see that you don't. What I want in return is the whole story, the whole story, on the Norman business. Is that a bargain?"

There was a long pause on the phone. Did he think I could hear a nod? "Well?"

"I agree to your terms, Mr. Ward. When this is over, you will know all of my secrets anyway. So, how can I lose?"

"Agreed, then. Don't look for me when you get to the amphitheatre. I'll see you and I'll follow her. I'll talk to you as soon as I have information."

I held on to the phone after hanging up, wondering how he could get this number without being able to help himself out of a simple case of blackmail.

I drew a hot bath to soak up my anxieties. An open-air concert hall, like the D.W. Griffith, is an ideal shooting gallery. Anyone in a place like that would be a sitting duck. How did I know that Emma Schneller would be there on her own? How did I know that Zavitz was telling the truth? I'd been a pebble in his shoe since I first arrived in LA. He was asking me to play the part of a clay pigeon in a shooting gallery. There wasn't much about the proposition that I liked. As Shakespeare or "Bugsy" Siegel might say, "How will this fadge?"

Before it had time to fadge or congeal or sort itself out, I called the home of the maid or housekeeper who had been packed off to Paris.

# CHAPTER TWENTY-ONE

*W*hen Jack got home that night, there was a hullabaloo down-stairs. For a moment, I felt aggrieved and hard done by, as any tenant might feel when awakened from a deep sleep. Then, snob that I was, I remembered that it was Jack Barrymore who had awakened me. The same Barrymore who used to fling a dead kipper into the jaws of a noisy audience when the coughing got him down and the kipper was available.

I climbed out of bed and put on manly readiness before descending to the studio, which seemed to be the seat of all collective activity. Jack was looking at my unfinished portrait on Decker's easel. "If only the picture could change, and you could go on living, forever young! Hello, Ward. *Wie geht'z?* Would you give your soul for that?"

"My sole and a tub of herring. But what I really need is a new identity."

"Hold on, Mike," Decker interjected. "You're exaggerating again."

"They've trapped me! I can't go anywhere. The cops have me surrounded. I'm in as bad a pickle as Dorian Gray ever was in."

"How so, old boy? Give us the truth of it."

"You don't want to hear. It's B-movie material and nobody in town will touch it," I said.

"You don't have my alimony situation. I have hungry ex-wives like a dog has fleas. Go ahead. Tell us. It'd take *Titus Andronicus* to make us sick. And pray make it improbable."

I told Jack all about my most recent adventures. He and Decker, who was sitting on a couch with a fat body stretched out behind him, listened carefully, taking in the details. Decker grinned, and wiggled his eyebrows; Jack gripped his chin which made me think of Rodin. But neither of them spoke. The voice, when it came, emerged from the couch.

"During my peregrinations in and out of the spirit realm, and in this world as well, I never heard such a story. It'd bring tears to the eyes of Jack the Ripper. It reminds me of *Uncle Tom's Cabin*, with the leads scampering over the ice floes and the dogs yapping after them like suppertime in the cat house. Yes, indeed."

"Go back to sleep, Bill. Mike is in hot water," Decker said to the body behind him.

"Water! Don't mention the stuff! I tried it once, and haven't touched a drop of the evil liquor since. It galvanized the lining of my innards."

The "Bill" referred to by the painter, if there could be any doubt, was W. C. Fields, who was struggling to sit up straight. Barrymore made the introduction, although he had done so previously.

His face was perspiring, his thin, lank hair looked damp. He regarded me through squinting little eyes. When finally he had hold of both ends of my name, he grinned. "I'm always happy to meet a man who doesn't come from Philadelphia."

"Glad to see you, Mr. Fields."

Fields nodded acknowledgment, but still eyed me suspiciously under his brows.

"Young man, how did you chance to pick D.W. Griffith as your rendezvous?"

"I didn't. That was Zavitz's doing."

"He'd steal the pennies off the eyes of dead Mormons. Trust him only with a lighted stick of dynamite."

"And you have to precede Zavitz into the amphitheatre and follow the woman out of there?"

"That's right."

"You'll have to be two people — first, someone invisible to catch the meeting, then, second, a totally different person to follow the woman. It won't be easy."

"We can make up your face, give you a wig —"

"And a limp, and an eye patch —"

"And it would work on stage or in a film, but —" The breath went out of him.

"Yeah! Real life follows different rules. I can't very well try to pass myself off as the Fool from *King Lear*, can I?"

"Nor as Long John Silver with a parrot on your shoulder."

"I have a makeup I once used in that thing by Mary Shelley. All scars and bad sutures."

"I could be a cleaner in the auditorium, sweeping the seating area with a big mop or broom."

"At six in the morning? No, that won't do at all. Even sweepers —"

"Maybe we should all go!"

"Yes! We might be rehearsing something!"

"Perfect!" snapped Barrymore. "We'll do a scene from a play!"

"Ah, yes! I'll muster Frank Morgan or Tom Mitchell or Carradine. They would never forgive us if we leave them out."

"This may be a circus full of fun for you gentlemen, but it's my ass that's out there!" They took no notice of me or my wet blanket.

"We'll run up a scene or two," Jack said, his eyes on the ceiling, giving us a view that showed off the famous profile to advantage.

"I always liked the 'key-cold' scene from *Richard III*. You know the bit, 'the key-cold figure of a holy king.' I once did it with my once-dear friend Ivana Janjic, before she changed her name and became famous on the screen. Dear child! Or we might try the closet scene from *Hamlet*."

"That would give parts for two, Hamlet and the Queen. What about the caterwauling scene from *Twelfth Night*?"

"Wonderful! I shall make a capital Sir Toby Belch," said Fields.

"And I'll play the Fool," Jack said. "The mighty hand of the Bard of Avon! I'm beginning to warm to the prospect. Our *Twelfth Night* will out-Boucicault Boucicault. I have some sides upstairs in my room. Six o'clock. We'll be ready. I'll call Tom Mitchell. He has a break from shooting *Mr. Smith Goes to Washington*. He'll give us an interesting reading of Malvolio. Decker will give us a superlative Maria. And you, of course," he said, looking straight at me, "will be Sir Andrew."

"Me! I haven't stepped on a stage since high school!"

"Don't fret. We'll see you right. I have a good wig for the part."

"But, Jack, that solves only half of the problem! I can't very well follow the suspect dressed in a rehearsal outfit. The rehearsal's a wonderful idea, but we need an encore."

"We could end the rehearsal in a scrap. A good fight would help Mike get away, out the stage door."

"Do you know where we're going, Mr. Fields?"

"Away with formality! From this moment on, you are my brother. I hope you don't gag at the name Dukenfield? There's a scrubbed urchin or two calls me 'Uncle Claude.' But 'Bill' will serve."

"But, Bill, do you know the backstage layout? You know how the performers get through the barriers. You know, the stage door?"

"My friend, trust me. There is a way, and I shall show it to you."

Decker had by now roused Hobart and together they had wheeled a tea trolley into the studio and begun to pour drinks. While I welcomed a glass myself, I had an apprehension that the matter of the last half-hour's conversation would certainly be drowned in conviviality and strong drink without any action.

## CHAPTER TWENTY-TWO

*T*wo-thousand-six-hundred-one North Highpoint Avenue, better known as D.W. Griffith Theatre, is located in a natural cirque in the Hollywood Hills, north of Hollywood Boulevard. In the pre-dawn darkness, it looked cold and unwelcoming. I'd attended a concert there some time ago, Rimsky-Korsakov's *Scheherazade*, but what little I had learned about the geography of the theatre left me ill-equipped to discover a place to hide while waiting to observe the meeting between Asa Zavitz and Emma Schneller. And, even if I could stand invisible between them, how could I follow the woman back to her car or whatever other clever means of transportation she had provided? I tried to draw a map of the place in my mind. I came up with a triangular space with the stage at one of the vertices. I was quite wrong, as I discovered.

Fields drove us in his big car — one of several. As I understood it, this one was called "the bone-crusher." Instead of driving into the usual lot, he parked well above the whole site, so that we were looking down on the rear of the bandshell that formed the back of the stage and the acre of seating for the paying customers. For about five minutes, we enjoyed the view, while waiting for a second car. There were few lights below; the audience area stood out as a dark black coal sack below the curved bandshell. There was a rosy glow on the horizon showing where the early morning city lay buried behind more hills. A slight breeze was blowing up here. When the car came, it was a dark Buick, out of which stepped Thomas Mitchell. "Is this thing going forward, Jack? I received an early call." Mitchell was holding a navy-blue overcoat around him, letting the belt hang down.

"Rest you fair, good signor," Jack called, clapping his shoulders.

"We'll see you home in jig time, when this is over," Decker added.

"I hear you're up for the Otis Skinner part in *Kismet*. You'll be great in the part, Jack."

"Bill Dieterle called me, but I haven't seen a contract. I'm not going to hold my breath. But I have hopes for Monty Woolley's part in *The Man Who Came to Dinner* in the fall. Bill Keighley said it's in the bag. And Bette Davis is lending her weight behind me. The Sheridan Whiteside part was based on Alex Woollcott and me, so I may continue to give imitations of myself at your favourite Bijou."

A short walk took us to a wooden booth near the rim of the cliff, about the elevation of the HOLLYWOOD sign on this or another of these hills. "Hollywood Bowl's just down the road a piece," Thomas Mitchell said to be helpful.

"Let's try there," said Fields. And we all grabbed him before he could turn around.

A few seconds later, Barrymore, Mitchell, and Fields greeted the watchman with familiarity. He was a nearly bald, clean-shaven man with a bad limp. The walls of his little realm were covered with signed photographs of conductors and soloists. I recognized Bruno Walter and Serge Koussevitzky. Mixed in with the music types, I spotted Betty Grable, Norma Shearer, and Barbara Lorrison, less formally attired. The watchman was greeted as Mr. Telling by the others. During a friendly banter of conversation, Telling handed Fields a letter, saying that he had been sitting on it for a week. Fields pocketed it and we boarded an elevator, which took us straight down to the backstage level.

"Mark my footsteps, gentlemen. I neglected to bring bread crumbs. We'd best not turn on the lights yet. But it isn't far."

Here, Decker brought out a flashlight, which he kept partly covered with a glove. We marched, one behind the other, to a set of steps leading up one level.

"This is the way to the dressing rooms, and through here we come out on the stage."

I could hear the sound of our footsteps, like cannon blasts on bare cement as we climbed. Fields turned back to Jack, as we came to the top. "Jack, did you bring the sides?"

"Right here, Bill." Jack was longer catching his breath than the rest of us. Although he looked fit enough, he was frail. "I think we should have brought your friend Edgar Bergen. He likes a merry romp like this," Jack whispered.

"That termite-infested imp who supports Bergen would have given us away. This is a serious and lofty enterprise, my friend, not for worm-eaten amateurs."

"I wanted to revive *Hamlet* here once," Jack said a little wistfully. He handed me what I thought would be a script of the scene, but it was only a few pages with just the lines for Sir Andrew recorded with the cues that came immediately before the lines. I saw that Decker was holding a bigger sheaf of lines than I had. And Jack and Tom held scripts larger than both of ours put together. I had by this time so forgotten the reason for this bizarre charade that I found room in my soul to envy those with the bigger parts.

A big full moon had come out from hiding; it looked down on us as we walked out onto the stage. Fields had found the lighting boy and had turned on the work lights, which managed to turn the view of the vast seating area into a black woolsack, thereby achieving exactly what I didn't need. Anyone in the rows of empty seats could see us, and we could see nothing but each other. "A fine how-do-you-do," as William S. Gilbert once observed.

"You didn't mention that Maria is a woman's part, Jack," said Decker, with some surprise.

"Tradition, old scout. The first Juliet, Lady Macbeth, and Cleopatra were men."

"You might have warned me." At about this point, I began looking for a better place to view the ghostly audience. I found it at the back of one of the shell-like arches that curved overhead from stage level. Here, I found a tiny window that looked out into the audience. From this corner, out of the light, I could make out a thousand empty seats, with a clear view of the flanking aisles all the way to the back of the amphitheatre, about a quarter of a mile away.

When I got back to the stage, Barrymore and Fields were already at it.

"Approach, Sir Andrew. Not to be abed after midnight is to be up betimes; and diluculo surgere, thou know'st —"

That was my cue, and I was not ready for it. Bill Fields repeated the line. My unpractised voice broke like a Ming vase as I did my best: "Nay, by my troth, I know not. But I know to be up late is to be up late."

I thought I heard something offstage, down in front, but I was helpless to investigate. My lines were coming thick and fast. I no longer envied the others with their bigger parts. Just before Tom Mitchell came on as Malvolio, I eased myself into the wings and peered out the cubbyhole again. A shadow was moving down an outside aisle towards us. It was Zavitz. He looked up at the stage, giving it a glance or two as he continued walking. He wore an open camel-hair coat over evening clothes. He stopped and glanced behind him. I tried to see what had stopped him, flattening my left ear, still seeing nothing more than the movie producer standing mid-aisle. A moment later, a woman's shape came into view. From this distance it was dark and indistinct. They cautiously approached one another. I watched them talk, without, of course, hearing a word. Envelopes were exchanged. That was part of the plot Zavitz and I had not discussed. Had he paid her to hush up the nasty piece she might pass along to the press, or would the contents of Asa's envelope shut her down for a time?

I heard my cue bellowed in my direction by Jack: "Beshrew me, the knight's in admirable fooling." Nearly out of breath, I delivered my line and ran back to my peephole.

Zavitz was walking up the aisle. The woman had disappeared from sight. I could see clearly now, but even with my sore ear pressed to the wall, I couldn't make out a trace of her. Then, there she was! Caught in a beam of light from the highway she was, just cresting the top of the encompassing wall of the amphitheatre. If I had had dentures, I would have dropped them. The light held her clearly for only a second, and then she was gone, escaping to the far side. Cursing, I returned to the stage in lots of time for my next cue. For once I delivered my line with some animation. Jack, as the Fool, who had left the stage with Tom, came downstage to me and said in a whisper, "I could see from the back! She went over the wall! I hope to hell she broke her pellucid neck."

"We're all done here. I'm on my way. And thanks!"

"Our mousetrap has been nobly sprung, but the mouse is on her way. You'd best be after her, old chap! Tally ho! We poor players will gobble up the remaining cheese."

# CHAPTER TWENTY-THREE

*T*he following morning saw none of me. When I first opened my eyes the sun was well over the yardarm. Normal people had been out and about for hours, shopping, driving to work, and meeting friends. I took a look at my pocket watch on the bedside table, and grudgingly rolled out of bed.

The rehearsal at the D.W. Griffith Theatre had ended on a lame note. Bill Fields wanted to continue. Tom Mitchell begged off because of an early morning start on a new movie. Jack, who was still game for anything, was as frustrated as I was when we found a mattress slung over the barbed wire fence that surrounded the perimeter of the outdoor concert complex. The mattress belonged in a ditch across the lane along with a rusty Norge refrigerator, a bed frame, and a big Alaska refrigerator with its wooden door hanging on a single rusty hinge. "She's taken cover," Jack said. It was chilly enough in the morning air that I could see his breath.

The boys looked depressed when we regrouped at an early-morning bar known to milkmen, other thirsty early-risers, and Jack Barrymore.

"There was a murder here one morning," Jack said. "A shooting," he added.

"Anybody we know?" quizzed Fields.

"A bit-player named Olga Sekulovich. She worked under the name Storm Williams. Did some fan dancing on the side. She was in my Sherlock Holmes epic. Sweet kid, but she had a jealous boyfriend. I forget his name. He came in here one night with a gun. Both of them were loaded."

"Interesting, but what is it to the purpose?"

"We're not rehearsing now. We can put the Bard aside. I'm sorry, Mike, our little charade didn't pay off as we'd hoped."

"What do you mean?"

"Well, we didn't catch anybody. There was no last act. If there was, they played it offstage."

"Oh, we did better than you think, Jack. True, we haven't seen the last act played to the curtain line, but we're better off than when we started."

"I don't see that. The villain is still at large. The boys in blue are still looking for you, and, excuse the indelicacy, you're out of work."

"True, Jack, but now I know who I've been chasing all over town. The fog is clearing. I'm still on my game. And I think I know the next step."

"Are you going to tell us or are you keeping it a secret? You have that look in your eye that Bill Powell gets at the end of his *Thin Man* movies: owlish and superior."

"There's little enough money in this business, Jack, don't grudge me my little flutter."

"Flutter all you want. Just let us in on it."

"Baldly put, I've met the woman we saw this morning twice before. I met her at the place where I have lunch, across from my old office. I know a little about her, and can start tracking her down later this morning."

"You think she'll stand still waiting for you to catch up?"

"Of course not. But I will be able to pick up more about her as the chase continues. She won't leave town; Asa Zavitz is too fat a plum for her to abandon. She'll try to get more out of him. And by now she may have other fish to fry. She's been working this blackmail scheme a long time, both here and across the water."

Decker drove us back to his place on Bundy Drive, where the group broke up into separate initiatives. Fields stretched out on a couch, Decker began stretching a canvas, when I declined to sit on the rostrum for him, and Jack buried himself in a memoir he'd been writing. For my part, I went to bed.

THE SINKING SUN CONTINUED TO shine through my window. A brisk shower prepared me for the sound of sizzling coming from Decker's kitchen.

Ever since I heard Zavitz say that he had cut Scott Fitzgerald off at the knees, Scott had lodged in my brain, like a piece of brisket between molars. I called the number Sheilah Graham had given me. She picked up the phone herself, and told me that they were both at home and receiving company. I checked the address again, and excused myself from the card game that wasn't likely to miss me.

I was looking for an apartment at 1443 North Hayworth Avenue, and found it after running north as far as Selma. Scott opened the door to the apartment himself. His face was pink, bloated, and wider than I remembered. There was a familiar odour of Aqua Velva. He was wearing a dark sports coat over light trousers. A gay cravat was tucked into the open neck of his shirt. He was holding a cigarette. Sheilah had transformed the man I'd last seen on the steps of the police station. He was well turned out.

"Come in, old chum! Sit down. Damn it all, Mike, it's good to see you. Meet my graduating class. Sheilah, this is one of the old gang who doesn't give me bad dreams, or kidnap me into his fiction. I don't even think I owe him any money. Do I, Mike?" Scott held Sheilah's hand, as we all settled down on pieces of the new sectional furniture, which could be reassembled in different combinations for different social occasions. Very modern.

"We're all paid up and even, Scott. What's this about a graduating class?"

"Scott's been tutoring me, Mr. Ward. I came away from London with the clothes on my back and not a full set of A-B-Cs. Scott's been sorting out Shelley and Byron for me. Before I met Scott, I couldn't tell Morley Callaghan from Jack London. Would you like to join the school? But I warn you, I'm the head of my class."

"Also the dunce," added Scott. "She doesn't play by Marquess of Queensberry rules."

"Ouch!" she said, fetchingly. She got up from her chair and walked to one of those bars on wheels you see in the movies, where she turned back to look at me. "Will you have something to drink, Mr. Ward?" She was a well-built, good-looking woman. She had an almost movie-star manner, a sense of herself being observed, and considerable poise.

"Oh, no thanks. I'm not —"

"Don't let Scotty stop you. Just because he isn't. I'm making highballs. Will you have one?"

"Okay, sure."

I didn't notice anything special about the scene when Sheilah got up to fix the drinks. Scott didn't seem to mind not getting one.

"Cheerio!" said the lady, hoisting her glass.

"Here's to the old days, Mike."

"Oh, damn your old days! I don't want to hear about you and Gertrude and Alice, or Sylvia and Adrienne, or Hemingway tonight. They're the spooks that haunt your life. Time to bury them all! I mean it!"

"Sorry, Sheilah; I'm truly sorry. You're right, of course, but until you came along, there hasn't been much to cheer about. What shall we talk about, then? Mike, you're newly arrived on the Coast. What do you make of us?"

Before I could say a word, he was off again.

"But this is no place for you. It'll suck the marrow out of your bones and walk away smiling. I hope you haven't run out of places to go, like I have. The movie people pay well, Mike, but the money evaporates. It's not real money. Not like it was in France. Hush, Sheilah! There, a ten franc note bought ten francs of food or drink, and you went away happy. Here? I'm just the middleman. I pass whatever money I make to my creditors. I owe my daughter's school for last term."

"Scotty, stop this! You're almost completely out of debt. You'll never know how hard he's been working on that, Mike."

"Mike, it won't be long. I'll be back on my feet again."

"Sure you will! Everybody knows that!" I said this with all the conviction I could muster, but I didn't convince anybody, least of all myself. Scott was into his leftover salad days. His clothes smelled of dry sweat and smoke. His cufflinks didn't match. There was a ghost of hopelessness in the air.

"'Fade out. The End. Print it!' Mike, that's exactly the kind of applesauce we live on out here. It's not the truth. Nobody tells the truth. People tell you what you'd like to hear, and then stab you in the back. This town is built on backstabbing. My early books have earned me a place in the pantheon of American letters. Out here, I'm just another writer nobody wants to sit with in the commissary. Failure rubs off on other people, Mike. It follows you home like a stray dog."

"Scotty, you exaggerate!"

"'Exaggerate!' I'm giving you the Breen Office cleanup job. This is the version suitable for children down at the Bijou Theatre, in Anaheim. This town is standing on its head, Mike. The more expensive your clothes, the more you need work. The gaudier the show, the more desperate the scrounger. It's beggar on horseback time; plus-fours and no breakfast. Go back to Canada, Mike. Go back to France, as soon as the Bosch have cleared out."

"Shut up now, darling. You're tiring yourself out. Mike didn't come for a lecture, Scotty. Besides, school's been out for an hour."

"I'm damned sorry, Mike. I let off a little steam when the boiler's about to burst. But imagine: Europe ablaze, and here we sit playing bingo and mah-jong, and clipping bank coupons as usual."

I DROVE TO THE DISNEY Studios in Burbank, using my handy street map. I recognized the big-eared mouse's head decorating the fence surrounding the lot. I left the car in a visitors-only space, and headed for the administration building.

Inside the main door, I was greeted by a young man wearing a badge marked MIKE. I should get myself one of those. I told Mike that I was looking for the employment records of Karen Roberts, who was an inbetweener and inker some time ago. I said that this was a routine credit search, and he went off in search of the person in charge. Soon, I was shunted into an inner office decorated with filing cabinets and populated wooden desks. Wherever I went in this new building, I saw older office furniture fitted into a spanking new space. The place struck me as only a year or two old. The walls were white and freshly painted. Everywhere the familiar faces of Mickey, Donald, and the Seven Dwarfs grinned at me from huge enlargements hung on every wall. All of the staff I saw wore badges with their first names affixed to them. Dress was less formal than in a department store. In my jacket, vest, and tie, I felt over-dressed. But I often get things like that wrong out here. Still, the informality of the staff made it easy to spot outsiders.

Eventually, a Mr. Hornby came to my rescue. His badge read STUART. "Let me see what I can find, Mike. Over here." He led me to a large filing cabinet, opened a drawer and began rummaging around.

"Ah! Here we are! Roberts, Karen Elizabeth. Yes, I remember her: a lively mite, full of energy. Good worker. She went off from here last October to another studio."

"To Schlesinger?"

"I really couldn't say. From glancing at her record here, she was a friendly, well-mannered colleague. I remember her farewell party. Yes, we gave her a big fruit bowl."

"You used the word 'mite.' Does that mean she was not tall?"

"Little bit of a thing. Good draftsman. Punctual. Can't say enough about her. She won a commendation from Roy himself, before she left us." I decided not to inquire who Roy might be; it might detract from my professional masquerade.

I made a note of addresses and telephone numbers. Stuart saw me out of the records department and again I was greeted by Mike, who saw me out the door. He gave me an envelope with notice of a sneak preview of a film later that week. I looked at it as I made my way back to the car.

I indulged myself in a quick break for lunch at a diner that looked as though it was trying to imitate Rough House's rundown saloon in *Popeye*, where Wimpy devoured his hamburgers. Thinking of Wimpy and the whole Thimble Theatre gang, I ordered a burger.

In the afternoon I repeated my morning steps at Schlesinger's animation studio. Luckily, it was in Burbank as well. Here, I actually saw artists working at illuminated glass-topped drawing boards. Here, too, I discovered the same information I'd already got from Disney, with the addition of a more recent address for Karen Roberts in Beverly Hills.

At 2348 West Alameda Drive, a house built well back from the curving, hilly street, I found Karen Roberts with a cast on her right arm and a nasty blue bruise on her forehead. She was about thirty, with brown hair showing the last traces of a permanent wave. She stood, all five feet of her, on the threshold of her house looking like a beagle and frowning. The frown was replaced by a cautious smile when I appeared to have no magazine subscriptions to sell, nor a shortcut to eternal bliss through giving support to a spurious religious foundation.

Unfortunately, the woman at the door was not the Karen Roberts I had met in the diner across from the news service office. My confusion when I saw her, and discovered my mistake, must have been visible on my face, for she invited me in and saw me seated in her art deco living room. She went to get me something to drink.

When I'd had a sip — it was a soft drink — she sat down opposite me, put her autographed cast on a foot stool, and asked, "Are you feeling any better now?"

"I'm sorry about this. When you told me your name, it gave me quite a turn. I don't usually have the vapours, or whatever the male equivalent is."

"You mean you thought I was somebody else? I don't think we've ever met."

"Right. But there's a woman out there using your name. She told me that she was an animator, first at Disney and then at Schlesinger."

"She gave you my name!"

"Yes. She was a good-looking woman of about your age. Taller and well put-together."

"Shirley! She's the woman who pushed me down the stairs."

"Shirley what? It's probably not her real name, but what did she tell you about herself? And why did she try to hurt you?"

"Shirley Warwick. That's the name she gave me. We met at Earl Carroll's place on the Strip. Somebody at the studio gave me an Annie to get in, so I — "

"An 'Annie'?"

"An Annie Oakley: a free pass including the cover charge. My friend Jack Bradley took me. We had a few drinks and were feeling pretty good, and got talking to this Shirley woman. We had a couple more drinks and when Jack passed out Shirley and I took him home in her car. She told me that she was looking for a place. She said that she'd just arrived from the Continent. I told her that I had a spare room. When we met for lunch the next day, she agreed to move in and help with the rent. She had contacts out here, but was still doing the rounds. Interviews, I mean."

"Did she tell you where she came from exactly, what she did for a living, who her friends were?"

"I guess I should be put away for being a bit simple, but I'm from a small town where we tend to trust people. She didn't talk a lot about herself. But when I pressed her, she told me volumes."

"Right off the top of her head, I'll bet. But most fiction is built on fact, so tell me, please, all you can remember."

"She told me right off that her name wasn't what she said it was. She said that she was a refugee from Soviet Russia, that she had escaped after the German-Russian pact, whatever it's called. She told me what a time she had crossing into the West with her brother, about her detention in Germany by the Nazis, about her run across France, after her brother was caught, and her passage in a fishing boat over the Channel to England. There, she says, she worked at the BBC translating broadcasts into Occupied Europe. Do you think any of this is true?"

"As I said, she has to have known some of this from her own experience. I have friends at Bush House. I'll get them to check on her for me."

"Bush House?"

"That's the shortwave and international service of the BBC. It operates out of a building near Trafalgar Square, in London. A short walk from a pub called The George, where I wasted many hours with poets and broadcasters. Sorry. Keep going."

"I think she stayed in London for some time."

"Where in London was she?"

"She mentioned a place called the Langham. I don't know what it is. Do you?"

"It's another hub of broadcasting. The BBC, Canadian Broadcasting Corporation, and other radio news services share the space. The Langham's an old storied hotel with as many ghosts as the Tower of London itself. This 'Shirley' seems to stay close to broadcasters. That's lucky for us, because I know a few of them. Some even owe me a favour or a fiver or both."

"She spoke a lot about the Piccadilly, the District, and the Circle Lines. That's a subway, isn't it?"

"They call it the 'Tube' or the 'Underground' over there. That tells us a little more. She wasn't stuck in central London, but got out west a bit, to Kensington High Street, Cromwell Road, or Earls Court, maybe Hammersmith. London's a big city. Not like LA."

"We're growing. This is a huge city already, but it's all cut up by lines on a map."

A sudden look came into her eyes. I was foolish enough to hope that she had the key to my quest. "Does the name 'Trebovir' mean anything? Is it a park or palace?"

"I think it's a street in Earls Court, but I can check on that. You're being a great help. How did she hurt you?"

"Day before yesterday. She was skipping out with her bags. She thought I was at work, but Leon let all of us take an early day. He does that sometimes."

"'Leon'?"

"My boss. Leon Schlesinger. He treats us all like family."

"But without name tags?"

"Oh, we're nowhere as big as that other place, and Leon hasn't tried to institutionalize a friendly working atmosphere. Anyway, when Shirley saw me on the stairs, she bumped me out of her way with one of her bags. She walked over me and went out the door."

"You could have been badly hurt!"

"This will do."

"You said she drove a car. Where did she leave it?"

"At the garage at the corner. It looks like a miniature castle. He has space in back for three or four cars overnight. That's where I keep my old Ford."

"You wouldn't happen to know —?"

"No, I don't, but Rory will have it written down at the garage."

I put the empty glass down on the low table between us and thanked her for her help. We shook hands when I got up, and I tried to stop her from seeing me out the door.

# CHAPTER TWENTY-FOUR

*R*ory, the garage owner, gave me a lesson in the practical side of free enterprise as he showed me over his "little gold mine," and I nodded politely until he gave me a slip of grease-stained paper with the registration number of the little English Vauxhall my quarry was driving.

"Fine thing," Rory said, "when the tenant drives a sweet little Vauxhall and her landlady drives a Ford!" He laughed at that, then added: "But, just wait 'til she needs parts! She won't be so free and easy then. That's why I always deal with the big Detroit carmakers. Still, this town's full of people going for the look of the thing. They'd rather be towed in a broken-down Rolls than pass the tow truck in a new Chevy. Know what I mean?"

"Plus-fours and no breakfast?"

"Damn it! Another Lime-juicer! As if we didn't have enough already!"

"I'm only English in that I like the beer over there. I'm really from up north, on the Great Lakes."

"Hollywood attracts Englishmen. Englishmen and Germans. The Germans are all on the run from the Nazis. We could do with a little of Hitler's housekeeping. He'd break a few heads and we'd have some order around here."

"I've seen some of that order. I wouldn't wish for it; you'll never know, until it's too late, whether you're one of the clubbers or one of the clubbed."

I asked him about "Shirley," but he wasn't able to add much to what I'd just learned from Karen Roberts.

From this point on, the day was filled with routine and familiar tracking down of the registration of a motor vehicle. I talked again to Bob Alton, my policeman friend, who had access to automobile registrations. That was the easy part. The rest was putting in the time waiting for a response. When it came at last, it sounded something like this: "They used to send a fox with a burning tail through the forest when they wanted to clear the land for seeding or settlement, Ward. You're lighting up the sky around here. I hope you have your ticket back to Canada. I wouldn't want to be in your shoes."

"Who's after me now?"

"Same old gang. Only I think the studio might be easing off a bit. But Swarbrick hasn't got wind of that yet. I wouldn't use your second-hand car anymore. We've got the number. And that dealer you got the last one from is being watched."

"I'll remember that. Thanks. Were you able to run the car registration number I gave you?"

"That's what you're paying me for, isn't it?"

"We're talking about public duty here, not pay. What's got you acting cute and playful?"

"This is like a Christmas cracker: you pull both ends and it goes bang!"

"Come on, Bob. What have you got?"

"The car belongs to one Ivana Janjic."

"I know the name. Jack Barrymore said he once worked with her before she became well known under a new name."

"She became well known, all right, under the name Barbara Lorrison!"

"Lorrison! Well I'll be damned!"

"Very likely. I'll talk to you later. Maybe in ten or twenty years. Bye."

Bob had a good nose for the dramatic. He couldn't have broken the connection at a better time. Max Reinhardt couldn't have improved on it. The effect of the news on me got me holding on to the wooden frame of the phone booth for support. I had the information. Now, what was I going to do with it?

But, first things first. I hired a battered Plymouth coupé from Rory, and drove off his lot, leaving in a dark cloud of poorly exploded exhaust. Rory waved me on my way, still grinning even when the car backfired three or four times.

"WE HAVE TO TALK," I said to Asa Zavitz over the phone, from Decker's house.

"You let me down, Mike. Nobody lets me down. You hear? I'm not likely to forget that."

"What do you mean? Nobody let you down. I was there! I watched you give her the money."

"What are you talking about? You couldn't have been there. You would have been seen. You can't hide in a place like that."

"I was with the bunch of actors rehearsing on the stage. What's more, I recognized your blackmailer." I could hear Zavitz take a breath or two. He needed room to turn around in.

"You better get over here right away."

He may have thought that he had ended the conversation, but I cut in before he disconnected. "No. That won't work. What's the name of the drugstore where they discovered Lana Turner?"

"Whatta you mean 'they' discovered her? I discovered her! At Schwab's on Sunset Boulevard."

"What about meeting there?"

"That's corny and crowded. Didn't you see *Footsteps on the Ceiling*? That's where they met. Besides, I'll be mobbed if I go there."

"Well, you name a place."

"There's a simple spaghetti place on Beverly, near Rodeo Drive."

"I know it! It'll be perfect. See you there in an hour."

"Make it half an hour later. I have to fire a big star first."

"I'll see you there. Don't tell anybody where you're going. Thanks to you, I'm on the Most Wanted list."

"I told them to fix that!"

"Maybe you're not God after all, just human like the rest of us. Goodbye."

I looked in my pocket for a piece of a torn menu. When I fished it out, I could see that it had been in service too long. It was showing its age. From it I picked a number I'd used only once before.

"Hello, Virginia?"

"Mike? Is that you? Where are you?"

"I guess you might call it a safe house. I'm fine. Nobody's tried to stop me for hours. How are you two?"

"Benny's in the desert. He's up there more than he's here. He's got me reading Shakespeare. Wants to improve my mind."

"As usual, Virginia, I need a favour."

"Okay, what is it? No more than half of my kingdom, though. That's the house limit."

"I've got to see Barbara Lorrison. Do you know the best place to do that? The studio's too public; I don't want to run into her mother at her house. What do you suggest?"

"This isn't as hard as you make it out to be. Ever hear of the Versailles Club? Very exclusive. She goes swimming and does her workouts there. Her mother never goes near the place. You might find her head poking out of a steam cabinet. It's on Melrose near Santa Monica Boulevard. Do you know it?"

"No, but I'll find it. Do you know her? What's she like?"

"Our circles don't overlap, Mike. But I hear that she's brighter than all those dizzy blondes she plays on the screen."

"Thanks. But do you think she might be there? She'd still be in mourning, wouldn't she?"

"Her new musical starts principal photography a week from this Thursday. If she has to lose weight before shooting starts, that's where you'll find her. Good luck, Mike."

"Thanks. I'll be in touch. Bye."

With a handful of change, I made some trans-Atlantic calls to old broadcasting friends. I felt self-conscious using real money. In the old days in London and Paris, I knew how to trunk expensive calls through the switchboards of large corporations. After a couple of dead ends, I reached Elwyn Thomas, a photographer and broadcaster, who knew as many of my secrets as I knew of his.

"Mike, you son of a bitch! I don't believe it!"

"It's really me, Johnny, and I need your help."

"You still owe me eighty quid."

"We'll not contest it. I need your help, Johnny. I'm serious." I filled him in on the few facts I had and what I could put together from the scraps I'd picked up from Karen Roberts. He told me how busy he was, and how this couldn't have come at a worse time. I reminded him of an altercation in a Soho restaurant involving the owner and three unhappy waiters. He promised to help after that. I gave him the Bundy Drive number, and promised him the moon with oak leaf clusters when I next saw him.

It wasn't all that hard finding the gym. It was a swanky place, no heavy sweat allowed. Members moved around the place in big white terry cloth robes. They looked like extras from a sequence set in heaven. All it lacked was the dry ice sending up clouds from the floor.

I told the woman at the desk that I was the reporter from *LIFE* she was expecting. Distracted, she began rummaging around for the note about my arrival. I explained that this was simply a survey. The photographer would be coming on his own and making his own arrangements. She was a dimpled blonde creature, easily flustered, but professionally agreeable. She told me what film personalities were in the gym or pool at the moment, and sent someone to fetch coffee for me.

While I was sipping that, I felt a heavy hand on my shoulder. The jig was up! Swarbrick had found me! Now I would be in for a beating at the very least. "Faith, it's an uncertain world entirely! How's your eye, old sport?"

It was Flynn, all dressed in white terry cloth with a sweatband around his forehead, and grinning like two Steinway pianos. He looked like a ballet dancer who'd strayed away from his barre. I remembered our last meeting on a yacht off San Diego during the post-wedding party. I'd caught some confetti in my eye.

"The eye's ship-shape now, thanks to you. My heirs will inherit your handkerchief. What are you doing in a place like this?"

"Like everybody here, I'm sweating the lard off my bones, old boy. What are you up to? They won't let you through dressed like that."

"I want to catch Barbara Lorrison for a minute, if I can."

"Ha! Another autograph-hunter in civilian dress. I thought better of you."

"I'm interested in her car."

"Her car! 'Aye, tell this to all the world, but to me you can say, she loves you not.'"

"When did you do *Cyrano*?"

"God help me! A literate bloke! A verse wallah! I don't believe it. What missed turning brought you here?"

"I'm looking for Barbara Lorrison. I'm no autograph-hunter; I need to talk to her."

"A newspaperman, I'll bet."

"That's right, but I'm working on my own now."

"A sleuth it is, b'dad! I should have known. Private investigations for one hundred down and ten bucks a day. I'm playing a sleuth in my next picture. No more boots and cutlasses. Just raw wits pitted against a misguided dentist. But Ralph Bellamy's a decent chap. We should have some fun."

"How well do you know Barbara Lorrison?"

"We did a picture six or seven months ago. She's a good sort. She's a wonder in a car. Drives like no other woman alive. Behind the wheel, she has *cojones*. And she's not hard to talk to."

"Not when you're Errol Flynn. I'm just Mike Ward from Toronto."

"Let's seek her out. Come with me." I followed Flynn through frosted glass double doors, down a corridor, around a bend, then up a short flight of stairs that brought us out onto a balcony overlooking the Olympic-size pool. "There she is!" Flynn shouted over the sounds of water echoing on tile walls. He'd pointed out a woman swimming in the far lane, wearing a white bathing suit. Her strokes were well timed and even. You could tell that she knew all there was to know about swimming lengths. Flynn and I watched her turn at the far end and head back in our direction. "Barbara's grown quite chubby with grief, old boy. Imagine trying to lose weight when you're worth what she is per pound."

I waited around watching Lorrison after Flynn begged off. He said there was a steam cabinet with his name on it awaiting. When Lorrison left the pool, I retraced my steps back to the double doors and lingered. She took about half an hour to reappear.

"Miss Lorrison," I yelled as I tried to catch up with her. She'd exploded out the frosted glass doors and was off through the hallway to the entrance. I yelled again, trying not to sound like a member of her fan club.

"Hello. What do you want? I'm in a hurry, I'm afraid."

Whenever reporters write about Barbara Lorrison they forget to say anything about the luminous glow of her skin. Wearing a simple white dress and with a turban-like towel around her wet hair, she was at once shockingly beautiful and irritated at me. She was shorter than I'd expected. The camera gave her inches. She'd stopped, waiting for me to make my case.

"I'm an investigator looking into the death of your husband, Miss Lorrison. Mr. Zavitz knows what I've been up to. I would like to talk to you. Please."

"I'm in a rush to get to the studio. Can't it wait?"

"We can talk in your car. That way you won't keep anybody waiting."

Lorrison didn't say anything, but by starting to move toward the door, I guessed she had swallowed my terms. "Thanks," I said.

She allowed me to open her car door, then reached across to unlock the opposite door from behind the steering wheel. There was something in the way she started the car and backed out of the narrow slot the roadster occupied that told me this was no ordinary driver. Flynn was right. She possessed that perfect calm rally drivers have. It's not simply that she was relaxed behind the wheel; she wasn't that, exactly: she was more like a coiled spring.

"You're a damned good driver," I said, as she headed down a street parallel to the one leading to the studio. Even with my full score of ignorance of the city, I knew that she knew what she was doing.

"Skip the flattery. You said you wanted to talk. So, talk." Blue eyes flashed anger at me. I tried to marshal my thoughts.

"Why would someone who might be implicated in the death of your husband be driving a car registered to you?"

"Which car?"

"The Vauxhall."

"How is she implicated in Mark's death?"

"I'm glad I came to the right place!"

"What do you mean?"

"You know the driver was a woman. If you know that, you know most of what I have to learn in order to settle up this business.

She's holding a nasty piece over Asa's head. He's paid her off, but she'll be back."

"How do you fit into all of this?"

I gave her the short version of my involvement, skipping the part about being wanted by the police for questioning. While running through all this, I found it hard keeping my eyes in neutral as those silky legs moved from clutch to gas and brake and back again.

"Mainly you're interested in the car?"

"Sure. And what it leads to. Asa's blackmailer isn't the sort to settle for a few hundred when there are thousands to be made from the same source."

"To the best of my knowledge, the Vauxhall hasn't been out of the garage."

"Right now it's not at your house."

"You're wrong!"

"Look, you know who borrowed the car, and you want to clear it with her before you tell me anymore. I understand that. I hope somebody will do that for me someday. But, Miss Lorrison, there have been two murders and a few attempted murders. If what you know could link a friend of yours to the crime, you're in danger. Real danger: not the sort that always comes out right before the lights come back up, but deadly danger. Please believe that."

"Look, Mr. Ward, I can't help you any more than I have already. I don't want to help a blackmailer dig her teeth deeper into dear Asa, but I'll have to manage it my own way."

"You don't believe the story of your husband's suicide?"

"Of course not. I knew Mark. Suicide wasn't something he'd ever consider. It's just another news story. I gave up believing in the papers about the same time I found out about Santa Claus. What I can't understand is why should you, a foreigner, be so interested in all this. You didn't believe the papers; you ignored the police. What's in it for you?"

# CHAPTER TWENTY-FIVE

*I*'m not sure where she let me off, exactly. I didn't recognize any landmarks. I decided not to worry about it, and gave the taxi I flagged down Decker's address, which was the closest thing to home I had in this city.

I'd been on this street now a dozen times, but the houses all looked new and strange. I was like Balboa discovering the Pacific Ocean, in spite of the poet's confused facts, but a Balboa cursed with a bad memory. In Los Angeles I was never sure what street I was on. I went quietly into the Bundy Drive house, climbing right into the shower on the second floor, thus avoiding the questions of my sometime brothers-in-crime. After my shower, I put on fresh clothes and brushed my hair. I even cut my fingernails before coming downstairs.

"Ah! You've heard, then?" Jack was holding something dark in a martini glass.

"What? Am I still a wanted man?"

"Heard about dinner. We're feasting forth tonight."

"Virginia called an hour ago. Hope you haven't made other plans," Decker was playing Mr. Interlocutor.

"Of course he'll come. He has the lean and hungry look of a lean and hungry man. Imagine coming from a place like Toronto. What do you use as a return address: Tomato, Can? Decker, have you no pity? Lacking in him is that wonderful quality my dear grandmother called 'bottom.' But he'll be put to rights by Virginia's groaning board."

"Cocktail, Mike?"

"Gladly, thanks."

"An old friend of yours from London called," Jack said, in a mock conspiratorial way. "Welshman, by the sound of him. Here! I wrote it all down."

"You mean I wrote from your dictation, Jack," Decker put in.

"'True art is nature to —' Never mind. Decker, art is the process of editing nature. As a painter, you ought to know that. We all edit life, leave things out that don't matter. What does it matter to Mike, here, who wrote down the words?"

The painter handed me a scrap of cardboard with the following written in block letters, which was as close to cursive script as Decker came:

Your girl went under several names, one known to you. She lived with a freelancer named Robert Kerr, in Earls Court, dumped him for titled bloke named Blair Seddon in the Boltons. She was well known in the French bar in Soho. Left trans-Atlantic phone bills behind her whenever she moved. Last seen last month with Lady Margaret Reynolds at Ascot.

Johnny.

The message included a couple of unfamiliar LA phone numbers in a postscript. I put the information aside for the moment. Barrymore frowned on me as Decker filled a glass.

"Well, now that you're freshly waxed and Simonized, what the hell have you got to say for yourself?" Jack demanded, Decker standing by with my drink in his hand. I told them, as well as I could, what had happened since our rehearsal of the scene from *Twelfth Night*.

When I'd done, Jack asked, "Why the devil can't you get Lorrison to tell you to whom she lent her car? It seems simple and straightforward to me."

"Yes, it's no skin off her pretty little nose."

"We each have a sense of loyalty, and they're each different. She wants to do it her own way. I couldn't stop her."

"Well, we'll have to leave it there. Virginia's expecting us for dinner later."

For those with an appetite, as well as for those with time hanging heavily, Decker made one of his famous Sunday brunches: eggs, French toast, two kinds of bacon, sausages, and coffee that did for me in the morning what no rare old Scotch could do for me later in the day.

To put in time on this sleepy Sunday, I bothered the San Francisco police for details of the Norma Fisher suicide off the ferry. I talked to the chief of detectives there and to the chief in Sausalito, across the Golden Strait. What they said only confirmed what Virginia had told me days ago.

DINNER THAT NIGHT AT VIRGINIA'S was a perfect delight. Not only was the roast welcome and tasty, but there were wine and spirits enough to raise the pulse of an Egyptian mummy. Virginia made an excuse to pardon Benny from joining us. He was entertaining Murder, Inc. at Ciro's, and wouldn't be home until later. Virginia herself was very much with us, making up for Benny's empty chair. She was gorgeously turned out in silky, silvery lounge pyjamas that added to her height. Under the chandelier, the necklace she was wearing sparkled like the real thing. Naturally, she wanted to know all about what I'd been up to, once Jack finished telling a story about how he lost his bicycle when he was living with two budding actresses at the Garden of Allah.

"Not only did I never see the two-wheeler again, but the women

I'd intended to visit were not at home to me forever afterwards. Ah, 'How happy could I be with either,/Were t'other dear charmer away ...'"

Jack sang the couplet in a light tenor voice, enhanced by rolling his eyes roguishly. We all laughed and had our glasses replenished.

"Now, Mike, it's your turn."

"Virginia, you told me all about this case when I first met you. I've been running around behind the scenes while you've been working under the blue and amber lights on stage. If I had papers, I should hand them in to the adjutant. It is the adjutant, isn't it, Jack? I'm slow on things military."

"The world would be a better place if we all were," Jack said. "But you make up for it in creating an Irish stew of your metaphors." We all laughed at that, and continued to demolish the roast.

Over coffee, we dug into the European war and the cold wind blowing this way from Japan. "Nobody will trust the Russians again. Stalin should not have got into bed with Hitler."

"Those would be very uncomfortable bedfellows!" Decker added. "But it's good for Hitler. He wouldn't fare any better on the Russian steppes than Napoleon in 1812."

"What a memory! What colour were Bonaparte's eyes? As a painter, I'm sure you'd remember?"

"Trouble is, nobody reads history."

"You don't have to go back to 1812. There's plenty going on right here in LA."

"As for instance?"

"A-Z-P had to close down a picture today and they don't know when or even if they'll be able to shoot it. Two hundred people are joining the bread line."

"What picture?"

"*Saratoga Bound*. Barbara Lorrison smashed up her car. She's in a coma. Don't you Olympians read the papers or listen to the radio?" When Virginia saw the effect of her news on the group, she quickly yanked her smile offstage.

"Mike, what's happened to your colour?" The painter noticed the effect of Virginia's news.

"Here, Mike, take a drink of this." Jack handed me a glass, which I emptied without tasting.

"I warned her, damn it! I warned her! Where is she?"

"Cedars," said Virginia.

HALF AN HOUR LATER — IT would have been longer if Decker hadn't driven me — I was waiting in the emergency ward at Cedars. I was told that a statement would be released to the press shortly. I sat down holding a copy of *Look Magazine*, but I was far from being able to read a word. I couldn't look the two Jacks in the eye.

"I don't understand this: she was one of the best drivers I know."

"You're right there. A mechanic friend of mine says that, behind the wheel, she has balls."

"I think I know that mechanic."

At this moment, while I was looking idly into space, and the two Jacks were being distracted by *Esquire* magazine, the less inspiring image of Swarbrick floated over my retina. He was with two plainclothes officers. The only good thing to say about it is that he looked as surprised to see me as I was to see him.

"Mike Ward. You're a fugitive from justice and I'm placing you under arrest. Damn it, Ward, you're lucky this is a Quiet Zone."

"Now, hold on!" Jack Barrymore shouted. Was he going to recite one of the great speeches from Shakespeare to save my bacon? I could almost see Swarbrick joining the three of us, waiting.

"Sir, this is none of your affair!" the cop shouted. "This man is wanted. Stay out of it. I'm not looking for you at present, so just mind your business."

I was surprised that the Great Profile had so little effect on the police. Jack was too.

"Ward, come along with us. And no funny business!"

I shrugged to Barrymore and Decker. It wasn't a moment for soliloquy or lengthy leave-taking. "I'll get one of my lawyers on this when I get home, Mike. He'll make such a racket as this town hasn't heard since I was accused of trifling with a minor."

On the way out of the emergency ward, we ran straight into Asa Zavitz and his man Friday, Jeff Swift. Asa and Jeff saw me walking with the policemen. Asa stopped in his tracks. "Swarbrick! What is the meaning of this?"

"But, Mr. Zavitz. He's wanted. On suspicion."

"Suspicion of what, may I ask? Picking the flowers in Forest Lawn?"

"Sir, you made the complaint in the first place."

"So, now I'm unmaking it. Haven't I got enough on my mind? A top star out of commission, and that son-of-a-bitch Goebbels has frozen our assets in Europe. I'd be living on Aspirin if my stomach could take it. Let him go, and find a place to bury this." He handed a limp Corona to Swarbrick. Then, he turned to me and said, "What do you know? Has she a chance?"

"They are going to make a statement in a few minutes. I wasn't able to learn anything else."

"Swarbrick, you'd better come along. You might be useful." The film producer was not smiling. Then he looked at me: "Make yourself useful! What are you standing on?"

"Certainly not ceremony. I was trying to figure out how a smart man like you can cut Fitzgerald loose. You know you owe him. We all owe him."

"Don't talk foolish. Is it a charity I'm running now?"

I returned to the emergency ward along with the others. My friends nodded at the newcomers. The newcomers sat across from us. No sooner had he been seated than Jeff was on his feet again interrupting the registration of a woman with a broken leg and a bleeding forehead. The nurse turned him away, saying that a statement would be made in a few minutes.

He sat down again, avoiding eye contact. We waited.

# CHAPTER TWENTY-SIX

*I*t was nearly an hour after Swarbrick had finished with us, and left, that a doctor appeared with the news that Barbara Lorrison was out of immediate danger and that her injuries appeared to be of a kind that would not interfere with the continuation of her film career. He went on to say that, nevertheless, her situation was serious, that she would remain at Cedars for a week or longer, and that, except for her immediate family, there would be no visitors allowed.

We, the waiting group, began to shuffle in our uselessness and got to our feet, going out into the night to our various cars, leaving a rather large hole in the visitors' parking area when we drove off.

Although I got into Decker's car, I did not stay. By the time the car came to the edge of the ramp leading back to the street, I had resolved to do some nosing around the hospital on my own. I said goodnight to the others, ignored their suggestion of making an early start in the morning, and shut the door between us. I listened to the car start its motor, after stalling, and watched it leave the lot.

Of course, I had no plan, but as I thought that my recent stay at Cedars might be worth something, I re-entered the building and pushed the button for the fifth floor. When the doors opened, I stepped out into familiar landscape. The nursing station was where it should be, and I knew where I could find a mug of hot coffee. In that meeting room, I found not only coffee, but, hanging in a closet, a white coat. I put it on and walked back towards the nursing station, past it, and down the corridor.

"Mr. Ward, what on earth do you think you're doing?" It was Nurse Crawford. Crawford was a leftover from my legitimate stay under this healing roof. She looked starched and antiseptic, and very real, standing in my path.

"Nurse Crawford! Just the person I'm looking for. I'm in luck." I tried on a pleasant grin to disarm her. It didn't work.

"You know you have no business —"

"I know, I know. But listen to me for a second before you press any alarm buttons."

"Come in here!" It was an order, not a request. "You were discharged weeks ago." We went into a small lounge for ambulatory patients and visitors. It had comfortable chairs and a radio. Luckily, at this hour, it was empty.

"Look, Crawford, I'm not stealing drugs or needles. I'm trying to save one of your patients from attack. I have reason to believe that the life of Barbara Lorrison is in danger. Her life!"

"It certainly is! She's not out of the woods by a long shot. I won't have you bursting in on her. I really will push that button."

"Just calm down! Listen, Crawford. She has more than her injuries to worry about. There may be an attempt on her life here tonight. I don't have to see her. All I need to do is to remove or change the name sign outside her room so that any attacker will not be able to find her."

"'Attacker'? What sort of crazy nonsense is this? Those signs aren't for decoration or primarily for visitors. The nursing and medical staff depend on them. You can't go moving her about or confusing the name signs. It doesn't take much to disrupt order around here, but that would be a start."

"Then what do you suggest? You can't move her to another room?"

"In her condition? Don't be silly! There are no empty beds."

"Could we rename her? Post a misleading sign? At this time of night, it can't do a lot of harm."

"We'll have to make duplicate charts under another name. That would be highly irregular. It's probably an indictable offence. And what about the listing downstairs in Reception?"

"I'm just trying to save her life. Is that indictable?"

Once she began to use the word "we," I felt my heart beginning to slow down a little. But her objections were solid, practical ones. I tried to think.

"Shouldn't the police know about this?"

"There was an LAPD sergeant here a while ago, but he drove off without leaving a guard. Look! If there's going to be an attack on her life, it will probably be tonight, before she regains consciousness."

Without further palaver, we removed the nameplate from outside Barbara Lorrison's hospital room. Crawford disappeared behind the counter into the nursing station, where she typed out a new name on the standard form. She was breathing harder than I was. It was gratifying to see that professionals can react in a human way to a human emergency.

"Here," she said. "Put this beside her door."

The new name read "E. Cinders."

"I couldn't think of anything else," she said, blushing about the name of a character in a comic strip.

"Can you leave a notice that Lorrison's in the room marked 'Cinders' at the nursing station?"

"I thought you wanted to hide her?"

"We're dealing with a clever assassin, Crawford. We need a follow-up, a second shot. Put the note about the name change where it can be seen. Is there a second bed in her room?"

"There is, but what are you thinking of?"

"Good! I'll climb into it and wait. Keep your eyes open from the nursing station. And remember: our villain, if I'm not way off the beam, may have found a white coat as I did. Or maybe he'll be in operating room scrubs."

"Are you sure it'll be a man?"

"Not one hundred per cent."

"You better get out of your clothes."

"What?"

"Your shoes and trousers will give you away. Here, put on these." She brought out a couple of cotton gowns, then slammed the cupboard door. I removed my shoes, and hoped that that would suffice, but I was urged out of my trousers as well. The nurse's only comment was, "Really!"

Crawford opened the door to Lorrison's room and pointed me to the empty bed. She removed the chart from the head of Lorrison's bed and placed it at the head of mine. There was no sound from the occupied bed. "Is she all right?" I asked.

"I'll check her vital signs," she said, drawing up the light coverlet around me. A moment or two later, she whispered:

"She's fine. I'm going to get you some bandages for your head. You don't look like a wounded movie star under those covers. Back in a minute." I heard the door close. Crawford was gone for a very long minute. I could now make out Lorrison's breathing.

I heard the door open again, and then felt Crawford's fingers wrapping my head with gauze. "Don't go to sleep!" she cautioned. "I'll be at the nursing station pretending to doze."

Then the silence closed in, deeper than ever. I could hear breathing, Lorrison's and mine. There was a sputtering fan someplace, and a steady electric hum. On the fifth floor, we were safe from the noises of traffic except for sirens of police, fire, and ambulances.

The time did not pass quickly. It hung about my loins like a young bride. I named my public school teachers and went on to the teachers at high school and university. I went through a short list of girls I've cared about, retracing the places where my marriages went off the track. Was it Jack who talks about his marriages as 'bus accidents'? I think it was something Fowler said about Jack. I thought about the funny group we made around Jack, as though he was a floating piece of timber with all of us clinging to the wreckage. I felt myself falling asleep, and fought against it. I tried blinking in the dark. I rolled my head around on my neck, getting a gritty feeling, as though my spine were lubricated with sand and gravel.

Then I heard something. Nothing you could put a name to. Nothing as loud as the creak of a floorboard or the scrape of a shoe on the tile. Then I heard it again, and a sliver of light fell across the venetian blinds covering the windows. I can't say I held my breath, because it wasn't a conscious act. My breath was held, without any action on my part. But my heart was stomping inside my ribs loudly enough to be heard at the end of the corridor.

I heard whispering. There were two of them! I felt a hand on my leg. Then a sudden stab of pain. My leg jumped compulsively. I thought of kicking whatever it was, but I wasn't sure that the bedclothes would allow free play to a kick. Instead, I leapt at whatever was on the side of the bed. I heard a sound that was half scream, half shout.

"Damn!"

It was a woman's voice. Unable to see the body from which it came, I grabbed at the sound. The person I was holding on to moved across the band of light falling through the door and I could see who she was. I felt arms around my chest.

"Help me, damn it!"

"Hold her still!"

Another arm was on my shoulders. I kept kicking. Then the light came on and blinded me. There was a thud somewhere around my knees. I heard a scream and a groan. My eyes were growing accustomed to the light now. I saw two figures on the floor. One was the woman I'd been looking for, the one from the diner. The other, rolled in a ball, was Jeff Swift. Nurse Crawford was standing over the bodies holding a Smith-Corona typewriter in her grasp. Some of the keys were broken.

## CHAPTER TWENTY-SEVEN

*T*wo days later, the inflammation in my leg had started to go down, but Dr. Murphy had said that the swelling was only natural in the circumstances. Swarbrick and his men had tidied away the two villains. Barbara Lorrison regained consciousness. Her injuries were healing well, and the studio had announced a new date for the beginning of principal photography on the film.

Decker had collected me at Cedars, after I had been jabbed in the arm and leg by several other needles. Nurse Crawford supervised.

"That was a damned close call, Mr. Ward," Dr. Murphy announced without the trace of a smile. He handed me three written prescriptions, which I pocketed.

The nurse, who had clobbered both Emma Schneller and Jeff Swift with her typewriter, saw me to the door and into Decker's waiting car.

"What's your name, Nurse Crawford? I should at least know the full name of the woman who saved my life."

"Jessica," she said.

"I think I like the sound of that."

"But you're not certain?"

"I'd like to kick the tires a few times to be sure."

She gave me a look, to which I replied: "I'm sure." She smiled, took out a pencil and wrote something on a scrap of Cedars stationery. I was glad to see that she had written out her whole name along with a telephone number. I didn't put that in my pocket until I'd placed it safely in my wallet.

Bill Fields's front room was largely occupied by a sturdy, antique billiards table. It filled the room with the colour of green baize, giving it the look of a painting by that Dutch painter from the 1880s who quarrelled with everybody. We'd come here from Decker's, because not only was his cleaning woman in a bad mood, but there were rumours that the poet Sadakichi Hartmann was prowling the neighbourhood.

All of us sat in the comfortable chairs, avoiding a collapsed folding chair that was part of Bill's schtick. Barrymore assumed a pose by a window to let his left profile show to advantage. It was the first time I'd ever seen him do something that showed any sign of vanity. Maybe he was feeling good. Decker helped Bill with some drinks.

"Place is going to the dogs," Fields said, handing me a glass. "Can't find what the Chinaman's done with my liquor."

"What's this?"

"Oh, that? Just something left over from last Christmas. Something that escaped the attention of the man in the red pyjamas. Have another."

"Well, Mike, are you going to leave us on tenterhooks until the Second Coming? We didn't come here to hear me recite *Lear*, for God's sake. Blast you, man, sing out!"

"There isn't much to tell, Jack. I just blundered around long enough for Nurse Crawford to save my long johns. She's the girl of the minute. We should be drinking to her."

"And so say all of us!" A toast was raised and drunk.

"Well, I did do some things," I said, moving the bouncing ball back to me. "Swift had to try to stop Barbara Lorrison from telling me to whom she had lent one of her cars. She lent it to Emma Schneller." The others looked at me as though the name O'Brien had suddenly appeared in a list of the dramatis personae in *Julius Caesar*. "She and her brother are the chief villains of this story."

"Brother? What brother?"

"Jeff Swift, Jack."

"Now how in hell can you know that?" Decker asked.

"Schneller and Swift mean the same thing. Well, almost. German and English. Both real surnames. She went by many names. The Brits and French knew her as Schneller. I don't know a lot about her background, but one name, Schneller, keeps cropping up. I'm sure that poverty played a big part in her early life. I'll leave that to her defending counsel. The fact is she had very little regard for human life. She murdered a policeman who had followed her from London; a man named Macdonald, an old friend of mine. She tried to kill me on several occasions, succeeding in putting me in hospital and killing another colleague.

"Schneller held a dirty piece about Asa Zavitz and his doings in Soho and other places in London a year ago, and used it to extort funds."

"Did she murder Mark Norman?" Before I could answer, Jack volunteered:

"No. That was his first wife." Jack smiled at me. "Then she jumped off the ferry from San Francisco to Sausalito."

"Sorry, Jack. That's what I thought, too, for a while. I think Norma, the first Mrs. Norman, thought she had shot her ex-husband. I mean, she arrived at his house with a loaded gun, saw the man who had thrown her over, and let fire. If the cops wouldn't swallow the suicide story, in spite of Zavitz and the power he wields, they had a perfect place to retreat to: 'Crazed ex-wife shoots newly married movie mogul.'

"Phoebe Wheeler was a friend of Norma's. She told Phoebe about shooting her ex. She pointed the gun and fired. She saw him fall, then she ran away. We know, from the same source, that Norman wasn't alone when Norma arrived. He'd been having drinks with someone who was out of sight when the gun went off.

"We know that Norman was about to tell his boss, Zavitz, that Swift was a Nazi sympathizer and fundraiser. He wanted to stop this from happening. And the smoking gun was still on the floor when Norman got up and dusted himself off, after an unexpected close call. The opportunity was too perfect. Swift picked up the gun, moved closer to Mark Norman, and fired the gun a second time."

"Well, I'll be damned!"

"But, 'vas you dere, Sharley?'" Fields did a good imitation of Jack Pearl, the radio character.

"The maid, Violet Bowden, who conveniently has been hustled offstage to Paris so she can't tell what she knows, told her son that she heard shots that day. She said 'shots,' not 'a shot.'"

"That's hearsay. Inadmissible."

"Hell, Jack, I'm no lawyer. I'm just trying to figure out what happened where no living witnesses are likely to tell us what took place."

"So," Decker added, "it was blackmail all along."

"No. Mark Norman's death had nothing to do with blackmail. He was killed because he couldn't be bought."

"Go on."

"A-Z-P had been a monument of the film industry. When Norman was murdered, Zavitz and his colleague, Jeff Swift, fed some ripe fiction to the cops. It was a juicy enough story so that the papers grabbed it, swallowed it, and never looked any further. A home run for the studio. The story Zavitz wanted hushed up was the story about Norman's first wife, who had worked closely with him at the studio. Any deep research into her life would reveal a lot of strange doings in the management of the studio going back to the early days. He would have had to resign, if all of that backstory came out. Swift's career too might have nosedived, since it's likely that he also knew where the bodies were buried. Maybe he might have succeeded Zavitz. Swift's not without ambition.

"We can see that Swift might have been trying to benefit himself by inventing the absurd story of the suicide. And there's another fact that we might overlook. Sure, Zavitz had to gain from the false story of Norman's death. But, as I've said, Swift had his own reasons for wanting Norman dead. Norman knew about Swift's playing about with the local National Socialists. He trained with them, marched with them, supplied them with funds. All very well; this is still a free country. Nobody would accuse him of being a premature anti-Fascist. Jack told me that Norman was about to tell Zavitz about all this."

"Damn it all! I do have a part in this epic after all!" Jack shouted. We smiled, and I kept on going.

"Zavitz was in private a strong supporter of American efforts to keep the US out of the European war. As Ambassador Kennedy has said, 'Nobody wants to fight a Jewish war.' After Chaplin's *The Great Dictator*, that became more difficult. Zavitz was under pressure to slow down any movement that might spark pro-war sentiments. That's why, so far, the only movies about the war have been made by studios whose heads aren't Jewish. Zavitz, himself, was sympathetic to the plight of European Jews, but he couldn't do anything publicly. He was caught. He was angry and frustrated."

"Norman talked to me a couple of days before his death," Jack Barrymore said, almost talking to himself. "He said that he was going to tell Zavitz about Swift's major part in supporting and promoting the Nazi position."

We all looked at Jack. "If he learned that his fair-haired boy was pushing for the other side, it would have ended his career then and there. So, my friends, the plot begins to jell."

"That's right. Swift killed Norman not to divert the police from digging into the things that his first wife knew, but to put a permanent lid on what Norman might say to Zavitz about his political activities."

We all drew in a fresh breath of air. The lid was finally off, and we could breathe again. It was maybe the last time I saw Jack laugh. I mean laugh without watching to see who was looking.

Then, after I had stopped talking, and had sipped from the drink I'd been holding, suddenly, there was a new, but not unfamiliar, face in the room. It was Hartmann. Sadakichi Hartmann, the philosophic gardener and poet. We froze to our seats. "What are you bourgeois peasants up to? Are you rebuilding the world from your easy chairs? It's too late; it's too late for that. Phooey! Double phooey!"

# EPILOGUE

*T*ime passes. Things change. The war came uninvited even to the City of Angels. Bugsy Siegel's gambling casino, named in honour of his mistress Virginia Hill, opened in Las Vegas, and became a great success, but not before Siegel's partners had rubbed him out in the living room I knew. I've lost touch with Virginia. She doesn't return my calls. William Dieterle offered Jack Barrymore a supporting role in *Kismet*. The lead went to dependable Ronald Colman. Monty Woolley was picked, over Jack, to recreate the role he had created on Broadway in *The Man Who Came to Dinner*.

It's funny, but in a crazy way, Jack, the has-been; Jack, the Monster; Jack, struggling under fathoms of debt, was the father of our little colony, our community of exiles and misfits, our community of innocents under Decker's roof on Bundy Drive.

Still, Jack's glory days were over. From then on he would play caricatures of himself on the stage and on the screen. He did these roles superbly. His friend Gene Fowler recorded his Götterdäm-merung. The waste.

And again: more waste. Scott Fitzgerald's passing was marked in all the papers. But it was in the notice in *The New Yorker* that the writers of those obituaries were called to task; all too young to have known him or ever to have read him. When I saw him last, he was kidding himself about the work that still remained to be put down on paper. He was far too good a writer to have really believed that.

# ACKNOWLEDGEMENTS

I acknowledge, with gratitude, the editorial help of Nancy N. Vichert and Griffiths Cunningham.

## ALSO BY HOWARD ENGEL

### Novels

*The Suicide Murders* (1980)
*The Ransom Game* (1981)
*Murder on Location* (1982)
*Murder Sees the Light* (1984)
*A City Called July* (1986)
*A Victim Must Be Found* (1988)
*Dead and Buried* (1990)
*The Whole Megillah* (1991)
*Murder in Montparnasse* (1992)
*There Was an Old Woman* (1993)
*Getting Away With Murder* (1995)
*Mr. Doyle and Dr. Bell* (1997)
*A Child's Christmas in Scarborough* (1997)
*My Brother's Keeper* (with Eric Wright, 2001)
*The Cooperman Variations* (2001)
*Memory Book* (2005)
*East of Suez* (2008)

### Non-fiction

*Lord High Executioner: An Unashamed Look at Hangmen,*
*Headsmen, and Their Kind* (1996)
*Crimes of Passion: An Unblinking Look at Murderous Love* (2001)
*The Man Who Forgot How to Read* (2007)

### Anthologies

*Criminal Shorts: Mysteries by Canadian Crime Writers*
(ed. with Eric Wright, 1992)

# ABOUT THE AUTHOR

Recently awarded the crime writers of Canada's inaugural Grand Master Award, Howard Engel is one of our best-known and best-loved crime writers. He has been honoured with the Arthur Ellis Award for Crime Fiction, the Derrick Murdoch Award, the prestigious Matt Cohen Award in Celebration of a Writing Life, the Jewish Book Award for Lifetime Achievement, and the Order of Canada. His novels have been adapted for radio and television and they have been translated into more than a dozen languages and published in fifteen countries.

Howard Engel was born in 1931 and grew up in St. Catharines, Ontario, which is the model for his fictional town of Grantham, where his detective Benny Cooperman plies his trade. He worked for the CBC for many years and from 1979 to the present has published seventeen novels and one with Eric Wright, three works of non-fiction, and edited, with Eric Wright, one anthology. He now lives in Toronto.